THE BARBA

Suddenly the Ter...
ing. The barge ...
water. Flame and smoke ...
ing vats of petroleum, swirls of red and
black across the midnight sky. Some of
the prisoners collapsed, their mouths open,
eyes wide. The boat floated toward them,
its oarsmen in black robes, faces hidden
within deep cowls. Only one other person
was aboard the boat. Her clothes were white
and silver, gleaming in the faraway spotlights.

Tatja Grimm had been transformed. Black
hair lapped smooth down to her waist, covering her perfect, even tan. All she wore
was ribbon armor, and that only around
her hips and breasts. She carried the blade
called *Death*.

Villagers began a soft chant, which slowly
gained force and numbers: "Hra-la. Hra-la.
Hra-la." A priest silenced the chant with a
single word. He spoke quickly to the trans-
lator. They would bow to the authority of
the Princess . . . if a slight formality was
observed. Nothing much. Just a little trial
by combat.

Other books by Vernor Vinge:*

THE WITLING
TRUE NAMES AND OTHER DANGERS
THE PEACE WAR
MAROONED IN REALTIME

VERNOR VINGE

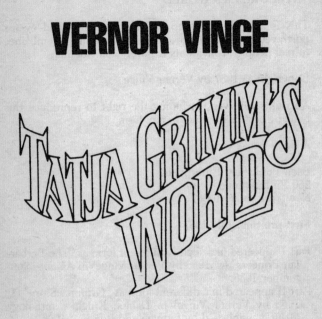

TATJA GRIMM'S WORLD

TATJA GRIMM'S WORLD

A Baen Books Original

Baen Publishing Enterprises
260 Fifth Avenue
New York, N.Y. 10001

First printing, July 1987

Part I appeared in a slightly different form as "The Barbarian Princess" (© 1986 by Vernor Vinge) in *Analog*, September 1986.
Part II appeared in a different form as "Grimm's Story" (© 1968 by Vernor Vinge) in Damon Knight's anthology *Orbit 4*, published by Putnam and Berkley, 1968.
Parts II and III appeared in a different form as *Grimm's World* (© 1969 by Vernor Vinge), published by Berkley Books, 1969.

ISBN: 0-671-65336-9

Cover art by Tom Kidd

Printed in the United States of America

Distributed by
SIMON & SCHUSTER
1230 Avenue of the Americas
New York, N.Y. 10020

TO ADA-GRACE TINGE
(1912-1959)

With love and admiration

PART 1

THE BARBARIAN
PRINCESS

Chapter 1

Fair Haven at South Cape was a squalid little town. Ramshackle warehouses lined the harbor, their wooden sides unpainted and rotting. Inland, the principal cultural attractions were a couple of brothels and the barracks of the Crown garrison. Yet in one sense Fair Haven lived up to its name. No matter how scruffy things were here, you knew they would be worse further east. This was the nether end of civilization on the south coast of the Continent. Beyond South Cape lay four thousand miles of wild coast, the haunt of littoral pirates and barbarian tribes.

Rey Guille would soon sail east, but the prospect did not bother him. In fact, he rather looked forward to it. For obvious reasons, there weren't many customers along the south coast run. The Tarulle Barge would put in at two of the larger barbarian settlements, villages with a taste for some of Tarulle's kinkier publications. There was also an author living in the coastal wilderness. His production was weird and erratic, but worth an extra stop. Except for these three landfalls, the barge would sail straight around the south coast, free of external problems. It would be thirty days before they reached the Osterlais.

Thirty days, sixty wake periods. Enough time for the translators to prepare the Osterlai and Tsanart editions, enough time for Brailly Tounse to recondition the Tarulle presses. Rey surveyed his tiny office. Thirty days. That might even be enough for him to dispose of his current backlog; Manuscripts were stacked from floor to ceiling behind him. The piles on his desk blocked his view of Fair Haven harbor—and more important, the breeze that seeped in from over the water. These were all the submissions taken aboard during their passage through the Chainpearls and Crownesse. There would be some first class stories here, but most would end up as extra slush in Brailly's paper-making vats. (Thus—as Rey had once pointed out in an editorial—every submission to *Fantasie* eventually became part of the magazine.)

Rey jammed open the tiny windows, and arranged his chair so he could sit in the breeze. He was about halfway through the desk stack: The easy ones he could decide in a matter of seconds. Even for these, he made a brief note in the submission log. Two years from now the Tarulle Publishing Company would be back in the Chainpearls. He couldn't return the manuscripts, but at least he could say something appropriate to the submitters. Other stories were harder to judge: competent but flawed, or inappropriate outside the author's home islands. Over the last few days, a small pile of high-priority items had accumulated beneath his desk. He would end up buying most of those. *Some* were treasures. Ivam Alecque's planet yarns were based on the latest research in spectrometry; Rey planned a companion editorial about the marvelous new science.

Alas, he must also buy stories that did not thrill him. *Fantasie* magazine lived up to its name: most of his purchases were stories of magic and mysticism. Even these were fun when the authors could be persuaded to play by internally consistent rules.

Rey grabbed the next manuscript, and scowled. Then there were the truly revolting things he must buy, things like this: another Hrala adventure. The series had started twenty years earlier, five years before he signed on with Tarulle. The first few stories weren't bad, if you liked nonstop illogical action with lots of blood and sex; old Chem Trinos wasn't a bad writer. As was Tarulle custom, Trinos had exclusive control of his series for eight years. Then Tarulle accepted Hrala stories from anyone. The fad kept growing. Otherwise decent writers began wasting their time writing new Hrala stories. Nowadays the series was popular all around the world, and was practically a cult in the Llerenitos.

Hrala the Barbarian Princess: over six feet tall, fantastically built, unbelievably strong and crafty and vengeful and libidinous. Her adventures took place in the vast inland of the Continent, where empires and wars had no need to conform to the humdrum world that readers knew. She was the idol of thousands of foolish male readers and a model for thousands of female ones.

6   *Vernor Vinge*

Rey paged slowly through this latest contribution to the legend. Hmph . . . for its kind, the story was well written. He'd have his assistant editor look it over, make it consistent with the background files she kept on the series. He would probably have to buy it. He tossed the manuscript under his desk and made a note in the submission log.

An hour later, Rey was still at it, the "in" pile fractionally smaller. From the decks below his windows came the continuing noise of supplies being loaded, crewmen shouting at stevedores. Occasionally he heard people working on the rigging above him. He had long since learned to tune out such. But now there was a different clatter: someone was coming along the catwalk to his office. A moment later, Coronadas Ascuasenya stuck her head in the doorway. "Boss, such a deal I got for you!"

Oh, oh. When Cor's accent thickened and her words came fast, it was a sure sign she had been swept away by some new enthusiasm. He waved her into the office. "What's that?"

"Tarulle magazines, they don't sell themselves. Other things we need to grab buyer interest."

Rey nodded. Jespen Tarulle had a small circus housed on the afterdecks. They put on shows at the larger ports, hyped all the Tarulle publications. Cor was fascinated by the operation; she was constantly trying to add acts representing stories and authors from *Fantasie*. She was good at it, too, a natural born publicist. Rey figured it was only a matter of time before higher-ups noticed, and he lost his assistant editor. "What have you got?"

"Who," she corrected him. She stepped back and waved at someone beyond the doorway. "I present you *Hrala*, Princess of the Interior!" She pronounced the name correctly, with a throat-tearing rasp that was painful even to hear.

The portentous intro brought no immediate action. After a moment, Cor stepped to the door and spoke coaxingly. There were at least two people out there, one of them a printsman from Brailly's crew. A second passed, and someone tall and lanky bent through the doorway. . . .

Rey rocked back in his chair, his eyes widening. The visitor was remarkable, though not in the way Cor meant. It was a female: there was a slimness in the shoulders, and a slight broadening in the hips. And she was *tall*. The ceiling of Guille's office was six feet high; the girl's tangled red hair brushed against it. But scale her down to normal size and she might be taken for a street waif. Her face and hair were grimy. A bruise darkened her face around one eye. With her arrival the room filled with the smell of rancid grease. He looked at her clothes and understood the source of part of the smell. She was dressed in rags. There were patches on patches on patches, yet holes still showed through. But these were not the rags of a street waif: these were of leather, thick and poorly cured. She carried a walking staff almost as tall as she was.

The circus people might have use for such a character, though scarcely as Hrala. He smiled at the girl. "What's your name?"

Her only reply was a shy smile that revealed even, healthy teeth. There was a nice face hiding under all the dirt.

Cor said, "She doesn't understand one word of Spräk, Boss." She looked out the door. "What did she call herself, Jimi?"

The printsman stuck his head into the office; there wasn't room for three visitors. "Good afternoon, Master Guille," he said to Rey. "Uh, it's hard to pronounce. The closest thing in a civilized name would be 'Tatja Grimm.' " The girl's head came up and her smile broadened.

"Hmm. Where did you find her?"

"Strangest thing, sir. We were on a wood detail for Master Tounse, a few miles south of here. Just about noon we came across her on the tableland. She had that there walking stick stuck in the ground. It looked like she was praying to it or something— she had her face down near the end of the stick's shadow. We couldn't see quite what all she was doing; we were busy cutting trees. But some boys from the town came by, started hassling her. We chased them off before they could do anything."

"And she was eager to stay with you?"

"She was when she saw we were from the barge. One of our crew speaks a little Hurdic, sir. Near as he can tell, she walked here from the center of The Continent."

Three thousand miles, through lands which—until very recently—had swallowed up every expedition. Rey cast a look of quiet incredulity at his assistant. Cor gave a little shrug, as if to say, *Hey, it will make great copy.*

The printsman missed this byplay. "We couldn't figure out quite *why* she made the trip, though. Something about finding people to talk to."

Rey chuckled. "Well, if Hurdic is her only language, she certainly came to the wrong place." He

looked at the girl. During the conversation, her
eyes had wandered all about the office. The smile
had not left her face. Everything fascinated her:
the carved wall panels, the waist-high stacks of
manuscripts, Guille's telescope in the corner. Only
when she looked at Rey or Cor or Jimi did her
smile falter and the shyness return. *Damn*. Didn't
Cor realize what she had here? Aloud he said,
"This is something I should think about. Jimi, why
don't you take this, ah, Tatja over to the public
deck. Get her something to eat."

"Yes, sir. Tatja?" He motioned her to follow him.
The girl's shoulders slumped for an instant, but
she departed without protest.

Cor was silent till their footsteps had faded into
the general deck clamor. Then she looked at Guille.
"You're not going to hire her." It was more an
accusation than a question.

"You'd find her more trouble than she's worth,
Cor. I'd wager she's a local girl; who ever heard of
an inlander with red hair? Watching her, I could
see she understood some of what we were saying.
Whatever Hurdic she speaks is probably in Jimi's
imagination. The poor girl is simply retarded; probably caused by the same glandular problem that's
sprouted her six feet tall before she's even reached
puberty. My guess is she's barely trainable."

Cor sat on one stack of manuscripts, propped
her feet on another. "Sure, she's no inlander, Boss.
But she's not from Fair Haven. The Haveners
don't wear leather like that. She's probably been
expelled from some local tribe. And yes, she's a
dim brain, but who cares? No need for The Great
Hrala to give big speeches in Spräk. I can teach

her to strut, wave a sword, make fake Hurdic war talk. Boss, they'll love her in the Llerenitos."

"Cor! She doesn't even *look* like Hrala. The red hair—"

"Wigs. We got lotsa nice black wigs."

"—and her figure. She just doesn't have, uh . . ." Guille made vague motions with his hands.

"No tits? Yes, that's a problem." The "true" Hrala danced through her adventures wearing next to nothing. "But we can fix. The vice magazine people have props. Take one of their rubber busts and wrap it in brassiere armor like Hrala wears. It'll fool an audience." She paused. "Boss. I can make this work. Tatja may be dim, but she wants to please. She doesn't have any place else to go."

Guille knew this last was not part of the sales pitch; Ascuasenya had a soft streak that undermined her pragmatism. He turned to look out at Fair Haven. A steady stream of supply lighters moved back and forth between the town's main pier and the deeper water surrounding the barge. Tarulle was due to lift anchor tomorrow noon. It would be two years before they returned to this part of the world. Finally he said, "Your scheme could cause real problems the next time we visit this dump. Come the night wake period, go into town and look up the crown's magistrate. Make sure we're not stealing some citizen's kid."

"Sure." Cor grinned broadly. Victory was at hand. Guille grumbled for a few more minutes: Hiring an actress would mean going up the chain of command to Overeditor Ramsey, and perhaps beyond him to Jespen Tarulle. That could take days, and much debate. Guille allowed himself to be persuaded to hire the girl as an apprentice proofreader. The move had a certain piquancy: how many writers had accused him of employing illiterate nitwits as proofreaders?

Finally, he reminded his assistant editor that she still had a full-time job preparing the issues that would sell in the Osterlais. Cor nodded, her face very serious; the Hrala project would be done on her own time. He almost thought he'd intimidated her . . . until she turned to leave and he heard a poorly suppressed laugh.

Chapter 2

It took Cor less than two days to understand what a jam she had talked herself into. The barge was back at sea and there were no distractions from shorefolk, but now she found herself working thirty hours a day, setting up the Hrala rehearsals with publicity, looking after the Grimm girl, and—most of all—getting *Fantasie* into shape.

There were *so* many manuscripts to review. There were good stories in the slush pile, but more science-oriented ones than ever before. These were Rey Guille's special favorites, and sometimes he went overboard with them. *Fantasie* had been published for seven hundred years. A certain percentage of its stories had always claimed to be possible. But only in the last fifty years, with the rise of science, could the reader feel that there was a future where the stories might really happen. Rey Guille had been editor of *Fantasie* for fifteen years. During that time, they had published more

stories of Contrivance Fiction than had been published in all the previous years. He had Svektr
Ramsey's permission to include two in every issue.
He found more and more readers whose only interest was in such stories; and he found more and
more readers who were creating the science that
future stories could be based on.

Cor knew that, in his heart, Rey saw these
stories as agents of change in themselves. Take the
spectrometry series: during the last five years, he
had written a dozen editorials advertising the new
science ("Spectrometry, Key to Nature's Secrets"),
and soliciting stories based on the contrivance.
Now he got one or two new ones at every major
stop. Some of them were salable, some were
mind-boggling . . . and some were wretched.

Ascuasenya had been working on the barge for
five quarters, and as Rey Guille's assistant for nearly
a year. She had read her first *Fantasie* story when
she was five. It was hard not to be in awe of the
magazine's editor, even if he was a crotchety old
codger. (Guille was forty-one.) Cor did her best to
disguise her feelings; their editorial conferences
were running battles. This morning was no different. They were up in his office, putting together
the first issue for the Osterlais. The slush pile had
been reduced to desk height and they had plenty
of room to lay out the pieces Rey had selected for
the new issue. Outside Guille's office, the bright
light of morning had slowly reddened. They were
well into the eclipse season; once every twenty
hours, Seraph blocked the sun or was itself eclipsed.
Every wake period was punctuated by darkness as
deep as night on the nether hemisphere. Guille

had set algae glowpots on every available hook, yet he still found it hard to read fine print.

He squinted at the Ivam Alecque manuscript Cor was complaining about. "I don't understand you, Cor. This yarn is *world-shaking*. If we didn't put anything else in the next issue, 'Pride of Iron' could carry it all."

"But the writing, it is so wooden. The characters have no life. The plot makes me sleepy."

"By the Blue Light of Seraph, Cor! It's *ideas* that make this great. 'Pride of Iron' is based on spectro results that aren't even in print yet."

"Phooey. There have been stories with this theme before: Ti Liso's Hidden Empire series. He had houses made of iron, streets paved with copper."

"Anyone who owns jewelry could imagine a world like that. This is different. Alecque is a chemist; he uses metals in realistic ways—like in gun barrels and heavy machinery. But even that isn't the beauty of this story. Three hundred years ago, Ti Liso was writing fantasy; Ivam Alecque is talking about something that could really *be*." Rey covered the glowpots and threw open a window. Chillness oozed into the office, ocean breeze further cooled by the eclipse. The stars spread in their thousands across the sky, blocked only by the Barge's rigging, dimmed only by mists rising from the pulper rooms below decks. Even if they had been standing outside, and could look straight up, Seraph would have been nothing more than a dim reddish ring. For the next hour, the stars ruled. "Look at that, Cor. Thousands of stars, millions beyond those we can see. They're suns like ours, and—"

"—and we buy plenty of stories with that premise."

"Not like this one. Ivam Alecque knows astronomers at Krirsarque who are hanging spectro gear on telescopes. They've drawn line spectra for lots of stars. The ones with color and absolute magnitude similar to our sun show incredibly intense lines for iron and copper and the other metals. This is the first time in history anyone has had direct insight about how things must be on planets of other stars. Houses built of iron are actually possible there."

Ascuasenya was silent for a moment. The idea was neat; in fact, it was kind of scary. Finally she said, "We're all alone in being so 'metal poor?' "

"Yes! At least among the sun-like stars these guys have looked at."

"Hmm. . . . It's almost like the gods, they play a big joke on us." Cor's great love was polytheistic fantasy, stories where the fate of mortals was determined by the whim of supernatural beings. That sort of thing had been popular in *Fantasie*'s early centuries. She knew Rey considered it out of step with what the magazine should be doing now. Sometimes she brought it up just to bug him. "Okay. I see why you want the story. Too bad it's such an ugly little thing."

She saw that her point had struck home. A bit grumpily, Rey unmasked the lamps, then sat down and picked up "Pride of Iron." It really was plotless. And—on this leg of the voyage, anyway—he was the only one capable of pumping it up. . . . She could almost see the wheels going around in his head: But it would be worth rewriting! He could have the story published before these ideas

were even in the scientific literature. He looked
up, grinned belligerently at her, and said, "Well,
I'm going to buy it, Cor. Assume 'anonymous colla-
boration' makes it twice as long: what can we do for
illustrations?"

It took about fifteen minutes to decide which
crew-artists would work the job; the Osterlai issue
would use slightly modified stock illos. Hopefully,
they could commission some truly striking pictures as they passed through that island chain.

The rest of the Osterlai issue was easy to lay
out; several of the stories were already in the
Osterlai language. The issue would be mostly fantasy, the new artwork would be from artists of
Crownesse and the Chainpearls. The cover story
was a rather nice Hrala adventure.

"Speaking of Hrala," said Rey, "how is your
project coming? Will your girl be able to give a
show when we start peddling this issue?"

"Sure she will. We get about an hour of re-
hearsal every wake period. Once she understands
about stage performance, things will go just fine.
So far, we work on sword and shield stuff. She can
memorize things as fast as we can show her. She's
awful impressive, screaming around the stage with
Death in her hand." In the stories, the Hrala
Sword was magical, edged with metal, and so heavy
that an ordinary warrior could not lift it. The Tarulle
version of *Death* was made of wood painted silver.

"What about her costume?" Or lack of one.

"Great. We still gotta do changes—ribbon armor is hard to fit—but she looks tremendous.
Svektr Ramsey thinks so too."

"He *saw* her?" Guille looked stricken.

"Don't worry, Boss. The overeditor was amused. He told me to congratulate you for hiring her."

"Oh. . . . Well, let's hope we're all still amused when you put her on stage with other actors."

Cor gathered up the manuscripts they had chosen. She would take them, together with the production notes, over to the art deck. "No problem. You were right, she understands some Spräk. She can even speak it a little. I think she was just shy that first day. Onstage she'll mainly scream gibberish—we won't need a new script for each archipelagate." Cor carried the papers to the door. "Besides, we get the chance to put it all together before we reach the Osterlais. We arrive at the Village of the Termite People in three days; I'll have things ready by then."

Guille chuckled. The Termite People were scarcely your typical fans. "Okay. I look forward to it."

Cor stepped into the darkness, shut the hatch behind her. In fact, she was at least half as confident as she sounded. Things ought to work out, if she could just find time to coach Tatja Grimm. The giant little girl was stranger than Cor had admitted. She wasn't really dumb, just totally deprived. She'd been born in some very primitive tribe. She'd been five years old before she ever saw a tree. *Everything* she saw now was a novelty. Cor remembered how the girl's eyes had widened when Cor showed her a copy of *Fantasie*, and explained how spoken words could be saved with paper and ink. She had held the magazine upside down, paged back and forth through it, fascinated by both pictures and text.

Worst of all, Tatja Grimm had no concept of

polemic; she must have been an outsider even in her own tribe. She simply did not accept that dramatic skits could persuade. If Grimm could be convinced of that single point, Cor was sure the Hrala campaign would be a spectacular success. If not, they might all end up with bat dreck on their faces.

The day they were to land at the Village of the Termite People, Rey took the morning off. He walked around the top editorial deck, looking for a place sheltered from the wind and passersby. This would be his first chance to play with his telescope since Fair Haven.

The marvelous weather still held. The sky was washed clean; widely spaced cumulus spread away forever. A Tarulle hydrofoil loitered about a mile ahead of the barge, its planes raised and sails mostly reefed. Guille knew there were others out there; most of the barge's 'foil bays were empty. The fastboats had many uses. In civilized seas, they ranged ahead of and behind the barge—making landfall arrangements, carrying job orders, picking up finished illustrations and manuscripts. In the wilderness east of Fair Haven, they had a different role: security. No pirates were going to sneak up on the barge. The catapults and petroleum bombs would be ready long before any hostile vessel broke the horizon.

So far, all the traffic was friendly. Several times a day they met ships and barges coming from the east. Most were merchantmen. Only a few publishing companies had Tarulle's worldwide scope. The hydrofoils reported that the *Science* was docked at the Village of the Termite People. That ship was much smaller than the Tarulle Barge, but it published its own journal. It was sponsored by universities in the Tsanarts as a sort of mobile research station. Rey looked forward to spending a few hours on the other vessel. It would mean some sales, and would give him a chance to make contacts; these were people who appreciated the new things he was doing with *Fantasie*. Notwithstanding Cor's Hrala project, seeing the *Science* would be the high point of this landfall.

Guille rolled the telescope cart into an open area at the rear of the editorial deck. Here the breeze was blocked by Old Jespen's penthouse, yet there was still a reasonable view. He clamped the cart's wheels and leveled its platform. Back in the Chainpearls—just after he bought the scope—this operation would have attracted a small crowd and begun an impromptu star- or Seraph-party. Now, passersby said hello, but few stopped for long. Rey had his toy all to himself.

He flipped the tube down and took a scan across the northern horizon. They were about fifteen miles off the coast. To the naked eye, the continent was a dark line at the bottom of the sky. The telescope brought detail: Guille could see individual rocks on the dun cliffs. Trees growing in the lee of the hills were clearly visible. Here and there were rounded lumps he recognized as wild termite towers. The village was hidden beyond a small cape.

Not a very impressive coast for the greatest landmass in the world. Beyond those cliffs, the land stretched more than ten thousand miles—over the north pole and partway down the other side of the planet. There was a hundred times more land there than in all the island chains put together. It was an ocean of land, and beyond its coastal fringe, mostly unknown. No wonder it had been the source of so many stories. Rey sighed. He didn't begrudge those stories. In past centuries, speculation about the Interior was a decent story base. The island civilizations weren't more than a couple of thousand years old. The human race must have originated on the Continent. It was reasonable that older, wiser civilizations lay in the Interior. Whole races of monsters and godlings might flourish in those reaches.

But during the last thirty years, there had been serious exploration. Betrog Hedrigs had reached Continent's Center. In the last ten years, three separate expeditions had trekked across the Interior. The unknown remained, but it was cut into small hunks. The myths were dead and the new reality was a dismal thing: An "ocean" of land is necessarily a very dry place. Beyond the coastal fringe the explorers found desert. In that, there was variety. There were deserts of sand and heat, deserts of rock, and—in the north—deserts of ice and cold. There was no hidden paradise. The nearest things to the "Great Lakes" of legend were saline ponds near Continent's Center. The explorers found that the Interior *was* inhabited, but not by an Elder Race. There were isolated tribes in the mid-latitude deserts. These folk lived naked, almost like animals. Their only tools were spears and hand axes. They seemed peaceful, too poor even for warfare. The lowest barbarians of the Fringe were high civilization compared to them. And all these years, the story writers had assumed that the Hurdic tribes were degenerate relatives of Interior races!

Yet Interior fantasies were still written. Guille saw hundreds of them a year, and worse, had to buy dozens. Ah, well. It was a living, and it gave him a chance to show people more important things. Rey stepped back from the telescope, and turned its tube almost straight up. It was Seraph he really wanted to look at.

"Hel-lo?"

Rey looked up, startled. He had an audience. It was the Fair Haven waif. She stood almost behind him and about ten feet away. He had the feeling she'd watched for several minutes. "Hello indeed. And how are you today, Mistress Grimm?"

"Well." She smiled shyly and took a step forward. She certainly looked better than when he first saw her. Her face was scrubbed clean. In place of rancid leather, she wore tripulation fatigues. If she had been five feet tall instead of six, she would have seemed a pretty pre-teener.

"Shouldn't you be rehearsing with Cor?"

"I, uh, that is la-ter."

"I see. You're off duty."

She bobbed her head, seeming to understand the term. Somehow, Rey had imagined that Cor or the publicity people would be looking after Tatja all the time. In fact, no matter how incompetent she was, there simply were not enough people to baby-sit her. The girl must have many hours to herself; no doubt she wandered all over the barge. By the Light, the trouble she could get into!

They stared at each other for a moment. The girl seemed so attentive, almost in awe of him. He realized she wouldn't leave unless he explicitly told her to get lost. He tried to think of an appropriate dismissal, but nothing came. Damn. Finally he said, "Well, how do you like my new telescope?"

"Good. Good." The girl stepped almost close enough to touch the scope, and Rey went through the usual explanations: He showed her how the wheels could be fastened to the deck. The oil bath in the cart's base damped the sea motion and kept the optics steady. The cart itself was an old drafting rig from the art deck. Rey had removed the drawing table and substituted clamps that attached to the base of his twelve-inch scope.

Tatja Grimm didn't say much, but her enthusiasm was obvious. She leaned close to the equipment to see the details Rey pointed out. When he explained something, she would pause for an instant and then bob her head and say, "Yes. So nice."

Guille wondered if he could have been wrong about her. In some ways, she seemed a more thoughtful and enthusiastic audience than crew people he had shown the gear to. But then he noticed the uniformity of her responses. Everything seemed to impress her equally. She took the same brief moment to absorb every explanation. Guille had a retarded cousin, mental age around five years, physical age thirty: after so much living, a retarded person learns to mimic the head movements and nonsense sounds that normal people make in conversation. Rey could imagine the blank look he would get if he asked Tatja something related to his explanations.

He didn't try such an experiment. What point was there in hurting the girl's feelings? Besides, she seemed to enjoy the conversation as much as a normal person. He aimed the scope at Seraph as he continued his spiel. The planet was in quarter phase, and the mountains of its southern continent stood in stark relief near the terminator. Wind and ship vibration jostled the image a bit. On the other hand, the line of sight was straight up, without lots of dirty air to smudge things. This was the clearest day-view he'd ever had. ". . . so my telescope makes objects seem much closer. Would you like to look?" Even a retard should be thrilled by the sight.

"Yes." She stepped forward, and he showed her how to use the eyepiece. She bent to it . . . and gave a squeal, a wonderful mixture of pleasure and surprise. Her head jerked back from the eyepiece. She stared upwards at the twin planet, as if to assure herself that it hadn't moved. Just as quickly she took another look through the lense, and then backed off again. "So big. So *big!*" Her smile all but split her face. "How can te-le-scope—" she reached up, as if to jerk the tube's end down to eye level.

Guille caught her hands. "Oops. Be gentle. Turn it around this pivot." She wasn't listening, but she let him rotate the tube so she could look in. Her eyes went wide as she saw the expanded image of her face in the main mirror. Rey found himself explaining about "curved mirrors" and how the diagonal directed the image from the 12-inch through the eyepiece. The girl hesitated the same fraction of a second she had after his other explanations. Then, just as before, her head bobbed with an enthusiastic imitation of total understanding. "Yes. Yes. So nice."

Abruptly, she grabbed Rey's hand. "And you think this thing? You make it?"

Tatja's grip was almost painful; her hands were slender but as outsized as the rest of her. "You mean, did I invent the telescope?" He chuckled. "No, Miss Grimm. The basic idea is two hundred years old. People don't invent telescopes just to pass the time on a dull morning. Things like this are the work of scattered geniuses. Part of an invention may exist for decades, useless, before another genius makes the idea successful."

The girl's expression collapsed. It might have been laughable if it weren't so pathetic. She had no concept of what was difficult and what was trivial, and so her attempt at bright conversation had foundered. Rey turned her gently back to the telescope and showed her how to adjust the focus. Her former enthusiasm did not completely return, but she seemed sincerely taken by the close-up view of Seraph. Rey gave her his usual spiel, pointing out the brown smudges across part of the southern continent. "Brush fires, we think. That land must be a lot like the grassy plains north of Bayfast. The religions have all sorts of visions of Seraph, but we now know it's a world much like ours." And the stories of hidden civilizations *there* might still be true. Rey had written more than one editorial about plans for detecting and communicating with Seraph's hypothetical inhabitants. One of the first steps would be to build an observatory in this part of the world, where Seraph could be observed with a minimum of atmospheric distortion.

A couple of people from Printing had stopped nearby, were watching intently. They were not the sort Rey would think attracted by skygazing;

one was Brailly Tounse's bombwright. Rey glanced at her questioningly.

"Sir, we've got a line of sight into the harbor now," the bombwright said, waving to the north. "We were wondering if you'd take a quick look at Termite Town through your scope."

Rey hid a sigh, and gave up any hope of having the device to himself this morning. The bombwright must have noticed his irritation. She hurried on to say, "Something strange is happening with the Termite People, sir. So far the officer types ain't talking, but—take a look, will you?"

Guille eased Tatja Grimm away from the scope and tilted it toward the horizon. He made a quick adjustment with the spotter scope and then looked through the main eyepiece. ". . . Looks about like I remember it." There were dozens of towers, from water's edge back up the hills around the harbor. The smallest ones were bigger than a house. The largest were over a hundred feet tall. The spaces between were like streets at the bottom of shadowed canyons. Even knowing the truth, one's first reaction was awe: this must be a city, the greatest one in the world. Krirsarque and Bayfast were insignificant, low-story affairs compared to this. In fact, there were only a few thousand humans in this whole "city." They dug their burrows and staircases through the termite mounds; they poked air holes through the walls, holes that also served as windows. "Hmm. There's something different. One of the towers by the moorage . . . it looks like it was burned, or stained with soot. The dark goes as high as the windows overhanging the water."

"Yes, sir. That's what got our attention, but we

couldn't see what made the stain. And there's something strange in the water, too."

Rey tilted the scope a fraction. A twisted pile of spikes and filaments stuck through the water, directly in front of the scorch-marked tower. Rey sucked in a breath. "It looks like ship's rigging, the fiberglass part."

The bombwright stepped closer, and he let her take a look. She was silent for a moment, then, "Unh huh. That's where they like visitors to dock. Looks like the gooks dumped pet' bombs out those windows, right onto the moorage. The guys they ambushed didn't have a chance."

A minute before, Rey had been feeling sorry for one retarded girl. Now. . . . He looked across the water. Without a telescope, the village was a barely distinguishable skyline, the scorch unnoticeable.

The guys they ambushed. . . . According to the advance reports, there had been exactly one ship tied up at the village: the *Science*.

Chapter 3

Crew and publishing folk spent the next few hours speculating: Why was the *Science* ambushed? What would Tarulle do about it? The barge stayed several miles offshore, but rumor held that fastboats were doing close recon under cover of the midday eclipse. The only word from the executive deck was that there would be no immediate landing.

Top management was not asleep—just terribly indecisive. Rey Guille bluffed his way onto the bridge shortly before eclipsend. All the biggies were there, both from Ownership and Operations. The atmosphere was that of an incipient brawl: consensus time had not arrived.

"—and I say, sail into catapult range and burn their filthy village to the ground! Barbarians must learn that ambushing merchants is a dangerous sport." The speaker was one of Tarulle's nephews, an arrogant pip-squeak who'd be scrubbing decks if it weren't for his relatives. The little man looked angrily around the room, daring anyone to disagree. Fortunately for the company, there were some strong personalities present:

Barge Captain Maccioso stood near the helm, facing the rest. His form was a vague, intimidating shadow in the eclipse light. Maccioso was a huge man; the bridge itself had been rebuilt to accommodate his six-foot eight-inch height. He was in his early fifties and only just beginning to go to fat. The first twenty years of his career had been spent in the Chainpearls Navy. The man had retired an admiral, and the greatest hero of the Loretto Bight affair. Now he crossed his ham-like arms and seemed to lean toward Tarulle's nephew. "Warlike talk coming from . . ." *a wee wimp who couldn't cock a bow,* the pause seemed to say, "from those who need customers to live. It's true, I could torch the village. It would be expensive; we wouldn't be left with much reserve. And what would we get for it? The Termite Folk are isolated, Master Craeto. There would be few to learn from the lesson. The Tarulle Company would lose one—admittedly minor—customer. The barge has visited here four times since I've been Captain. We've had less trouble than in some civilized ports. These people are not pirates. The *Science* crew did something, broke some taboo. . . ."

Maccioso turned to look into the harbor; sunbreak was almost upon them. The land was bright with washed-out pastels. When he continued, his voice held more frustration than certainty. "Sure. We have the power to raze the place. But we could never bring off an assault landing. There's no way we can rescue the survivors and find out how to avoid such a debacle in the future."

Survivors? Someone had lived through the pet'
bombing. Rey felt a surge of joy. No one else
seemed moved by the news; they already knew.
This must be a major point of the debate. "We
can't just leave them there!" The words popped
out of Guille's mouth without conscious thought.

Dead silence greeted his words. The people closest to him moved slightly away, but didn't look at
him; it was as though he had made a bad smell.
Maccioso turned and his gaze swept the bridge.
"Master Tounse!"

"*Sir!*"

The barge captain pointed at Rey Guille. "Take
this man out and . . ." Rey's guts went cold; there
were stories about Ked Maccioso's command of
the Chainpearl Armada, "*brief* him."

"Yessir!"

Brailly Tounse emerged from the crowd and
hustled Rey onto the open walkway beyond the
bridge. The printmaster shut the hatch and turned
to face him. " 'Brief you?' The commercial life is
turning Ked soft." It took a moment for Rey to
realize that the other man was suppressing laughter. "Don't you understand that a rescue is what
Ked is dying to do? For almost an hour, he's been
trying to trick these flightless bats into backing
one."

"Oh." Rey was both embarrassed and encour-
aged. "Maybe my, uh, little outburst will start
something."

"I hope so." Brailly stopped smiling. "But even
by Ked's standards, it would be a risky operation
pulling those *Science* people out."

He led Rey to the forward end of the walkway.
All around them, twilight brightened suddenly into

day as the sun came past the edge of Seraph.
Swarms of daybats rose from the harbor. They
swept around the towers, their cries coming clear
and reedy across the water.

Brailly gestured at the bridge binoculars. "Take
a look to the left of the harbor towers. That's
where they're holding the survivors." It was some
kind of pit, probably the root of a fallen tower.
Rey saw Termite Folk camped around the edge.
Tounse continued, "They're in that hole, out of
sight from this angle. See how the locals have set
petroleum vats along the edge? They could light
and dump those in a matter of minutes . . ."

. . . incinerating the prisoners. The Tarulle people would have to sneak in a large party, and
overpower the guards at those vats all at once.
One slip and a lot of company people would share
the fate of those in the pit. "We could offer a
ransom, Brailly. It might be expensive, but the
Science home universities would probably pay us
back. . . . And there'd be lots of good publicity."
The spinoffs from such an adventure could fill
several issues of the Tarulle magazines.

"You don't understand: the *Science* people aren't
hostages. The only reason they're still alive is that
an appropriate method of execution hasn't been
decided on. The local bosses tell us that no ransom
will save the prisoners. They won't even tell us
what 'blasphemy' the poor suckers committed. The
whole matter is closed. And you know, I think the
gooks actually expect to continue business as usual
with the rest of us!"

"Hmm." Rey had dealt with the village's rulers.
Their interest in certain types of pulp fiction had
always made them seem relatively civilized. They

had not seemed religious—and now he saw that
was just a sign of how damned secretive their
religion must be. He stared through the binocs a
moment more. Beyond the edge of that pit were
some good people. "We've got to do something,
Brailly."

"I know. Ked knows." The printmaster shrugged.
After a moment, the two men walked back to the
command bridge. Inside, Rey saw that the tension
had drained from the meeting; consensus had finally been reached. Brailly smiled sourly and whispered, "But we also know how it's going to turn
out, don't we?"

Rey looked around, and with a sinking feeling
he understood. The Tarulle Publishing Company
had existed for seven hundred years. Few island-
bound companies were that old—and yet Tarulle
had been sailing the oceans of Tu all that time,
contending with tempests and pirates and religion-
ists and governments. There had been disasters;
three hundred years earlier, the old barge was
burned to the waterline. Yet the company had
survived, and prospered. One doesn't last seven
hundred years by rushing into everyone else's fight.
The barge and its hydrofoils were well armed, but
given a choice they simply avoided trouble. If a
village or even an island chain turned to religious
nuttery, they lost Tarulle's business. The years
would pass, and the regime would fall—or decide
that it needed trade more than its crazy convictions.

Kederichi Maccioso had done his subtle best to
bring another outcome, but it was not to be: The
talk now was of delivering a few threats and—if
that did not help the *Science* people—weighing
anchor and sailing off.

There must be some way to stop this! Then he had it: Brailly said the Termite Folk wanted business as usual. For the second time in fifteen minutes, Rey interrupted the meeting. "We can't simply take off; we have magazines to sell here, and customers who want to buy."

This outburst was greeted with the same silence as before. Only this time, it was not Ked Maccioso who responded. There was a croaking sound from somewhere behind the Tarulle in-laws. The owners looked nervously at each other, then stood aside. Out of the shadows came a very old man in a wheelchair: Jespen Tarulle himself. He rolled far enough past his relatives to get a look at Rey Guille. It was only the third time Rey had seen the man. He was wrapped in blankets, his hands clasped and shivering in his lap. Only one eye tracked and it was starred with a cataract. His voice was quavery, the delivery almost addled. "Yes. These folk haven't done us harm, and our business is to *do business*." He looked in Rey's direction. "I'm glad someone still understands this."

Maccioso didn't sound quite so enthusiastic. "It's risky, sir, not your average sales landing. . . . But I could go along with it, if we can get the volunteers." Volunteers who might wangle the prisoners' freedom, or at least discover their exact situation; Rey imagined the wheels turning in the Barge Captain's head.

"Sirs. I volunteer for the landing." It was Brailly Tounse, barely hiding a smile.

"I—I volunteer." The words were coming from Rey's own mouth. He mumbled the rest, almost as a rationalization to himself: "I've handled sales landings here before."

Old man Tarulle tilted his head at the other owners. "Are we agreed?" It was not quite a rhetorical question; the explicit recommendation of Jespen Tarulle counted for a lot, but he was not a majority stockholder. After a moment, there came mumbled acquiescence. Tarulle looked across the deck. "Operations? Are there any objections from them?"

"I have a question." It was Svektr Ramsey. He looked at Guille. "Have you finished your work on the first Osterlai issue of *Fantasie*?"

"My assistant can handle what remains, Master Ramsey." He had just finished the rewrite of "Pride of Iron."

"Ah." A smile split the gaunt Overeditor's face. "In that case, I have no objections." And if things didn't work out, there would be plenty of time to put a black border around the editorial page.

They didn't go ashore until ten hours later, in the night wake period. It had been a busy time. The landing was to look like the previous ones here. There would only be one boat, less than a dozen people. Except for Rey—who was probably known to the locals—those twelve were not the usual sorts for a commercial landing. Maccioso picked people with military and naval backgrounds. The barge captain had imagined many contingencies. Some involved simple gathering of information, perhaps an attempt at diplomacy; others would mean quick violence and a frantic effort to get back to sea ahead of the Termite People. From the beginning, it was agreed that no obvious weapons would be taken. Braily Tounse produced explosive powder that could be carried in their jackets; that should pass any inspection the Termiters might make.

Though it was probably a futile contribution, Rey Guille took his telescope. It had impressed Tatja Grimm; it might have some effect on the locals. On the other hand, he thought, such high technology might be what got the *Science* in trouble. Rey broke the scope into its components and stored them in different parts of the landing boat.

Coronadas Ascuasenya had been furious. She wanted to take her Barbarian Princess act ashore and pretend that Tatja Grimm was *truly* Hrala. Maccioso rejected the plan—and Rey agreed with him. Ascuasenya claimed the girl had absorbed the role these last couple of days, that she was the most convincing Hrala ever produced. It really didn't matter. Rey doubted that the local rulers believed the Hrala stories. In any case, using the act to intimidate could cause the prompt massacre of both prisoners and would-be rescuers.

So Cor stayed behind, and Guille found himself on the landing boat surrounded by some very competent fighters. Except for Brailly, he knew none of them.

They were only a hundred yards from the shore. Seraph was at first quarter, and its blue light lay serene across everything. The loudest sounds were the splash of oars into water, and the occasional grunt of a rower. Beach bats and flying fish swooped low around the lighter. The smell of char and oil was stronger than the salt tang of the water. They were passing a ragged jungle of black glass: what was left of the *Science*. The bats swarmed through the twisted rigging: one creature's catastrophe is another's new home.

The termite mounds were awesome at this distance. Hundreds of air holes lined their sides. A few of the towers actually broadened with height so that they hung over the water. It was like some artist's vision of a city of the future. Even knowing what the towers really were, it was hard not to feel intimidated.

Early seafarers thought the Termite Folk were nonhuman. Alas and fortunately, this was not the work of gods. The locals were normal humans, using mounds that occurred all through this region. They brought in extra materials for the termites, then guided and pruned the structures. Basically the Termite People were Hurdic folk taking advantage of local circumstance. And strangely, they had no special pride in the towers. They seemed much prouder of the heritage they imagined having lost when they left the Interior.

Brailly Tounse kicked at the crate that was their cargo. "Still don't see why the gooks are interested in *Fantasie*."

Rey shrugged. "We don't sell them the whole thing, just stories of the Interior. My guess is, they see themselves as a great people fallen on hard times. Stories about Inner Kingdoms stroke that vision. We don't sell more than a few dozen copies per visit, but they pay several coppers for each."

Tounse whistled softly. "Gods, if only our other customers were that eager." He turned to look at the towers. On the other hand, the Barge's usual customers bought in much larger quantities . . . and didn't incinerate visitors.

The landing boat slid up to a crude pier. Some thirty guards stood along its length, their spears held in salute. The local bosses were in a group just above the landing point. As the Tarulle people climbed from the boat, low-ranking priests came down to help carry Rey's crate. So far everything seemed normal.

The tallest of the locals advanced on Rey, and gabbled something in a singsong cadence. This was the priest they usually dealt with; the guy had an excellent reading knowledge of Spräk but little chance to speak it. His vocabulary was straight out of an old-time adventure novel. After a second Rey got the avalanche of mispronounced words sorted out: "Master Guille, happy we are to see you again." The priest bowed in the direction of the magazines. "And happy we are to learn more Ancestor Truth. You and your crew are welcome in the hall. We will examine the new truth and decide on fair payment."

Rey mumbled something appropriately pompous, and they walked toward the Village, Guille and the Termiter priests in the lead. Behind him, the landing party hung together, their tenseness obvious. This was the third time Rey had been here. He marveled that he had not been afraid before. In fact, the place had been a comic relief. *Then* when the locals spoke of "Ancestor Truth" it seemed a light turn of phrase. *Now* he had the wild impulse to run: what if there was some blasphemy in the stories? It put him in a cold sweat to think how casually he published new twists on traditional themes, or allowed small inconsistencies into story cycles. And just a few days ago, he'd looked forward to testing the Hrala skit on these people!

The tall priest's tone remained friendly: "You

have come at an appropriate moment, Master
Guille. We have confronted blasphemers—who may
be harbingers of the Final Battle. Now is a time
when we must consult all sources of Truth." Another priest, an older fellow with a limp, interrupted with something abrupt. The tall guy paused,
and looked faintly embarrassed; suddenly Guille
knew that he was more than an interpreter, but
not one of the high priests. "It will be necessary to
inspect both your boat and your persons. More
blasphemers may come in fair forms. . . . Don't
be angered; it is but a formality. I, we recognize
you from before. And if the writings you bring
speak to our questions, you can expect payment
even more generous than usual."

Away from the pier, the smell of burned petroleum products faded, replaced by a barnyard smell
and the acrid stench of the tiny insects that built
the mounds. Up close, the tower walls were not
smooth sweeps. Glabrous patches were surrounded
by warty growths. The "windows" were holes hacked
in the irregular surface. Even Seraph's blue light
could not make such things beautiful. Behind the
front tier of mounds, stone corrals held a few
dozen skoats: the source of the farm smell. The
place really was a village, similar to backward villages the world over. Without modern science,
they had no way of making strong or hard materials. Their spearheads were fire-hardened wood and
obsidian. Where the termites did not build for
them, their structures were simple piles of stone.
. . . It was no wonder travelers had seen no dan-
ger from these people; a squad of crossbow-armed
troops could take them over. No one guessed they

had access to petroleum or the knowledge to produce flammables.

They walked some distance through the shadows between the towers. The Great Hall was cut into the side of one of the largest mounds. The resulting talus was pressed into steps as broad as in front of any government building in Crownesse. At the top of the steps, carved wooden barricades blocked the entrance. Rey's guide called out something Hurdic and ceremonial-sounding. Spear-toting priests slid aside the barricades.

Their porters carried the crate of *Fantasies* toward the altar at the back of the Hall. The place was exactly as Rey remembered it: at least one hundred feet from entrance to altar, but with a ceiling that was nowhere more than seven feet high. It seemed more like a mine than a building. Twelve-foot-wide pillars stood in a rectangular grid across the floor. The pillars were native moundstuff, painted white. The only light came from ranks of candles that circled each of them. As the Tarulle people walked toward the altar, they saw hundreds of Termite Folk standing quietly between the farther pillars. The room couldn't be more than one hundred feet across, but the pillars seemed to go on forever. On his last visit, Rey had walked to the side of the hall (an act of unknowing bravado, he realized now), and discovered that the pillars there were smaller, more closely spaced, and the walls were painted with the image of more pillars stretching off to a faked infinity; cleverly placed flecks of glass simulated hundreds of faraway candles. Like a lot of primitive folk, the Termiters had their own subtleties.

Rey expected the threatened body searches would

come next. Instead, the Tarulle people were gestured to sit before the altar. There was a moment of near silence after Guille was asked to open the crate. Now he could hear a faint buzzing that came from all around, the sound of the real termites. They were, after all, inside an enormous hive. He pulled up the lid of the crate, and the insect sound was lost behind the villagers' soft chanting.

The high priests lifted the top sheets from the crates. These were color illustrations that would be inside/outside covers on normally bound editions. The color didn't show well in the candlelight, but the Termiters didn't seem to mind; the best pictures from previous issues were mounted in the walls behind the altar. The priests pored over the illos, just like ordinary fans thrilled with the latest issue of their favorite magazine. Before, Rey would have smiled at their enthusiasm. Now he held his breath. At least one of those pictures showed Hrala carrying a spring-gun; could that be blasphemy?

Then the tall priest looked up, and Rey saw that he was smiling. "Wonderful, friend Guille. There is new Insight here. We will pay double." The others were lifting typeset galley proofs out of the crate and solemnly laying them on velvet reading stands. There couldn't be more than a handful of locals who knew Språk; did they *preach* from the stories? Rey let out a carefully controlled breath. It didn't matter now. The Tarulle people had passed the test and—

—outside the hall, someone was shouting. The words were indistinct, but Hurdic. The priests straightened, listening. The shouts came louder; people were rushing up the steps to the hall's

entrance. The barricades slid aside and Seraph's
light shone on the arrivals: they were spear carriers from the pier. They rushed down the aisle,
still shouting. Their leader was waving something
over his head. Everyone was shouting now. Rey
saw that Brailly's men had slipped into a circle
formation. Some of them were reaching into their
jackets.

Then the newcomer reached the altar, and one
of the priests—the old one with the gimp leg—
gave an incredible warbling scream. In an instant,
all other cries ceased. He took two objects from
the guard and held them close to the candles.
Strange reflections shifted across his face and the
ceiling. . . . He was holding the main mirror and
the diagonal bracket from Rey's telescope.

*How can he know what these are, much less
think them blasphemous?* The thought hung for an
instant in Rey's mind, and then everything went
crazy. The old man threw the mirror to the floor,
then turned on the Tarulle visitors and shouted in
Hurdic. No translation was needed; his face was
contorted with hatred. Spearmen ran forward, weapons leveled. Brailly tossed something onto the altar; there was an explosion and swirling gouts of
chokesmoke. Rey dived to the floor, tried to belly
crawl out from under the choke. He heard Brailly's
men fighting their way toward the entrance. By
the sound of it, they had some sort of weapons—
strip knives probably. There were screams and
ugly ripping sounds, all against a background of
coughing and nausea. It sounded as if all the villagers had thrown themselves into the fight. They
could never get past such a mob!

He had underestimated the Printmaster. From

out of the smoke and shouting came Brailly's voice. "Down! We're gonna blast!" Rey tucked his head in his arms. A second later there was a flash of light and invisible hands crashed upon both sides of his head. He looked up. There was blue light ahead! Tounse had knocked the barricade over.

Guille came to his knees. If he could move while the locals lay stunned. . . .

His poor ears couldn't hear the rumbling; it came through his knees and palms. All around them, the hive was shaking. He saw now that the pillars near the entrance had been smashed. Avalanches of moundstuff—first small, then engulfing, spilled down from above.

With that, the tower collapsed on the Great Hall, and Rey saw no more.

Chapter 4

Consciousness returned in patches. There were unpleasant dreams. Something was banging his head; it wasn't the knock of his alarm clock. They were dragging him feet first, and his head was bouncing off uneven ground. The dream faded to pleasant grayness, then came back in a new form: he was rolling down a hillside, the rocks cutting into his body.

Rey came to rest in foul-tasting water, and wondered if he would drown before he woke up. Strong hands pulled him from the water. Through the ringing in his ears he heard someone say, "There. A moment of sitting to catch the breath."

He coughed weakly, and looked around. No more dreams: the nightmare was reality. He was sitting by a shallow pond, near the bottom of a pit. The edge of the pit was ten yards above his head, except on one side, where it broke low and gave a view of the harbor. He was not alone. There were dozens of people here: all that remained of the *Science* crew. They clustered around the newly fallen. Looking up at their faces, Rey saw hope in some, fear and despair in others.

"You're looking bad. Can you talk?" It was the woman who had pulled him from the pond. She was in her late fifties, an Osterlai by her accent. Her clothes were neat but stained. There was a matter-of-fact friendliness in her voice. In a moment he would remember who she was.

"Y-yes," he croaked. "What happened?"

The woman gave a short laugh. "You tell us. Five minutes ago it just started raining people. Looks like the Termite Folk have found new blasphemers."

Rey swallowed. "You're right." And it was his fault.

Most of his companions were in worse shape than he. The *Science* prisoners were trying to help, but two of the Tarulle people looked freshly dead. Nowhere did he see Brailly Tounse. He glanced at the Osterlai woman and made a wan smile. "We came to rescue you." He gave his captive audience a brief account of the sales landing. "Everything was going fine. I was beginning to think they might listen to us, that we'd at least learn more about your situation. Then they found the mirror from my telescope. How could they know what it was, much less . . ." He noticed the look on the woman's face.

"And how do you think we got in trouble, my sir? We thought to do some observing from the peaks Inland. We had a twenty-inch mirror; the Seraph-seeing should be better here than—" She broke off in surprise. "Why you're Rey Guille!"

Rey nodded, and she continued, "So I don't have to tell you the details; you've written enough about the idea. . . . I'm Janna Kats, Seraphist at Bergenton; we met once a couple years back." She waved a hand as recognition slowly dawned on Rey. "Anyway. We dragged that mirror ashore, gave the Termiters a look. They thought it was great stuff, till they learned what we wanted to look at." She laughed, but it was not a happy sound. "Lots of religions worship Seraph. You know: home o' the gods and such garbage. Turns out the Termiters think Seraph is something like the gods' bedroom—and mortals mustn't peep!"

So that was how they learned what the parts of a telescope look like. "It still doesn't make sense," Rey said. "In everything else, they seem to be ancestor worshipers; I've sold them dozens of Interior fantasies. How did Seraphidolatry get mixed in?"

The question brought a fit of coughing from the little man sitting beside Kats. "I can answer that." The words were broken by more rasping coughs. The fellow's face seemed shrunken, collapsed; Rey wondered that he could talk at all. "The Termite Folk are intellectual pack rats. For three hundred years they've been here, picking up a little of this, a little of that—from whoever was passing through." More coughing. "I should have seen through 'em right off; I've spent my whole life studying coastal barbarians, learning Hurdic. But these folks are so secretive, I didn't understand what was driving them . . . till it was too late." A smile twisted his thin face. "I could get a nice research paper out of what we've learned here. Too bad we gotta die first."

Rey Guille had years of experience finding loop-holes in impossible situations—on paper. "Maybe we don't have to die. I never thought the Termiters were killers. If their religion is such a hodgepodge, they can't take the taboos too seriously. You've been here for several days. Maybe they just want a graceful way out." It really made sense. Then he remembered Brailly's bomb, and continued more quietly, "If there's anything they'd kill for, I think it would be what my people did to the Village Hall."

"You don't understand, fellow," a third *Science* person spoke, a sharp edge in his voice. "Knock-ing over a termite mound is a peccadillo in their eyes, compared to invading the gods' privacy. They've kept us alive this long because they're having trouble devising a torture-death appropri-ate to our crime!"

"How can you know that for sure—"

"We know, Master Guille," Janna Kats's tough exterior broke for an instant, and she looked just as frightened as the others. "In the last two days they've taken three of us from the pit. W-we could hear the screams; one we could see. Each took longer to die than the last."

There was a moment of silence, and then the cougher said, "I think the Termiters are scared, too—of their Seraph gods. If they can't come up with the proper death for us, they think the gods will apply that death to *them*. The three they killed were . . . little experiments."

"But there will be no more." The toughness was back in Janna's voice. "The next time they come, one big surprise we'll show them. We won't be skoats waiting for the slaughter."

Rey looked up, at the rim of the pit. There were Termite Folk all around. Most carried spears, but that wasn't the most deadly thing; spears kill one at a time, make a slow thing of a massacre. Much more ominous were the priests carrying torches. They stood near the three petroleum vats Brailly had spotted earlier. Each tank was mounted on a crude swivel. Should they choose, the torchbearers could drown their prisoners in flame. A few hours before, that prospect had filled him with sympathetic dread. For Janna and the others, it had come to be the only imaginable out.

The hours passed. At the top of the sky, Seraph widened toward full, its western ocean turning dark and reddish with the start of the midnight eclipse. The villagers marched steady patrols around the edge of the pit. Mostly they were silent. The *Science*'s anthropologist said they had long ago stopped responding to his shouted questions.

There were no more "experiments," but Rey gradually realized the pit was in itself a killing place. The only water was in the shallow pool at the bottom of the pit, and that became steadily more foul. The only food was what the villagers threw into the pit: slabs of skoat cheese and balls of what turned out to be pressed termite larva. Rey had eaten some exotic things in his years with Tarulle, but the larva patties were half rotted. Hungry as they were, only a few of the prisoners could keep them down. Three of the Tarulle prisoners were dead, their bodies broken by the explosion. Two of the survivors had compound fractures; their moans came less frequently with each passing hour.

The prisoners were not alone in the pit. The true builders of the village were here, too. In the silence that dragged between conversations and occasional screaming, Rey heard a *scritching* sound coming from all directions. At the corner of his vision, a pebble would move, something would scuttle from one hole to another. The termites were no bigger than a man's thumb, but there must have been millions of them in the sides of the pit. They avoided the humans, but their activity was ceaseless. The sides of the pit were not ordinary earth. All the way down to the pool, this was moundstuff. It had to be old, the detritus of thousands of years of towers, but it was still used by the tiny creatures. The stones in this "soil" must have washed down from the hills to the north. The coming of humans was a recent event in the hives' history.

The towers of the village crowded around three sides of the pit, but beyond the broken southern lip, they could see the harbor. The Tarulle Barge was less than a quarter mile out. Deck piled on deck, loading cranes sticking out in all directions, masts and rising windmills into the reddish blue sky—the barge had never seemed so beautiful to Rey as now. Safety was just twelve hundred feet away; it might as well be on the other side of Seraph. An hour earlier, a hydrofoil had arrived from the ocean and docked in a starboard slip. There was no other boat activity, though Rey fancied he saw motion on the bridge: another meeting? And this time, a final decision to leave?

Most of the prisoners huddled on the north slope of the depression; the corpses were carried to the other side of the pit. The prisoners were

bright people. They'd had plenty of time to try to
figure a way out, and no success in doing so. The
arrival of Rey's group brought new hope, even
though the rescue had been a failure. For an hour
or two, there was renewed scheming. When it
became clear that nothing had really changed, the
talk gradually petered out. Many of the prisoners
drifted back to inward-looking silence.

There were exceptions. One thing Rey loved
about scientists was *their* love for speculation. Take
Tredi Bekjer, the little guy who spent the hours
coughing his lungs out. Tredi was a sickly fellow
who should never have been on the *Science* expedition in the first place. He was an anthropologist,
and the only captive who spoke fluent Hurdic. He
might be dying, but between spasms of coughing
he argued about the origin and future of their
captors. He predicted that—no matter what the
prisoners' fate—the ambush had doomed the
Termiter culture. Now, outsiders knew there was
petroleum nearby. When that news got to the
archipelagates, the Termiter Folk would have lots
of visitors. Even if the locals were not booted off
their land, they would be forced to make big
changes. In thirty years, there would be a *real* city
here.

There were others like Tredi, folks who could
walk through the gates of death, still arguing about
ideas. When the planning and the scheming was
done, these few still had something to talk about.
Rey found himself drawn in.

Janna Kats was the most interesting. Before spe-
cializing in Seraphy, she'd had lots of experience
with other branches of astronomy. And U Bergenton
had the best atronomers in the world—if you

excepted the Doo'd'en fanatics on the other side of
the world. Kats was just the sort of person he'd
been hoping to talk to, back when he thought
they'd find the *Science* in one piece. For minutes
at a time Rey could forget where he was, and what
his fate must be. Kats had had great plans for the
Seraph observatory. There should be good seeing
from the mountains behind the harbor. Ground
resolutions better than one hundred yards would
have been possible with the twenty-inch mirror.
The issue of intelligent life on Seraph might finally
be resolved. . . . Instead, the project had brought
them all to this pit.

Rey grunted. "Other things are happening in
astronomy. Things that aren't so dangerous. There
have been some fantastic discoveries at Krirsarque."
He described "Pride of Iron" and the spectroscopic observations it was based on. "Can you
imagine! With spectroscopy, we can know what
things are like on planets around other stars." He
sat back, waiting for Janna's reaction to this news.
It was one of the occasional pleasures of his job, to
be the first person in an entire archipelagate to
report a breakthrough.

Janna grinned back at him, but there was no
surprise in her expression. "Ha! That's one of the
results the U Tsanart people sent west with *Science*. During the last year, they've got good spectra on twenty stars in our sun's class. Every damn
one of 'em is metal rich. And we have other results too. We can measure radial motions with
this spectro stuff—" She laughed at the expression
on his face. "You've written a lot of high-flown
editorials about 'Spectroscopy, Key to the Universe.' Well, you may have understated the case.

Combine the spectral shift data with proper motion studies, and it's obvious our solar system is an interloper, just passing through the local star stream."

Outcast Star. The title flashed through Rey's mind. There were writers who could run with that idea—and surely would, if he got out of this alive. "You know, it's almost as if someone were picking on the human race," he mused. "Out of all the solar systems, that we should be on the low-metal one, the outsider." He didn't like the idea. It smacked of the theistic fantasy Cor Ascuasenya so loved: humanity as doormat to the gods.

"You've got it backward, my sir. Ever hear of the anthropic principle? Most likely, intelligent life exists on Tu *exactly because* we are different from the others. Think what an abundance of metals would mean. It's not just a matter of wealth, millions of ounces of iron available for large-scale construction. My guess is such concentrations of metals would change the surface chemistry so much that life would never develop."

Janna's middle-aged features were filled with a happy smugness, but Rey did not feel put down. He was imagining deadly, treasure-house worlds. "Or life might develop, but different than here. Why, there might be—"

Janna abruptly grabbed his arm. She was looking past him, her expression intent; his speculations were suddenly of zero interest. There were scattered gasps from the prisoners. He turned and looked into the harbor. The barge had lowered a boat to the water. It glowed with white light, a jewel in the reddening dimness. Then he realized that Tarulle had lit a flare at the focus of the bridge's signal mirror. Its light fell dazzling on the boat, which was nothing more than a freight lighter painted silver and white. Before the flare guttered out, two more were lit at other mirrors. They tracked the boat as it started toward shore.

The Termiter priests were suddenly shouting. One group of spear carriers ran to the south side of the pit, while others moved to the pet' vats and slid the covers aside. Priests dipped their torches into the vats—and the night exploded. The thunder went on and on, drowning the shouts of prisoners and villagers alike. Flame and smoke rose from the petroleum, swirls of red and black across the midnight eclipse. Hundreds of bats swarmed drunkenly in the superheated air, burning, falling. The stench of pet' was everywhere. The Termiters cowered back from the pyres they had created, but Rey saw a few priests near each, setting long poles against the sides of the vats. A few good pushes, and the prison pit would be wall-to-wall fire.

Some of the prisoners collapsed, their mouths open, eyes wide. They must be screaming. Beside him, Janna Kats had caught his arm in both her hands. Her eyes were clenched shut, her face averted from the fires. Something in Rey's mind retreated and suddenly he wasn't frightened. He wasn't brave; he simply couldn't grasp the reality of his imminent torch-hood. He looked back to the harbor. The firing of the vats hadn't stopped the boat. It floated serenely toward them, still lit by the Barge's flares. He strained to see what it was carrying. The oarsmen wore black robes, their faces hidden within deep cowls. Those weren't Tarulle uniforms, yet they were somehow familiar.

There was only one other person on the boat. She
stood at the bow, scorning all support. Her clothes
were white and silver, gleaming in the faraway
spotlights. Black hair cascaded around her face
and shoulders.

Now Rey understood this latest rescue attempt.
He damned and thanked Cor all at once for trying.

Tarulle doused the flares the instant the lighter
touched shore. In the roaring red dimness, the
figure on the boat was a vague thing. She did
something to her robes and suddenly was near
naked, and incredibly female. When she swung
over the railing, reddish silver glinted from her
breasts and thighs. The oarsmen followed, clumsy
black beetles by comparison. They started up the
hillside, and were lost to Rey's view beyond the
south side of the pit . . .

. . . but not lost to the Termiters'. The spear
carriers hadn't moved, but every face was turned
toward the approaching party. The priests by the
fire vats had dropped their poles, and stared in
shock. Janna's grip loosened. She tried to ask him
something, but even shouting mouth to ear, she
couldn't talk over the flames' roar. Rey could only
point to the rim of the pit.

A minute passed. Villagers at the southeast corner of the pit backed away . . . and the newcomers appeared. *By the Light*, what a job Cor had
done! It was strange to see—in the middle of
terrible, deadly reality—the incarnation of a hundred fantasies. This *was* Hrala, complete with a
contingent of the Sibhood Sinistre. The Sibhood
followed Hrala through most of the stories. Their
motives were beyond knowing, but seemed more
evil than not. Sometimes they were Hrala's deadli-

est enemies, sometimes her allies. When they were her allies, the rest of the world better watch out. The black-cowled figures hung silently behind her, looking a dozen times more deadly than any Termiter priests.

The fraud would have been nothing without its central character. Tatja Grimm had come to Tarulle an outsized waif. The makeup people had transformed her. Black hair lapped smooth down to her waist, a perfect copy of all the illustrations. Her body was evenly tanned, though all she wore was ribbon armor, and that only around her hips and breasts. If he hadn't seen the girl before, Rey never would have guessed that bosom was faked. She carried the blade named *Death*. Crafted of "magic metal," edged with diamonds, it was a living creature and one of Hrala's earliest conquests. Without her control, it would take up its original mission: to corrupt the powerful and scourge the Continent. In fact, the prop was carved from puffwood painted silver and edged with quartz. Any sharp blow would shatter it.

Tatja Grimm walked forward, *Death*'s flat resting on her shoulder as though it weighed pounds and not ounces. Cor had coached her well. Every motion was fluid, arrogant. She walked straight to a high point on the pit's rim. For a long moment, she surveyed the flaming vats and the priests. Not once did she look at the spear carriers. The villagers stared back, eyes wide. Rey could see the fear mounting in them.

Abruptly, Hrala's hand flashed out. She pointed at the vats and clenched her fist. The Barbarian Princess wanted those fires *out*. The Termiter priests scrambled to push the lids back onto the vats. Flames burst sideways, searing the priests, but one by one the lids were forced into place. There were scattered explosions; one of the vats trembled in its cradle. Then a great silence replaced the violence. For a long moment, everyone listened to the ringing in their ears.

Rey couldn't believe his eyes or ears. Did the Termiter priests actually believe the stories? Of course, the instant the girl opened her mouth the illusion would be broken.

The Grimm girl turned, gestured the chief Sib to stand close behind her. The cowled figure slid forward, servile and sneaky at the same time. That must be Coronadas Ascuasenya; she might be just close enough to prompt the girl. There was a hissing conversation between the two, broken off by an imperious gesture from the Princess. She looked back at the Termiters and finally spoke. The words rattled fast, diamond hard. They were not Spräk.

Tredi Bekjer gasped. He crawled the few feet that separated him from Rey. "That's Hurdic!"

Janna and Rey dropped to their knees beside him. "What's she saying?"

Bekjer listened a moment more. "Hard to follow. She speaks a deep Interior dialect. I've only heard it a couple times." He choked back a coughing spasm. "Says she's angry as . . . the hot pits of the earth. Termiters have no business holding her . . . property? prey? She means us, in any case. She demands reparations, replacements for the dead, and—" Tredi laughed and coughed at the same time "—and the return of the survivors."

The sharp-voiced speech ended. The Barbarian Princess stood waiting a reply. *Death* twitched in her hand, impatient to forego these diplomatic niceties.

A voice came from the priests. After a second, Rey recognized it as belonging to the tall Termiter. The words were tentative and quavery, totally lacking the menace Tatja/Hrala put into hers. Tredi continued his translation: "Local guy is explaining our blasphemy. Case you can't tell, he's practically wetting his pants. . . . If he doesn't punish us, the High Gods will torture-kill his people. And now Hrala is threatening to skewer his guts if he doesn't let us go. He's caught between two dooms."

Hrala had a reply. She swung *Death* from her shoulder and thrust it skyward. The fake metal gleamed red-silver, "diamonds" glittering. Her speech was as angry and decisive as before. Tredi's translation consisted of a single, soft-spoken, "*Wow.*" Janna punched his shoulder, and the little anthropologist remembered his listeners. "Whoever she is, she's wonderful. . . . She told the Termiter to remember his place, that he's too *low* in the scheme of things to *presume* upon the High Gods' vengeance. . . . I can't translate it any better; she packed a freight-load of hauteur into a couple sentences. She's telling him, if her property is offensive, then that's something between Hrala and the Gods."

Rey Guille looked from Tatja Grimm to the clustered priests. Hope was a sudden, wonderful thing. Every state religion he'd ever seen had a core of hypocrisy. That was why he'd been against bringing "Hrala" ashore—he knew the priests would never accept their theology suddenly incarnate. But Cor and the Grimm girl had taken the risk, and now, incredibly, the plan was working.

For several minutes the priests had no reply. They stood in a tight group, speaking in low voices. Around them, the spear carriers held their weapons loosely, their eyes never leaving Tatja Grimm. From beyond the rim, an anonymous voice called, "Hrala." After a moment, one of the spear carriers repeated: "Hra-la." The word was passed back and forth among the low-ranking Termiters. They pronounced the guttural "H" with a force and precision that made Rey wince. "Hra-la. Hra-la. Hra La. Hra La." The chant spread around the pit, a soft drumbeat.

One of the priests shouted; the chant stumbled, guttered out. After a moment, the priest continued. His voice was placating, but without the quavering fear of before. "New guy," said Tredi. "He's talking humble, sweet as sugar. Says that for sure Hrala's claim takes precedence over theirs, but. . . ." Tredi sucked in a breath. "*Bastard!* He says, in dealing with beings so deadly as the High Gods, his people need at least to go through the motions . . . of verifying Hrala's identity."

Another priest spoke up, his voice high-pitched and not nearly as confident as the first. " 'A mere formality,' the second jerk says."

"S-so what's the *formality*, Tredi!" Janna all but shook the little man.

Bekjer listened a second longer, then caught back a sob. "Nothing much. A little trial by combat."

Chapter 5

Rey's eyes stayed on Tatja Grimm all through this speech. She didn't flinch. If anything she stood taller now, her chin raised at the impudence of the "request." No amount of coaching could have taught her to do that; the girl was as gutsy as anyone he'd ever known. When the priest finished, her reply was immediate, a sharp three syllables filled with anger and arrogance.

" 'Certainly,' she says," Bekjer translated unnecessarily.

And Rey's hope fled as quickly as it had come. The girl looked down at *Death*, and for an instant he saw the gawky youngster who had come aboard Tarulle just a few days before. She wasn't afraid, just uncertain, feeling her way in a strange situation. The puffwood sword was a magnificent bluff, but they were beyond bluffs now. It couldn't cut butter, and it would shatter at the first blow.

The girl gestured imperiously at the chief Sib,

the one who must be Coronadas Ascuasenya. The Sib slid forward, and spoke hissingly into Hrala's ear. The rescue party was about out of options. No doubt they were heavily armed. If they acted quickly, while the tattered bluff had some credibility, they could probably fight their way back to the landing boat—and at least save themselves.

Hrala listened to the Sib for a moment, then interrupted. The two were arguing! It was consistent with all the stories, but why now? Cor's hissing broke into full voice for an instant, and suddenly he realized this was no sham. Hrala shook her head abruptly, and handed her sword to the Sib. Cor sank beneath the pretended weight of *Death*. She didn't have much choice now. She slunk back to the other Sibs, her fear obvious but suddenly in character: She held *Death* in her hands. As a Sib Sinistre, she could not be perverted by it (the Sibhood was already pretty perverse), but possessing *Death* and being possessed by it were very close things. It was a theme Rey himself had insinuated into the series.

Hrala turned back to the Termiter priests. She was smiling, and the anger was gone from her words; mocking arrogance remained.

"Says she's happy to fight, but it's no . . . fun . . . wasting *Death* on such easy prey as the Termiters. She'll fight with whatever weapons her opponent chooses."

That almost started the chant again. The priests shouted it down, and after a moment one of them carried a sword-club toward Hrala/Tatja. This fellow was no fighter, just an errand boy. He laid the club on the ground ten feet from the girl, then scuttled back to safety. Hrala let him depart, then stepped from the high ground to inspect the weapon.

"If she's from deep Inland, she's never seen a sword-club," said Tredi. "Spears and pikes are all the Inlanders have. Even on the coast, it's a cere-monial weapon."

This one was clearly for special occasions; the wood was polished, unmarred. Without metals or composite materials, true swords were impossible. It looked deadly all the same. In overall shape it was something between a club and a pike. Elabo-rate hooks and blades—of bone or obsidian—were set along its length. There was a spike of glassy blackness at one end, and a hilt at the other. A second grip was set halfway down the pole; per-haps the thing could be used like a quarterstaff.

Hrala/Tatja picked it up, clearly as mystified as Rey. Somehow the puzzlement didn't take her out of character: she smiled her curiosity, seeming to say *how interesting, how clever*. He couldn't tell if she were acting or if this were the same frank wonderment he'd seen in her before. She swung it through a couple of clean arcs, then paused, glanced hesitantly at Cor and the others. Rey understood; this was her last chance to cut and run. Cor started toward her, but the girl turned away and shouted at the priests.

"She says she's ready."

Rey scarcely realized he was holding his breath. The girl *could win*. The spear-carriers were al-ready sold on the fraud; none of them could fight effectively. The more cynical priests weren't fooled, but they were exactly the sort that let others do their fighting. Who did that leave? Mental subnor-mals, too stupid to be afraid?

The crowd of priests parted and someone very broad and heavy started up the incline toward Tatja Grimm. The man's gait was slow, almost shambling. Even from here Rey could see the dullness in his features. *Thank the Light!*

Then he saw the second one.

They were nearly identical: giant, stupid . . . and armed. They carried their sword-clubs before them, both as threat and shield. Each was dressed in heavy leather. It was primitive armor, but at least real; Tatja Grimm was virtually naked, what armor she wore a gaudy fake.

Together, they outweighed her three to one.

The two separated as they approached the girl. They stopped ten feet from her, and for a moment the combatants stared at each other. Rey thought he saw traces of anxiety in the dullards' manner; you'd have to be a vegetable to ignore the mood of the villagers and the deadly confidence that came from the enemy.

Twenty years of fantasy collided with reality tonight—and for an instant the fantasy seemed the truer vision. The scene would have made a perfect cover painting: Hrala standing straight and fearless before a pair of subhuman attackers, a city of towers spreading on and on behind her. The last blue had disappeared from Seraph's eastern ocean. The disk shaded from brighter reds to darker. The cloud of tarry smoke from the pet' vats still hung in the air, roiling Seraph's continents out of all recognition. Everything—towers, prisoners, priests, fighters—was lit with shifting reds. It was the color of blood, *Hrala's color,* the background color of her most chilling battles.

A priest shouted at the swordsmen, and the

moment passed. They came in from opposite sides, their bladed clubs swinging. The girl grabbed her club at the hilt and foregrip and whirled between them. They were slow, and Tatja Grimm was terribly quick. That could only save her from quick death. She danced backwards, up the rise. She used the club like a staff, blocking. Blade fragments flew from every blow.

She bounded back three great steps, and moved both hands to the hilt of the club. She swung it in a quick sweep, her greater reach keeping the two back—till they separated again and came at her from the sides. Even so, she wasn't retreating now.

"She learns very fast," Tredi said to no one in particular.

But some lessons are learned the hard way. The bladed hooks were good for more than terror and disemboweling. One of her parries brought a crashing halt; her club had locked with the attacker's. The swordsman raised his club, swinging her slender body against him. Tatja kicked and kneed him. Even in his armor, the fellow staggered beneath the blows. The second attacker ran forward, rammed the point of his club squarely at the girl's torso. Somehow she sensed the attack, and threw herself backwards. The impaling thrust was turned into a deep slash across her chest.

She hit the ground and bounced instantly to her feet. For a moment the action stopped and the antagonists stared at each other, shocked. In the smoky red dimness, details were vague . . . yet the fake bosom still seemed to be in place. Everyone could see that the armor around her chest had been slashed open. Everyone could see the ripping wound across her breast. Everyone could see that Hrala *did not bleed*.

The second swordsman stepped backwards and whimpered. His tiny brain finally realized that he should be terrified. He dropped his club and ran from both priests and Hrala.

The first fellow didn't seem to notice. He flipped Hrala's club over his head and advanced on her. She didn't retreat, didn't try to rush around him to the discarded clubs; she stood with knees slightly bent, hands held open. Only when the bladed club swung toward her middle did she move—and then it was too fast for Rey to follow. Somehow she caught the foregrip of the club, used it as a brace to swing her body up and ram her foot into the other's throat. The blow jarred the club loose, and the two fell in an apparently random tangle. But only one combatant rose from that fall. The other lay twitching, the point of a sword-club struck through his skull.

The girl stared at the dying man. A look that might have been horror passed across her face; her arms and shoulders were shaking. Suddenly she straightened and stepped back. When she looked at the priests, haughty pride was back in her features.

"Hrala. Hra-la. Hra La. Hra La. . . ." The chant began again. This time, no priest dared shout it down.

Coronadas Ascuasenya had plenty of contact with the rescued during the next few days. Some recovered from the horror better than others. Janna Kats could laugh with good humor within ten hours of the rescue. The little anthropologist, Tredi

Bekjer, was almost as cool, though it would be some time before his body recovered.

But four days out from the village, some of the *Science* people were still starting at shadows, crying without provocation. And for every survivor, there would always be nightmares.

Cor had never considered herself especially brave, but she hadn't been trapped in that pit; she hadn't seen friends torture-murdered. Once they returned to the barge, and the village was irrevocably behind them, it was easy to put the terror from her mind. She could enjoy the Welcoming Back, the honor given her and Rey Guille and Brailly Tounse, the greater honor given Tatja Grimm.

It was as close to a storybook ending as could be imagined. Thirty-six from the *Science* had died. But nearly one hundred had survived the adventure and would return with the barge, much to the surprise of their sponsoring universities, who hadn't expected to see them for two years. When Tarulle sailed into the Osterlais—and later the Tsanarts—everyone would be instant celebrities. It would be the story of the decade, and an immensely profitable affair for the Tarulle Publishing Company. Whatever their normal job slot, every literate participant in the rescue had been ordered to write an account of the operation. There was talk of starting a whole new magazine to report such true adventures.

And management seemed to think that Cor and Rey had masterminded their publishing coup. After all, he had suggested the landing; she had produced Tatja/Hrala. Cor knew how much this bothered Rey. He had tried to convince Svektr Ramsey that he had fallen into things without the

least commercial savvy. Of course, Ramsey knew
that, but he wasn't about to let Rey wriggle free.
So Guille was stuck with producing the center-
piece account of the rescue.

"Don't worry about it, Boss. They don't want
the truth." Cor and the *Fantasie* editor were standing at the railing of the top editorial deck. Except
for the masts and Jespen Tarulle's penthouse, this
was as high as you could get on the barge. It was
one of Cor's favorite places: a third of the barge's
decks were visible from here, and the view of the
horizon was not blocked by rigging and sails. It
was early and the morning bustle had not begun.
A cold salt wind came steadily from the east. That
air was so clean; not a trace of tarry smoke. White
tops showed across miles of ocean. Nowhere was
there any sign of land. It was hard to imagine any
place farther from the Village of the Termite People.

Rey didn't answer immediately. He was watching something on the print deck. He drew his
jacket close, and looked at her. "It doesn't matter.
We can write the truth. They won't understand.
Anyone who wasn't there won't understand." Cor
had been there. She *did* understand . . . but wished
she didn't.

Rey turned back to watch the print deck, and
Cor saw the object of his interest: The man wore
ordinary fatigues. He wandered slowly along the
outer balcony of the deck. He was either lonely,
or bored—or fascinated by every detail of the railing and deck. Cor suspected the fellow wasn't
bored: Part of the Hrala fraud had been the demand that the Termiters replace her damaged
"property" (the dead from Brailly's party and the
Science). It seemed unwise to retract the demand

completely, so five unfortunate villagers were taken aboard.

This was one of them; he had been a Termiter priest, their spokesman/interpreter. Cor had talked to him several times since the rescue; he made very good copy. He turned out to be a real innocent, not one of the maniacs or hard-core cynics. In fact, he had fallen from favor when the cynics pushed for trial by combat. He had never left the village before; all his Språk came from reading magazines and talking to travelers. What had first seemed a terrible punishment was now turning out to be the experience of his lifetime. "The guy's a natural scholar, Boss. We drop the others off at the first hospitable landing, but I hope he wants to stay. If he could learn about civilization, return home in a year or so. . . . He could do his people a lot of good. They'll need to understand the outside world when the petroleum hunters come."

Rey wasn't paying attention. He pointed further down the deck.

It was Tatja Grimm. She was looking across the sea, her tall form slumped so her elbows rested on the railing and her hands cupped her chin. The ex-priest must have seen her at that instant. He came to an abrupt halt, and his whole body seemed to shiver.

"Does he *know?*"

Rey shook his head. "I think he does now."

In many ways the girl was different from that night at the village. Her hair was short and red. Without the fake bust, she was a skinny preteener—and by her bearing, a discouraged one. But she was nearly six feet tall, and her face was something you would never forget after that night.

The priest walked slowly toward her, every step a struggle. His hands grasped the railing like a lifeline.

Then the girl glanced at him, and for an instant it seemed the Termiter would run off. Instead, he bowed . . . and they talked. From up on the editorial deck, Cor couldn't hear a word. Besides, they were probably speaking Hurdic. It didn't matter. She could imagine the conversation.

They were an odd combination: the priest sometimes shaking, sometimes bowing, his life's beliefs being shot from under him; the girl, still slouched against the railing, paying more attention to the sea than to the conversation. Even during the Welcoming Back she had been like this. The praise had left her untouched; her listless replies had come from far away, punctuated by an occasional calculating look that Cor found more unsettling than the apathy.

After several minutes, the priest gave a final bow, and walked away. Only now, he didn't need the railing. Cor wondered what it must be like to suddenly learn that supernatural fears were unnecessary. For herself, the turn of belief was in the opposite direction.

Rey said, "There's a rational explanation for Tatja Grimm. For years we've been buying Contrivance Fiction about alien invaders. We were just too blind to see that it's finally happened."

"A visitor from the stars, eh?" Cor smiled weakly.

"Well, do you have a better explanation?"

". . . No." But Cor knew Tatja well enough to believe her story. She really was from the Interior. Her tribe's only weapons were spears and hand axes. Their greatest "technical" skill was sniffing out seasonal springs. She'd run away when she was eight. She moved from tribe to tribe—always toward the more advanced ones. She never found what she was looking for. ". . . She's a very quick learner."

"Yeah. A quick learner. Tredi Bekjer said that, too. It's the key to everything. I should have caught on the minute I heard how Jimi found her 'praying' to the noontime shadow of her quarterstaff. There she had reproduced one of the great experiments of all time—and I put it down to religion! You're right; there's no way she could be from an advanced civilization. She didn't recognize my telescope. The whole idea of magnification was novel to her. Yet she understood the principle as soon as she saw the mirror."

Cor looked down at the print deck, at the girl who seemed so sad and ordinary. There had been a time when Cor felt the start of friendship with the girl. It could never be. Tatja Grimm was like a hydrofoil first seen far astern. For a while she had been insignificant, struggling past obstacles Cor scarcely remembered. Then she pulled even. Cor remembered the last day of rehearsals; sympathy had chilled and turned to awe—as Cor realized just how *fast* Tatja was moving. In the future, she would sweep into a faraway Coronadas Ascuasenya could never imagine. "And now she understands us, and knows we are just as dumb as all the others."

Rey nodded uncertainly. "I think so. At first she was triumphant; our toys are so much nicer than any tribe's. Then she realized they were the product of centuries of slow invention. She can search the whole world now, but she won't find anything better."

So here she must stop, and make the best of things. "I–I really do have a theory, Boss. Those old stories of fate and gods, the ones you're so down on? If they were true, she would fit right in, a godling who is just awakened. When she understands this, and sees her place in the world. . . . She talked to me after the Welcoming Back. Her Spräk is good now; there was no mistaking her meaning. She thanked me for the Hrala coaching. She thanked me for showing her the power of fraud, for showing her that people can be used as easy as any other tool."

For a long while, Rey had no response.

PART II

THE IMPOSTOR QUEEN

Chapter 6

The tavern was old, luxurious—even respectable.
Its sloping floor and high ceiling created the illusion that the hall was an open bowl. Crystal spheres
cast an even, unwavering twilight over tables and
patrons. Svir Hedrigs squinted gloomily at the
newly polished table surface. Barely visible beneath the varnish were three centuries of minor
vandalism. Krirsarque had been a university city
for almost ten generations; unnumbered students
had carved their names in the durable furniture of
the Bayside Arbor.

It was still early and not a third of the tables
were occupied. The jongleurs were up on their
platform, playing songs and doing acrobatics. So
far their amusements had not drawn a single couple onto the dance floor. Svir grunted his disgust,
and extended long legs under the table. He absently caressed the furry body of the creature sitting on the table. The animal turned its outsize

71

head toward him and regarded him with limpid black eyes. A deep purring sound came from its wide, pointed ears. Then it turned away and scanned the hall. The ears that were not ears flicked this way and that. Far across the hall, a waiter looked severely in their direction, began walking toward them. When he got to within three tables of Svir, he stopped, puzzled, with the air of someone who has forgotten his purpose. The waiter shook his head confusedly and headed back to the bar.

"Good boy, Ancho," murmured Svir. Tonight he didn't want to argue with anyone about his pet's presence in the tavern. He had come out for one last fling before sailing tomorrow. Fling—hah! He knew he would just sit lumpishly till closing time. For the thousandth time he cursed his bad luck. Who'd have thought that his thesis topic would require him to sail all the way to Crownesse? Because of the season, that was more than ten days sailing time, unless one could afford hydrofoil passage—which he certainly could not.

The hall was filling now, but there weren't many unattached girls. Svir concluded with sick self-pity that this night he didn't have the courage to play either side of catch-and-be-caught. He slouched back and made a determined effort to finish his drink in one draft.

"May I join you?" The soft voice came from behind and above. Svir choked violently on his skaal. He looked up to see that the speaker was as pretty as her voice.

"Please do!" he gasped painfully, trying to re-gain some shred of poise. "Miss, uh . . . ?"

"Tatja Grimm." The miracle lowered herself

gracefully into the chair next to his, and set her
drink on the table next to Ancho's forepaws. Svir
felt himself staring. He constantly daydreamed of
encounters like this, but now that he was confronted by reality he didn't know what to do. In
fact, Tatja Grimm was not pretty: she was beautiful, beautiful in an especially wonderful way. From
a distance she would have appeared to be a slender girl with a superb figure and reddish-brown
hair. But Tatja Grimm was more than six feet
tall—nearly as tall as Svir himself. Her hands were
slim and delicate—and larger than the hands of
most men. But the most wonderful thing of all was
the look of genuine interest and intelligence in her
gray-green eyes.

"And your name?" Tatja smiled dazzlingly.

The wheels went round and Svir remembered
his name: "Svir Hedrigs."

Tatja rubbed Svir's pet about the neck. "And
that," spoke Svir, happy at finding something to
say, "is Ancho."

"A dorfox? They're awfully rare, aren't they?"

"Uh-huh. Only a few can survive ocean voyages."

Tatja played with Ancho for a few seconds. The
dorfox responded with satisfied humming. The human female was accepted.

But Svir's hopes were shattered almost as quickly
as they had crystallized. Three men came over and
sat down, without a word to him.

"Miss Grimm, did you . . . ?" one began. Then
he noticed the dorfox. The newcomers sat silently
and watched her and the animal. Svir didn't know
what was going on, but there was obviously more
competition here than he could handle.

Tatja Grimm looked up from the dorfox. "Men,

this is Svir Hedrigs. Svir, meet Brailly Tounse, Svektr Ramsey, and Kederichi Maccioso. They are respectively the printmaster, overeditor, and barge captain for Tarulle Publishing Company. I serve as the science editor for *Fantasie*."

Like hell. Svir knew he was naturally gullible. Once, in this very tavern, a couple of netscrapers managed to convince him they were hot-air balloonists. Since then, he had always been on guard. No way could his new "friends" be what they claimed. The Tarulle fastboats weren't due in the Krirsarque area for another three days. Svir had been very upset to learn that his ship would stay a day ahead of the Tarulle fleet as the publishing company sailed east through the Chainpearl Archipelagate. He wouldn't receive the latest copies of *Fantasie*—all two years' worth—until he reached Bayfast in Crownesse. In any case, people like Svektr Ramsey and Ked Maccioso were far too important to sail ahead of the barge, just for the sake of slumming in a Krirsarque dance hall. The frauds at his table had aimed far too high in their impersonation. Of all the literary corporations in the world Tarulle was the most prestigious. In a very real way, *Fantasie* had molded Svir's life: as a teenager, it had been stories like "Pride of Iron" that turned him to astronomy. Svir had long admired Rey Guille and the Overeditor, Svektr Ramsey. But never had he seen a Science Department in *Fantasie*, nor heard of Tatja Grimm.

Well, he determined, *I can trade you lie for lie.* Aloud, "So happy to meet you. I find a lot of your stuff especially provocative since my specialty is astronomy."

"An astronomer?" The over-muscled bruiser identified as Ked Maccioso seemed impressed.

"That's right," Svir affirmed. And, actually, he *was* an astronomer. But the others might assume from his unmodified assertion that he worked with the Doomsdaymen who manned the sixty-inch High Eye on the Continent. Life in the Doomsday mountains was a constant struggle against asphyxiation, cold, mountain apes, and Hurdic tribesmen. "I'm out here to deliver some speeches at Krirsarque University." This last was an inversion of the truth. Svir was a graduate student in astronomy at Krirsarque. For the last two years he had worked with the thirty-inch telescope at the university. The most recent journals from the Continent had brought news that the priests of Doomsday had duplicated some (or—gods forbid—*all*) of Svir's work. Now he had to journey to the coast to meet with the Doo'd'en and thrash the problem out.

"What's your preference in astronomy?" asked Tatja. "Seraphy?"

"No," replied Svir. Seraph was not visible from Doomsday. "I'm in positional astronomy. Using very delicate trig techniques, we measure the distances to some of the nearer stars." *And someday I'll do much more.*

"Really! I bought an article on that very subject for the latest issue." She snapped her fingers. "Brailly Tounse" reached into a side pouch and handed Tatja a magazine. She gave it to Svir. "See."

Svir gasped. There was the familiar masthead of *Fantasie*. In small letters beneath it were the words: "Issue of the 162nd Meridian. Whole Number 5,239." Here was physical proof that the Tarulle fleet had already arrived.

The cover was a Togoto pastel, at least the equal of that artist's Lindolef study. Svir opened it to the table of contents. Beneath the magazine's famous motto, "Things are not as they seem," were listed ten stories by authors from all over the world, including new works by Ivam Alecque and Enar Gereu. Svir flipped through the pages and came across one that caught on his fingers. It wasn't made of the usual seaweed pulp, but of some heavier, lacquer-coated material. At the top of the page was written: "Meet the *Fantasie* staff." There were six portraits, done in tones of green. They weren't acid-etch prints, or even paintings. Though green tinted, these pictures seemed realistic beyond all art. And one was a perfect likeness of . . . Tatja Grimm.

Svir wondered if he looked as embarrassed as he felt. These people were everything they claimed to be. And now Tatja Grimm was even more desirable—if that were possible—than she'd been before the others appeared.

Tatja placed her hand on his arm as she saw what he was looking at. "How do you like those pictures? It's something we picked up in the Osterlais. Those pictures are made by a machine that looks at its subject and instantly 'paints' the picture, just like in the Diogens stories." Her hand slipped down onto his. For a moment Svir's vision blurred. A warm glow spread through his body. "My picture is at the bottom there because the Science Department was only introduced last year, when Svektr here gave in to the increased popu-

larity of Contrivance Fiction. . . . How long have
you been acquainted with *Fantasie*?"

"Ever since I was in triform school. Ten years.
The Tarulle Barge has come through the Archipelagate five times in that period. I've looked forward
to each arrival more and more eagerly. I've worked
part time for the University Library's Restoration
Department, seen all the issues they have."

Tatja laughed, a friendly, intimate chuckle. The
men at the table receded into the far back of Svir's
consciousness. "Such restoration is a worthwhile
job. Did you know that in all Tu, there is only one
complete collection of *Fantasie*?"

"You mean the proof copies on the barge?"

"No. Not even the Tarulle Company has a complete version. Remember, there was a fire on the
Old Barge three hundred years ago; all the copies
to that date were lost. Up to twenty years ago
there were several complete collections, but a series of accidents has destroyed all but one." She
put a faint accent on the word "accidents."

Svir had never thought about it, but it was
possible that only one complete collection existed.
As the Tarulle Company toured the world, they
sold their magazines and printed extra copies to
drop off at later island chains. Delivery was quite
unreliable compared to a subscription service—such
as some island magazines used. Thus it was very
difficult to get a continuous sequence of issues.
And *Fantasie* was seven hundred years old. Even
though most issues had been recopied and their
stories anthologized—any major library contained
thousands of stories from the magazine—there
were still "lost" issues unavailable on the Chainpearls.

The person or government that possessed the complete set must be very wealthy and dedicated to culture. "Who has the collection?" asked Svir.

"The regent of Crownesse, Tar Benesh," Tatja answered.

Svir frowned. Tar Benesh had never impressed him as a man with deep cultural roots. He almost missed what Tatja Grimm said next. She wasn't looking directly at him, and her lips barely moved. She seemed to be preoccupied with something far away.

"It's too bad Benesh is going to destroy them."

"*What!* Why? Can't he be stopped?" His shocked questions tumbled over each other. Why would anyone want to destroy seven hundred years of *Fantasie*? The epic cycles, the ingenious short stories—all those glimpses into worlds-that-are-not—would be lost. Half the faculty of Arts and Letters at Krirsarque University would suicide.

Tatja's hand tightened around his. Her face came near to his. "Perhaps there is a way to stop him. With you and your dorfox perhaps—"

"*Please*, Miss Grimm, not here!" Ked Maccioso leaned forward tensely, at the same time glancing around the tavern. Svir's circle of attention expanded. He realized that now the Arbor was half full, the dance floor overflowing, and the jongleurs in fine form on their resonation platform. Tatja's presence had made him completely unaware of the changes.

She nodded to the barge captain. "I suppose you're right, Ked." She turned back to Svir. "When were you planning to return to the Continent?"

Return? Then Svir remembered the lie he had

implied. But he couldn't reveal his fraud to her now.

"I sail tomorrow for Bayfast."

"Would you like to come on the Tarulle Barge? It's slower than hydrofoil, but we'll get you there just the same."

"I certainly would." The words came spontaneously, but he felt no desire to retract them. Imagine sailing off with a beautiful, famous girl—into adventure. His previous reality seemed pale indeed beside these prospects.

"Why don't you come out to the Barge with us tonight. We'll show you around." She looked straight into his eyes. The men with her watched carefully, too. They couldn't talk here.

"Okay." Svir set Ancho on his shoulder. They stood and worked their way to the door. The music and party sounds faded as they descended the ancient stone stairs that led from Highrock to the wharves of the Krirsarque harbor.

There were people waiting by a lander. Soon the silent crew was paddling them out to sea. Apparently the landing was a secret. It was well into the night sleep period and no other craft were moving. A breeze swept across the water, splashed luminescent algae into the boat. The crew shipped their oars and raised a sail.

Half an hour passed. No one spoke. Ancho shivered quietly, fearful of the water. They left the glowing waters of the harbor behind. It was cloudy, so even the light of Seraph was denied them. Gradually Svir convinced himself there was a greater darkness on the water ahead of them. And then he was sure. The huge pile of the Tarulle Publishing Barge rose tier upon tier out of the ocean. Beside it floated the smaller forms of scout hydrofoils. All were without lights.

They pulled over to the hulk, and a group of company sailors hauled the little boat into a lighter bay. A section leader saluted Maccioso. She said, "XO's compliments, sir, and no exterior activity noted."

Maccioso returned the salute. "Have him take us out past the shelf."

Svir was escorted up a zigzag of stairs, into the heart of the vessel. They entered a luxurious, brightly lit room. Just maintaining the algae pots must have cost several man-hours a day. The five seated themselves around a table, on which was fastened a detailed map of Bayfast, the capital of Crownesse.

"This must all seem a bit melodramatic, Svir," spoke Tatja, "but Tar Benesh has an efficient spy system extending from Crownesse on the Continent all the way to the Osterlai Archipelagate. The regent is ambitious without limit. He—"

Ancho began nibbling at the map. As Svir pulled him back, the animal keened an almost inaudible whistle. For an instant everyone in the room felt stark terror. Then Svir patted the little animal, and the dorfox relaxed. The feeling of panic disappeared. Ancho turned his large eyes toward Svir as if to ask forgiveness.

Tatja smiled shakily. "Tar Benesh is an extremely intelligent, capable individual. He is also perverse . . . and mad. Since he came to power in Crownesse, he has been a collector of *Fantasie*. We believe that, to enhance the value of his collection, he has sabotaged the others."

"We know for a fact that he has destroyed other collections," Brailly Tounse interrupted.

"Every five years Benesh holds the Festival of the Ostentatious Consumption. You may have heard of it . . ."

Svir gulped. "You're not telling me that the *Fantasie* collection is going to be one of the sacrifices?"

Tatja nodded her head slowly. "Yes, that's it exactly. The Festival is scheduled to begin ten days from now. We plan to arrive in Bayfast on the night wake period of the Consumption." She gestured to the map of the Bayfast area and the detailed floor plans of the Crown's keep. "I can't go over the details of the plans now, but we are going to try to save that collection. Our magazine has the unconditional backing of the entire Tarulle Company—" she glanced at Maccioso "—in this venture. It's not going to be easy. But I think we could succeed if we had Ancho's help. And we need you too. You know Ancho best, and can persuade him to cooperate."

Svir glanced down at the little mammal, who sat licking his paws, unaware of the plans being made for him. "Yes," he answered, "dorfoxes are strange that way. It takes years to gain their loyalty."

"Svir, this will be dangerous. But we need you. And some of the stories Benesh has exist nowhere else. Will you come with us and help?" She was pleading.

Svir suddenly realized what he was being asked to do. He could get *killed*—and all for some magazines. Before now he had been uneasy at the mere thought of traveling to Crownesse, and now he was going to risk his life in a plot against the government of that country. Some sensible element within him was screaming *No, no, no!* But he saw the pleading in Tatja's eyes. He was hooked. "Yes," he quavered, then continued more strongly, feigning confidence, "I'll do anything I can."

"Wonderful!" said Tatja. She stood. "You'll want to go ashore and get your stuff together. Ked will have a boat take you back." The group left the room and walked toward the outer hull. About halfway there, Tounse and Ramsey left them for the typeset area. The walk gave Svir time for some heart-stopping second thoughts. He had a vivid imagination and it was working overtime now. Ancho responded to his fright, moving nervously on his neck.

They reached the landing bay, and Maccioso went off to get a crew. Tatja turned to Svir. She grasped his hand gently and moved close. "Thank you, Svir. *Fantasie* is the most valuable artwork in the world. I want to save that collection very much." She slipped her arms around him. He felt her body against his, her lips against his. His fears and half-conscious plans to junk the whole project were erased. He would be back.

Chapter 7

It was well past midmorning. Svir stood, with Ancho on his shoulder, at the edge of the deck that reinforced the barge's bowform. Tatja had said she'd meet him here and take him on a tour.

The Tarulle Barge was especially impressive by day. Over the centuries, it had grown without any overall plan. New barge platforms had been added and built upon, then built over again until the mass resembled nothing so much as a man-made mountain of terraces, cupolas, and cranes. The rigging and much of the hull were of spun glass— the most modern construction material. Yet some of the inner hulls were braced by timbers three hundred years old. From the top of the main mast to the bottom of the lowest hold was almost three hundred feet.

Now the filmy sails were stretched taut as the barge tacked across the Monsoonal Drag that blew steadily off the Continent.

Svir grabbed the railing to steady himself in the
wind. Just looking up at those masts was enough
to make him dizzy. He turned back to the ocean,
the whitecapped waves that stretched out to the
horizon. Two company fastboats cut through the
farther waters as they sailed out to minor ports of
the Chainpearl Archipelagate.

And the Tarulle fleet was not alone on the main.
Svir could pick out three cargo barges at various
distances. The Chainpearls lay along one of the
busiest trade routes on Tu. For all their cultural
importance, the publishing lines accounted for only
a small fraction of total ocean tonnage. Most publishing enterprises were operated landside, and
contracted with shipping companies to serve other
islands. Relatively rare were the huge publishing
barges, like Tarulle, which toured the entire world
and printed a variety of books and magazines.

"Hey, Svir!" Tatja's voice came clearly over the
wind. He turned to see her striding toward him.
Her hair was caught in a soft reddish swirl tied
with a clip to the front of her tunic. The wind blew
it back and forth to caress the side of her face. She
seemed small and delicate even in her coveralls,
but when she came near, her eyes were level with
his. Her smile sent a long shiver down his spine.

"I'm sorry we couldn't get together earlier in
the morning," she said, "but things are really moving around here. The Chainpearl run is always the
busiest of the circuit, and when we have monsoon
winds, every press is running at the breaking point."

"Uh, that's all right; I've had plenty to see," he
replied. As a matter of fact, the wake period had
been something of a bore so far. Since lunch he
had wandered about the decks. The crew was

distinctly hostile toward nonessential personnel. His ears still burned from insults received when he walked in a door marked TRIPULATION ONLY. These people weren't really stranger-haters. They just didn't want nonprofessionals messing up their work.

Tatja reached out to pet Ancho's neck fur. Ordinarily the little animal didn't enjoy being fondled by others, but he had taken a shine to Tatja. He didn't retreat from her hand, and after a moment began purring satisfaction. "Hello, Ancho. You don't look a bit seasick. . . . Keep a careful hold on him, Svir. Some of the areas I'll show you could upset him. But I want to see how hardy he is."

Ancho had recovered from his initial fear of sailing, though he clutched at Svir's shoulders more tightly than was necessary to maintain his perch. Dorfoxes came from a single island far around the world. They were long-lived and relatively infertile. Most became mortally seasick when taken aboard a ship. Ancho was an exception. Betrog Hedrigs, the great explorer and Svir's grandfather, had brought the animal to Krirsarque forty years before. Ancho was probably the only dorfox in the Chainpearls. Perhaps it was just as well, for if dorfoxes were common, they would have turned society upside down.

Svir and Tatja descended two flights of stairs, to the vat holds. This was a different world: the inside of a claustrophobe's nightmare. The wind was no longer audible, but there was an ominous creaking from the hulls. Dim orange light filtered from half-dead algae pots. Worst of all was the smell. Svir had been raised near the ocean, and generally enjoyed the odors of the sea. But here, the essence of those smells was being distilled.

Some of the workers actually smiled at them: Tatja's presence was safe conduct.

Tatja pointed to where the water was coming through the bowform. "The whole papermaking operation runs at just the speed that water can flow through these hulls. Not much vegetation in this part of the sea—that's good for the fastboats, and bad for papermaking. It's still worth seeing, I think."

The seawater flowed through the underpart of the barge like a subterranean river. Narrow catwalks hung inches above the dark water. Every forty feet they had to climb up a short flight of steps and then down again, as they moved from the hull of one barge platform to the next. They walked about two hundred feet through the gloom. Svir admired the graceful way Tatja moved along the catwalk, and cursed his own fearful, halting pace. Below them, the channels narrowed, and the stench of concentrated seaweed was overpowering. Workers dribbled reagents into the sludge, thickening it even more as it approached the pressing drums and its new life as paper.

Tatja gave a running account of what was going on. She also kept a close eye on Ancho for any signs of nausea or disorientation. But the dorfox seemed quite calm. It was a different story for Svir. The stench was beginning to get to him. Finally he asked, "How can the hull take these chemicals? I should think it would rot inside of a few quarters."

"That's a good question," Tatja responded. "The processing seems to have just the opposite effect. The carbonates in this sludge seem to replace the wood fiber. Over the years, the timbers actually become stronger. And what we discharge beneath the hull is so concentrated it kills any parasites that might nest there. Oops!"

She slipped on the walk. Svir's arm reached out and grabbed her waist as Ancho caught for his hair. The three of them teetered precariously for a moment. Then Tatja laughed nervously. "Thanks."

Svir felt obscurely proud. He might move more slowly than she, but when it came to a test, his caution paid off. He didn't remove his arm from her waist.

At last they reached the stern. Here the remaining water was pressed from the bleached sea mass, and the paper was actually formed. The fine sheets hung for several days before they were wound about drums and taken up to printing. They walked up to the next deck, where tons of newly printed magazines were stored. Here there was only a faint musty smell. Thank the gods the final product didn't smell like seaweed.

Tatja hung close on his arm and became more talkative. The Tarulle Company put out five different magazines every eighteen days. *Fantasie* and a couple of vice magazines accounted for three hundred thousand copies per issue and provided the bulk of the Tarulle income. Since some copies were stocked for as long as two years before they were sold, the barge carried two hundred tons of magazines. Over the centuries, it had been a race to keep up with world population increase. The barge was ten times as large as its first platform. All the latest machinery was employed. But even with increased landside printing and the prospect of automatic typesetting equipment, they were still falling behind.

They came to one of the loading slips. The sound of the wind was strong; beyond the huge hole in the hull was a bright panorama of sky and sea. A fastboat was moored here, its sails reefed and booms raised. A fifteen-ton load of magazines was being hoisted onto the hydrofoil by one of the barge's cranes.

They watched the scene for several minutes. Finally the operation was complete, and the boat pushed away from the barge. Its booms were lowered and the boomsails—like sheets on a clothesline—were hung out. As it moved out of the barge's wind shadow, it gathered speed, and the booms tilted into the wind. The whole affair lifted up on the slender stilts of its hydrofoils, and the boat moved away at nearly forty miles an hour. Then the barge's crewmen closed the loading port and everything was dim again.

Tatja frowned. "You know, I've always wondered why they tilt the boomsails like that."

Svir grinned broadly and gave her an explanation of Dertham's pressure theories, complete with an analogy to tacking. Her eyes showed scarcely concealed admiration. "You know, Svir, that's the clearest explanation I've ever heard of that. You ought to write it up. I could use some decent articles."

"Okay!" said Svir. Then he noticed the dorfox. "He's glazing over," he said, indicating the animal's eyes.

Tatja agreed, "So I see. We better cut things short. It's almost supper time anyway. Let's take a quick look at the print deck, and leave the editorial offices for later."

They went up another stairway and entered a low room filled with noise and whirling machinery. Svir wondered if all vessels were this crowded. It destroyed the romantic air he had always associated with far sailing. He kept a close hold on the dorfox and petted him comfortingly. This was no place for Ancho to run about unprotected.

There were two printing presses in the room, but only one was in operation. At one end of the machine, a yard-wide roll of sea-paper unwound and slid between rotating drums. The upper drum was inked, and with every swift revolution it pressed print on at least twelve feet of the flowing paper. Beyond this first pair of drums, a second pair did the same for the underside of the sheet. The paper finally moved under a glass flywheel that chopped it into neat, yard-square sheets that landed in a small dolly, ready to be taken to the cutting and binding section. The machine was driven by a spinning shaft that connected to windmills outside.

One of the printmen looked up angrily and started toward Svir. Then he noticed Tatja, and his manner changed. Up close, Svir saw that the ink-stained face belonged to Brailly Tounse. "Day, ma'am," Tounse shouted over the din. "Anything we can do for you?"

"Well, if you have a couple of minutes, could you describe your operation, Brailly?"

Tounse seemed momentarily surprised, but agreed. He took them down the print line and traced the progress of the paper through the machine. "Right now we're doing almost five thousand impressions an hour; that's about one hundred thousand pages after cutting. Sometimes we go for days scarcely idling, but when we move into the Drag we have to make up for every minute of it. I'm pushing these machines at their limit now. If you could get us a hundred ounces of iron, Miss Grimm, we could make more steel bearings, and run these things as fast as the wind can blow." He looked at Tatja expectantly.

She smiled and shouted back, "Brailly, I'll bet there isn't a thousand ounces of iron in the whole barge."

Svir was confused. Since when did a printmaster ask an editor for mechanical help—and for something as ridiculous as iron! Perhaps the fellow was just teasing, though he certainly looked serious enough.

Tounse grimaced, wiped a greasy hand over his bald head, leaving a broad black streak. The man was obviously exhausted. "Well," he said, "you might stick around and watch us install new boards on the other machine." He waved at the idle printing press.

Tounse's crew brought in sheets of rubbery printboard. The elastic base made it possible for them to stretch the type across the drum and fasten down the edges. The dur-sap type gleamed dully in the light. In a few moments it would be black with ink. When the first sheets were properly tied down, the workers moved down the line and tacked four more on the underside press. Then they hand-fed twenty feet of paper through the machine.

Tounse nodded to the man at the clutch. The gearing engaged. Perhaps the fellow released the clutch too fast. Or perhaps the gearing was fatigued. Whatever the cause, the machine was transformed into a juggernaut. Gears splintered and paper billowed wildly about him. The first print drum precessed madly and then flew off its spindle, knocking Tatja and Tounse against the first machine. The glass blade at the far end of the room shattered, and slivers flew everywhere. Whirling chaos lasted several more seconds.

Tounse seemed on the verge of breaking down himself: he had schedules to keep. Svir stepped around the wreckage to help Tatja.

"Svir—where's Ancho!"

The dorfox was gone. Tatja bounced to her feet and swore. "Tounse! Forget your damn machines. We've got to find that animal." Soon Tounse and his whole crew were searching the print deck for Ancho. Svir wondered briefly if the dorfox could be deceiving them with an "I'm-not-here" signal. Ancho hadn't pulled a trick like that in five years, though gran'ther Hedrigs claimed it was the dorfoxes' most common defense in the wild. If Ancho had not been killed in the mangle, he was probably scared witless. Panic would drive him outside and to some higher deck.

Svir left the others and ran outside. He glanced quickly about and ran up to the next level. Soon he had reached a deck of masts and windmills. He stopped, gasping for breath. From the sails and rigging above him came a continuous, singing hum. He was alone except for a single sailor in a short semiskirt. She was climbing a rope ladder that stretched down from the tallest mast. Svir wondered what she was doing. The rigging should be adjustable from the bridge; besides, it was too windy to climb safely. Then he looked past the girl. Almost forty feet above her, he saw Ancho's furry form. Svir ran toward the mast.

The dorfox continued up the rope. He had panicked completely. Ancho was trying to retreat from all the things that frightened him, and up was the only direction left. Svir debated whether he should follow the sailor, then saw that it would just upset her precarious balance. The wind blew the ladder into a clean catenary form. As the sailor rose higher, she was forced to climb with her back to the ground and the rope above her. Ancho was radiating helpless distress—even down the deck it made Svir faint with fear. For a heart-stopping instant it looked as if she were going to fall. Her feet slipped from the rope and she hung by one hand from beneath the ladder. Then she hooked her leg around the ladder and inched forward. She was no longer climbing. One hundred fifty feet above the deck, the ladder was blown horizontal.

Finally she reached Ancho. She seemed to coax him. The dorfox clutched at her neck. The two came slowly down the long, curving ladder.

The girl collapsed at the base of the mast. Ancho released his tight hold on her and scuttled over to Svir.

Svir held the whimpering animal as he helped the sailor to her feet. She was a bit taller than average, with black hair cut in short bangs. At the moment her face was very pale. "That was a brave thing you did," said Svir. Without doubt, she had saved the animal's life. "You really know how to handle those ropes."

The girl laughed weakly. "Not me. I'm a translations editor. Llerenito editions mainly." She spoke in brief, anguished spurts. Her mind knew she was safe now, but her body did not. "That's the first time I ever climbed them. Oh gods! Every time I looked down, I wanted to throw up. Everything looked so far away and hard."

She sat back down on the deck. She was shaking as much as Ancho. Svir put his hand on her shoulder.

"I like to come up here on my free time," she said. "Your animal came running across the deck like his tail was on fire. He just grabbed the ladder and climbed. I could tell he didn't want to climb, but he was terrified of whatever chased him. Every few rungs, he'd stop and try to come down. I—I had to do something."

As she spoke these words, Tatja arrived. She ran over and inspected Ancho with a careful, expert eye.

She didn't say anything for several seconds, though she favored the girl with a long, calculating glance. *Could Tatja be jealous?* thought Svir, surprised. Finally Tatja turned to Svir and smiled. "Svir Hedrigs, be introduced to Translations Editor Coronadas Ascuasenya. Coronadas Ascuasenya, Astronomer Svir Hedrigs."

"Pleased." The girl smiled hesitantly.

"Tatja, Coronadas climbed almost to the top of the mast to save Ancho."

"Yes, I saw the last of it. That was a brave rescue." She petted Ancho. "I just hope we haven't wrecked the dorfox. We were fools to take him along this morning." She looked up at the sun, which was just past the zenith. "We might as well get some dinner. It's too late to start any training. We can begin this evening." Svir wrapped Ancho in his jacket, and they returned to the lower decks.

Chapter 8

The sun was three hours down before they began. The night was clear and Seraph lit both sea and barge in shades of blue.

Tatja had used paperboard partitions to simulate a hallway within Benesh's keep. She had constructed the mock-up on a deck out of the wind and hidden from the view of other ships. "I'll admit it's pretty crude, but we don't need anything elaborate just yet," she said. "The dimensions are the same as inside the Keep. You can see side passages opening off the main one."

Svir walked to the entrance of the maze. It certainly wasn't very convincing. The ceiling of the passage was purple sky. Company sailors were to simulate the Royal Guards of the Keep. They didn't seem too certain of just what was expected of them.

Tatja reached past Svir's shoulder to pet Ancho. "We want Ancho to make these 'Guards' hallucinate. It's going to take some practice, but I want him to convince whoever he points those pretty ears at that you constitute an authority figure."

Svir tried to break the news gently: "I doubt if that's possible. Dorfoxes aren't very bright. It seems to me that in order to generate a detailed illusion, Ancho would have to be humanly bright."

Tatja shook her pretty head. "Nope. The intelligence of the victim provides all the background detail. I've spent some time on Dorfox Island, and I know things like that are possible. C'mon, let's start, or we'll still be at it when we pull into Bayfast."

Ancho was usually sluggish at night, but he perked up noticeably when Tatja had a large bowl of rehydrated *klig* leaves brought on deck. He strained to push his nose past the bowl's cover, but it was securely fastened. The dorfox would have to earn his treats. Svir's father had often played games like this with Ancho, and had managed to teach him a number of tricks.

Svir stepped back from the *klig* leaves and put Ancho on his shoulder. The "Royal Guards" had assumed their posts in the passageway. He saw Cor Ascuasenya standing at the far end of the mock-up.

Tatja stood behind Svir. In this position she could watch what happened with relative impunity, since Ancho was not likely to turn around and broadcast in her direction. "All right, Svir, give it a try. Let's see if Ancho will give us a demonstration."

Svir walked slowly through the mock-up. Everything seemed quite normal. But then, Ancho rarely aimed his illusions at his master. . . .

When he was through, Tatja asked the first sailor what he had seen.

The fellow looked at her a little blankly. "What do you mean? When are you going to start the test?" The others were similarly confused. None of them had been conscious of Svir or Ancho as they walked down the hall. Tatja unfastened the lid on the *klig* bowl.

"That was a good performance," she said. "Ancho managed to scan every person as you walked past. Now we have to make him try other effects, till he produces exactly what we're looking for." She fed Ancho two leaves. The little mammal sucked on them greedily, momentarily enraptured. When he was done he reached out for more, but Tatja had already relocked the basket.

Svir petted Ancho, who appeared to enjoy the game. "You know, Tatja, Ancho is really dependable with that I'm-not-here signal. And he can scan a lot of people at once. Why can't you settle for that?"

"Being invisible isn't enough. You'll be going all the way to the center of the Keep—to the vault where the most precious sacrifices are kept. With Ancho's I'm-not-here, you *probably* could steal the Guards' keys. But what if some of the doors have combination locks? You need more than the Guards' passive acceptance. They must actively help you. And there are more than five thousand volumes in the *Fantasie* collection. That comes to at least two tons. You'll need help getting them out." She picked up her noteboard and pen. "Let's try it again."

And again. And again.

Ancho soon learned that anything he tried would

earn him some reward, but that if he repeated a previous performance, the prize was smaller. So he tried to come up with a new effect on each try. They soon exhausted the natural dorfox responses, the projections which served so well on the dorfox's native island. Some of these could drive away predators or dull their senses. Others attracted insects and lulled their suspicions.

Ancho also tried the tricks he had been taught since arriving in civilization. On one pass all the crewmen in the passage broke into fits of hysterical laughter. Cor Ascuasenya had the giggles for fifteen minutes after Ancho came by. What they saw was hilariously funny, though they couldn't explain to Tatja and Svir just why.

Each trial was a little different than the last. Tatja had innumerable variations to suggest. But after the first half hour, the project was awfully boring. For the sailors it was also uncomfortable. Ancho had put them through an emotional wringer. In one twenty-minute period he made them laugh and cry. He had responded eagerly to all the attention showered upon him, but now was beginning to lose interest. And he had yet to display any behavior Svir had not seen previously. What Tatja was asking of Ancho was quite unrealistic. A half-guilty feeling of relief grew in Hedrigs. He really wanted to help Tarulle Company with the rescue. Even more, he wanted to help Tatja. But it was beginning to look as though he would not have to risk his life, after all. He wasn't exactly eager to stick his nose into the business of Tar Benesh.

For the hundredth time, Svir started down the mock passageway. He was still surprised by the respect and obedience these sailors showed Tatja.

She must have more authority on the barge than her title indicated. When she made a suggestion in her low, pleasant voice, people hustled. It was evidence of how the best people rose to the top in any organization. What had he done to deserve her?

"Damn it, man, stand up straight when you walk!" It took Svir an astonished second to realize that Tatja was speaking to him. "Come back and start over. How can you expect the dorfox to cast an illusion of authority if you drag about like an addled tri-form student?"

Svir bit back a sharp reply. He walked to the beginning and started over. He almost swaggered down the passageway, imitating the gait of a Crownesse bureaucrat he had once seen at a university dinner in Krirsarque. The effect was subtle. Suddenly he was no longer pretending. He actually felt important and powerful, the way he had always imagined politicians and generals must feel. It seemed only natural that the sailors should snap to attention as he passed them. He returned their brace with an informal salute. The feeling of power disappeared when he came to the end of the passage.

Tatja smiled. "Wow! Cor, what did you see when Svir walked by you?"

Ascuasenya looked confused. She glanced from Tatja to Svir and back again. "When I first looked at him coming down the hall, I could swear it was my father—but my family is in the Llerenito Archipelagate! Closer, I saw that it was Captain Maccioso. I mean, I knew it was Svir—it had to be. But it was Ked Maccioso at the same time. Even now when I look at him, I see Maccioso—

and yet I see Svir, too." Svir glanced at Ancho's ears. They weren't pointing at Cor. The illusion persisted even after the dorfox stopped radiating.

Tatja didn't say anything for a second. She made a note in her book and looked up. "Can you see Ancho sitting on Svir's shoulder?"

Cor squinted. "No. All I see is that queer double image I just described."

The others had similar reactions. About half saw Svir as Tatja. These people were especially confused, since they were seeing *two* Tatja Grimms. Every one of them realized that Ancho's trickery was involved, and all but two could see Svir behind the illusion.

Svir was amazed. Even Gran'ther Betrog had never mentioned anything like this. But what practical use was it? A half-baked illusion that wasn't even uniform. It would never fool the Royal Guards.

But Tatja seemed to feel otherwise. She finished writing in the notebook and looked up, smiling. "Well, we've done it. The illusion is one of the strongest I've ever seen. It persists even in the face of contradiction-to-fact situations. See, Svir, all you have to do is *act* confident. Ancho knows you and will radiate the same thing. I really didn't mean to jump on you."

Svir nodded, still blushing from the unexpected attack. Her technique worked, but it was shocking.

Tatja continued, "We'd better knock off now. Ancho's losing interest; by now he's crammed full of *klig* leaves. And most of you look pretty dragged out. Let's have another session after lunch."

During the rest of the voyage they had three hours of practice in every wake period. Toward the end, Ancho was able to broadcast the authority signal even better than he could the I'm-not-here. He also grew fat on the *klig* leaves, assuming an almost spherical form. Tatja had him perform his new trick under every conceivable condition—even in the dark, down in one of the holds. They found that if a single authority figure were suggested to all the "victims," then they all saw that same person. It took Ancho only a fraction of a second to set up the illusion in the human mind, and it persisted without booster treatment for almost ten minutes. Ancho could detect people hiding behind bulkheads, and could even project the illusion through many feet of stone.

One experiment was a mystery to Svir. Tatja produced a flat *balsir* box and strapped it to Ancho's back. He didn't seem to mind; the box was light and apparently the straps didn't chafe. The contraption looked vaguely like an oversize cookie cutter—its profile was an irregular set of semicircles and lines. Stubby cylinders of glass and wood projected from either side of the box. On top was a little hole, like the keyhole in a clock. And the device clicked almost like a clock when it was mounted on Ancho's back.

Tatja refused to reveal the purpose of the contraption. She said it was a last precaution, one whose usefulness would be impaired if Svir knew its purpose. He couldn't imagine what sort of precaution would have such properties, but he accepted her explanation. Perhaps it was empty— a placebo to give him the false confidence necessary to trigger Ancho's authority signal.

The drag kept Tatja busy—even busier than the general run of the crew. Outside of their practice sessions, Svir was with her only two or three hours in every wake period. He actually saw more of the translations editor, Coronadas Ascuasenya. It was surprising how often he found her eating at the same time and in the same meal hall as he. He came to enjoy those meals more and more. Ascuasenya was older than she looked. She'd been with Tarulle almost seven years. She'd actually worked with Rey Guille, and had met most of the authors who had shaped Svir's world view. She was no competition for Tatja—how could anyone be?—but Cor was pretty and intelligent and very nice to be with.

Svir spent the rest of his free time in the barge library, where Tatja's influence had opened some otherwise locked doors. Only fifteen or twenty people out of the thousand on board were allowed in the library, but once inside there was no restriction on use of materials. Here Tarulle kept copies of all available issues of magazines published by the company. That amounted to about twenty thousand volumes. Jespen Tarulle was in the publishing business to make money, but he had a sense of history and the barge library was the most luxurious part of the craft that Svir had yet seen. Here was none of the cramped stuffiness of the lower decks. Virtually none of the sea or ship noises were audible through the thick glass windows. Deep carpets covered the floor. During the night wake periods, well-tended algae pots supplemented Seraph's light. The librarian was a strange old bat. He was helpful enough, showing Svir how to find just what he wanted in the stacks. But he treated the magazines with an awe that went beyond Svir's. You'd think he was a priest in

a temple. Wherever Svir went in the stacks, the
gangling librarian was sure to follow, lurking in
wait for some desecration.

Maybe the guy wasn't nuts. To a confirmed
Fantasie addict, the library was halfway to heaven.
The Tarulle collection was nearly three quarters
complete—more than four thousand issues. That
was better than any library on the Chainpearls.
There were several copies of the first issue, printed
just forty years after the invention of movable
type. In those years the magazine was sold in
yard-square sheets, folded into quarters. Only rarely
was a story illustrated, and then with crude wood-
cuts. But that was part of the enchantment. On a
single barge—the predecessor of the present compound vessel—they had printed such works as
Delennor's Doom and *Search for the Last King-
dom,* novels that after seven hundred years were
still studied by poets and read with enjoyment by
near illiterates. And here he could see the origi-
nals, genius seen direct across the centuries.

That first barge had been owned by an ambitious trading family distantly related to the present
publisher. In the beginning, the barge carried general trade between the islands of the Osterlai group,
at the same time providing regular and vital communication between those islands. As the publishing sideline became more profitable, the family
gave up their other trading operations and visited
islands further and further asea. The lands beyond
the horizon provided ever more enchanting themes
and original authors. *Fantasie* readers were the
first, and for a long time the only, cosmopolitans
on the planet.

The magazine's success was not without repercussions. The effects of the first interplanetary fantasy were shattering both for the magazine and for the rulers of the Tsanart Archipelagate. Ti Liso's *Migration* foreshadowed the rise of contrivance fiction. Liso's hero discovered a species of flying fish, which during the winter season in the northern hemisphere migrated to the southern hemisphere of Seraph. The hero captured several of the vicious creatures and taught them to pull his sailing boat. After an eight-day flight the fish deposited him, half-starved, on the south polar continent of Seraph. The story went on to describe the civilization he found there. It was an unfortunate coincidence that Liso's Seraphian government was an absurd dictatorship founded on Tu-worship—for the tyrannical government of the Tsanarts was just such a farce in reverse. In plain fact the story had not been intended as satire. It had been written as straight adventure. Liso, a native of the Osterlais, had honestly conceived the most ridiculous autarchy imaginable. The Seraphiles of the Tsanarts did not take it as a joke, and for the next fifty years, until the fall of their religion, Tsanart waters were forbidden to the barge. This was an especial hardship, since the technique for sailing to the windward was not fully developed at that time. Avoiding the Tsanarts cost many tens of days sailing time.

Each day brought Svir closer to the coast of the Continent, closer to Bayfast. Back in Krirsarque, the prospect of invading the Crownesse Keep had seemed a faraway adventure. But now he was coming to realize that it was a reality which he personally would have to face. More and more he spent his time in the library, in retreat from the nightmare that approached. He had always found refuge in *Fantasie*, and now he dived into the more recent stories with a vengeance. Sometimes he could avoid thinking of his own problems for hours at a time. Despite the literary past, he enjoyed the recent stories most. The straight fantasy themes had been handled in every conceivable way in the past seven hundred years. It was only in the last two hundred that the idea of physical progress had emerged; the idea that there could be mechanical means of achieving fantastic ends. In the last fifteen years nearly half of *Fantasie*'s output had been cf.

Hedrigs read straight through Enar Gereu's new serial. Gereu was a biologist from the Sutherseas. His science was usually strong and this novel was no exception. Like many authors, he assumed the discovery of large metallic deposits on the Continent. Such deposits made possible the construction of huge metal machines—machines powered by the same as-yet-unexplained mechanism that made the sun shine. As far as Svir could tell, this story contained a genuinely original idea—one that he wished he had thought of first. Instead of going directly to Seraph in his metal "ships of space," Gereu set up way-stations, artificial satellites in orbit about Tu.

The ultimate landing on Seraph produced deadly peril. Gereu populated the other planet with a race of intelligent animalcules. Svir choked—this fellow was supposed to be a biologist? But on the next few pages the author justified the alien life form in a manner quite as logical and novel as his space-island idea. Svir found himself totally caught up in the story as the human race fought to protect itself from the menace brought home by the explorers. The struggle was one of the most suspenseful he had ever read. Things looked hopeless for humankind. . . . He turned the last page.

The dirty bastard! Svir's feeling of warm anticipation was suddenly shattered. Gereu let the human race fall before the invaders! He suppressed a desire to rip the magazine up into small pieces. The shock was like finding a snake in *schnafel* pastry. Wasn't there enough tragedy in the real world? He had seen far too many stories of this type lately. Feeling quite betrayed by Messrs Ramsey and Gereu, the young astronomer stood up and stomped out of the library. He scarcely noticed the librarian rush forward to secure the abandoned magazine.

Svir stopped on the deck near his cabin. It was past midday. Far above him the wind whistled through the empty rigging and mastwork. Just two miles away the brown and gray cliffs of Somnai rose abruptly from the ocean, hiding Bayfast from view. Where the surf smashed into the base of Somnai, the coastal plankton formed a glistening green band. In this longitude Seraph hung almost thirty degrees above the horizon, its bluish crescent wraithlike in the daytime sky.

The scene had no appeal. Svir cupped chin in palm and morosely inspected the pitted guard railing he leaned against. Even in *Fantasie* there was no escape. Reality could not be ignored: For all practical purposes they had reached Bayfast. He'd heard Kederichi Maccioso was treating with the Port Commander for permission to land. There was some problem about getting pier space, but that would be cleared up, and come this afternoon they would be sailing right past the Regent's Keep into the Hidden Harbor. And tonight he, Svir Hedrigs, would be risking his life to save some damned collection of old magazines.

Chapter 9

Coronadas Ascuasenya had made a careful analysis of the astronomer from Krirsarque: Hedrigs was a wimp, a naive kid who was following his libido straight to destruction. So why was she hung up on him?

The kid was tall, too skinny to be really good-looking. But he was bright, with an imagination that sparkled as she remembered Rey Guille's had. And if he lived long enough, he might eventually grow up. She knew he was Betrog Hedrigs's grandson; that should count for something. Old Betrog was the first to trek across the Continent, and the story of that expedition was a hair-raising thing.

So Cor watched and waited and wondered how directly she dared interfere. Finally there was no time left. The dope would be dead if she waited another day.

She found him at the railing just outside his

cabin. He didn't look up till she was at the railing beside him.

"Hi, Cor."

"Hi." She smiled. They stood for a moment silently, watching the sparkling sea. Then she said, "It's tonight, isn't it?"

"Yeah," casually.

"Svir . . . don't go through with this thing." So much for the subtle approach.

"Huh?" He looked at her in some confusion. "Why not?"

"Magazines are *things*; they are not people. They are not worth dying for. And I think you would die. Crownesse is the most powerful country in the world. When we move into port, we'll pass Hangman's Row. They play rough here."

"I agreed to do it, Cor. And I owe it to Tatja." But there was fear on his face.

She took a deep breath and started over. "You don't owe her one thing. Tatja Grimm is . . ." *what?* Cor stumbled on the question that had haunted her the last five years, the question that had eventually driven Rey Guille from the barge. "You've been used. Can't you understand that? Tatja Grimm is not a very nice person." The first statement was true; the second was beyond Cor's knowing.

Svir scowled. "You can't expect me to believe that. I've watched the crew working with her. She gets more wholehearted cooperation and respect from them than any officer."

Cor sighed. "Yes, she is truly popular." Five years ago Grimm could barely understand Språk. After the Termiter incident things changed and changed again. Her vision, her invention, her

scheming had increased Tarulle wealth more than
it had grown in the previous century. "So popular
she is, you should guess that she runs everything
of importance here. The people you think are
boss—Jespen Tarulle, Ked Maccioso, Svektr Ramsey—love and fear her. They've benefited by everything she's done.

"And she's at least as talented when it comes to
mechanical things. She designed the power trains
they use in printing. She invented the special
sailing rigs we have on our hydrofoils."

Svir looked up sharply at this last claim, and his
face reddened. After a moment, he said, "And
you? How are you free of this 'spell'?"

Another mystery Cor had spent five years trying
to understand. When she didn't answer, Hedrigs's
tone became angrier. "And if she has done all you
say, why do you think the plan to save the *Fantasie*
collection will fail?"

"Before, increasing the wealth of the Barge increased Tatja's power. Now . . . now I think she's
run us as far as she can. She's never before messed
with groundside politics. And even if the scheme
succeeds, *you* may not.

"I . . . I don't want you hurt, Svir. Tatja is not
precisely evil. But she is beyond my understanding. And I know that if it would further herself,
she'd put your life in jeopardy. Besides, I . . .
want you myself." Her voice dropped almost to a
whisper.

Svir seemed to soften. The things Cor had said
became more understandable and more excusable.
"I'm sorry, Cor. I didn't know you felt that way.
But you're wrong. Tatja is wonderful. And I love
her."

Wimp. "No! Just let me show you. Can you make Ancho broadcast that I'm-not-here signal?"

"Yeah." Svir petted the animal sitting on his shoulder. "He's almost seemed to enjoy things these last couple of days. If he knows that something is expected of him and yet I don't pull that confidence act, he'll generally broadcast the I'm-not-here."

"Fine. Let's use him to do eavesdropping. I'll give you odds five-to-one that Tatja Grimm will be doing something you will find out of character."

Svir seemed shocked by her vehemence. He suddenly seemed in search of excuses. "It's kind of late, you know. She's probably asleep."

"Sleep? She does very little of that." She caught his arm. "C'mon." Cor led him fifty yards aft and down a couple of flights. They were well into the day sleep period, and hardly anyone was about. The mast watch could detect any hostiles approaching the vessel, but they were not well placed for observing the deck itself.

Finally Svir and Cor stood below the balcony of Tatja's office. This was Cor's last chance to back down. A terrified chill enveloped her. She had never crossed Tatja before, never really wanted to. Those who had—or who couldn't accept what Tatja was—were all gone now. None had been killed; most had been left better off than before. Rey Guille had been set up with a cute little vice editor, and left with a groundside publishing career. But those earlier antagonists were never immediate threats to Tatja's interests.

Svir cuddled Ancho. "Stay close, Cor." He climbed one of the pillars, then gave Cor a hand up. Anyone outside Ancho's range could see them, but it was too late to worry about that; they were committed.

They crawled to the office window and peeked over the sill. The office was almost as large as the barge library. These last five years, the Tarulle Barge had used a considerable fraction of its new fortune to support Tatja Grimm's strange hobbies. Walls and racks were piled high with Grimm unintelligibilia: floor plans of the ruins at Alt-Llerenito were draped over copies of the earliest writing found in the Tsanarts. Dozens of boxes held sea floor core samples Grimm had collected from all over the world. Black cloth hooded her daytime/nighttime experiments.

Tatja sat at her desk, her face in profile. Cor sucked in a breath, and grabbed Hedrigs's arm. His mouth hung open, but he had the sense to know this was not the time to ask questions.

This was not the Tatja Grimm known to the world outside. There was the same face, that same red hair. But gone was the shapely body that no doubt had been such an attraction for Svir Hedrigs. Her jacket draped flat across slenderness. For the real Tatja Grimm was pre-menarche; nearly eighteen years old, yet still with the body of a twelve-year-old. Cor guessed there were only three—now four—people on the Barge that knew this secret. The past five years had proved it to be dangerous knowledge.

Tatja slumped forward, studied a large sheet of paper on her desk. Her face had none of the familiar animation and good nature. Her eyes were wide and staring, and a tear glistened on her cheek.

Hedrigs petted Ancho, and the two interlopers leaned close to the window. What was she reading that could be so depressing? The paper on her desk was a detailed engineering diagram of—what? Then Cor recognized it as one of the Osterlai plans for a steam-driven turbine. The engine was ingenious and quite workable, but many thousands of ounces of iron were necessary for its construction. Attempts to make boilers of nonmetallic materials had been comical, and occasionally disastrous, failures. *Why would an engineering diagram cause someone to cry?* Cor could imagine the question rattling around Hedrigs's brain.

Tatja looked up suddenly, not at the window, but at the door to her office. Someone was asking admittance. She moved with amazing speed to cover the diagram and compose her features. She did nothing to disguise her figure. Cor realized there were secrets within secrets here.

The visitor was Brailly Tounse. Their conversation was mostly inaudible. "Your people took fifteen ounces . . . iron. My iron. Why?"

". . . needed steel." Grimm's expression was haughty.

Tounse was not put off; in all the years, he was the only one left with active hatred for the mistress of the barge. It didn't affect his performance— and perhaps that was why he was allowed to stay. "So? I . . . too. We can't run the presses without *some* metals, you . . ."

"Tough. We're . . . lee of the Somnai now, so it doesn't matter . . . return it after we leave Bayfast . . . need it to rescue . . . *Fantasie* collection."

This last promise seemed to mollify Tounse somewhat, but he still asked, ". . . really think . . . will go through with it?"

Tatja laughed, and Tounse's face went red. Her

words were lost to the watchers. Footsteps sounded on the gangway across the next deck up. Another few seconds and they would be in clear view of people beyond Ancho's range.

They backed to the edge of the balcony, slid awkwardly down the pillar. Seconds later a trio of crew appeared on the deck above, but by then Svir and Cor had recovered themselves and were casually walking away. Five minutes later they were on the other side of the barge.

This close to the Somnai, the wind was a tiny thing, but Cor found herself shivering in a film of sweat. She hadn't realized how frightened she had been. They stopped a few feet from the entrance to Hedrigs's cabin. Cor looked at him. "Well?"

Hedrigs was silent, looking at his feet. Then, "I don't know, Cor. I made a promise. Perhaps if I knew more, what we saw wouldn't be incriminating. I'm all confused."

"When do you have to make up your mind?"

"Sometime this evening. I'm going to have a final briefing before lunch in the night wake period. I don't know how long after that I'd be leaving."

"Don't go; at least think about what I said and what we saw." She looked at him. "Please."

Svir laughed harshly. "That's one thing you can be absolutely sure of."

She touched his hand briefly, then turned and walked away. She had done what she could. And somehow, for the first time in five years, she felt that Tatja Grimm had been outmaneuvered.

Svir didn't get much sleep that afternoon. He lay on his bunk in the shuttered cabin and stared

into the darkness. What was Tatja Grimm? To him
she had been a miraculous discovery, an escape
from loneliness. And until now he had never
doubted her sincerity. To the crew she was an
immensely popular leader, one who could solve
any problem. To the top officers on the barge she
could be a tyrant, a bitch-goddess. Where did that
leave the Tatja Grimm who sat silently, crying
over an engineering diagram?

In any case, Tatja was not what he had imagined. And that revelation put the present situation
in a new light.

Though it was past sunset, he didn't go down
for breakfast. For one thing, crew came around
and asked him to move to another cabin—something
about painting the first one. Afterwards, he paced
tensely back and forth in the new cabin. On the
bed, Ancho chirped and croaked in misery.

Rescuing the *Fantasie* collection *was* an important project, but, as Cor said, not one worth dying
for. Only now did he realize how weirdly he had
been influenced by Tatja. Svir had agreed to do a
job, but the promise had been extracted by means
of fraud. What else was on Grimm's agenda? If he
went through with the plan, Svir Hedrigs would
probably die tonight. And that death would not be
the adventurous, romantic death of a hero, but an
empty, final thing. Just thinking about it gave him
the chills. How close he had come to sacrificing
himself for . . . nothing. If it hadn't been for Cor
he would have, too. She was as true as Tatja was
false.

He would turn Tatja down—the most she could
get him for was his passage. She would have to
find another sucker and another dorfox. He would

see the Doomsday astronomer and get that situation cleared up. And, *and* he would see Cor again,
and ask her to come back to the Chainpearls with
him.

Svir fed the dorfox, then went down to the
main chow hall. He didn't see Cor. That was
unusual, but not surprising. They were still
working extra shifts. He would see her later in
the evening, after he confronted Tatja. Now that
the decision was made he felt so relieved, anxious
only to be done with telling Grimm of it. He
walked quickly up the steps to the briefing room,
trying to imagine what Tatja might do when he
told her he wasn't going to help her.

The barge was entering Bayfast Harbor now.
That entrance was a narrow gorge cutting through
the Somnai cliffs. Seraph was nearly full, and its
brilliant blue light transformed the normally brown
cliffs into shimmery curtains of stone. Svir had to
crane his neck to see the top, where the Bayfast
naval guns were mounted, pointing down at him.
The Tarulle Barge was almost half as wide as the
entrance.

His stride broke as he noticed a landing boat
pulling away from the barge. That girl with the
helmet of short black hair—she looked like Coronadas Ascuasenya. He rushed to the terrace rail.
She was a hundred yards away and not facing him,
but he was almost sure it was Cor. On her lap she
carried a small suitcase. What was going on? He
ran along the rail, shouting her name. But the
wind, channeled by the gorge, threw back his
words. The boat rounded the curve of the gorge,
disappeared. Perhaps it wasn't Cor after all. But

the old *Fantasie* motto came to mind: "Things are not as they seem."

His mood was considerably subdued by the time he reached the executive deck. He confronted one of Tatja's secretaries and was ushered into the briefing room.

Tatja smiled faintly as Svir advanced on her. "Have a seat, Svir. Ready to begin the briefing?"

Svir didn't accept the proffered chair. He stood awkwardly before the table. Tatja's physical presence made him suddenly ashamed. After all, he had given her a promise. And his spying had revealed nothing overtly evil. "Tatja—Miss Grimm, I've been thinking, uh, about this . . . project. I know it's important to you—to everyone here. But I, uh, I don't think that I'm the right, uh . . ."

Tatja picked a crystal letter opener from her desk. She flashed him a broad smile. "To make a long story short, you've decided you would rather not go through with it. You're willing to pay for your passage, but you feel no obligation to risk your neck on this scheme. Is that what you are trying to say?"

"Why, yes," Svir said, relieved. "I'm glad you see my point of view."

Tatja didn't say anything. She inspected the letter opener, tossed it into the air in a glittering whirl, and caught it just before it would have struck the table. A strange gurgly sound came from behind her lips. Svir realized she was laughing.

"You know, Hedrigs, you are the most gullible person I ever met. Correction: the second most gullible. You're a provincial, overgrown adolescent, and how you thought you could fool anyone into thinking you had ever been off the Islands is beyond me. I need that dorfox. Did you think our encounter on Krirsarque was an *accident*? I've been studying those animals a long time. If I had you killed, I'm certain I could become Ancho's new master. Only my . . . high moral character prevents me from taking that course."

She smiled again. It was almost a sneer, revealing a hostility that seemed to transcend the subject at hand. "If I had known Ascuasenya could be such a nuisance, I would have kept her out of your way. Yes, I know of your activities this afternoon; no one gets on that balcony unnoticed. No matter. For my plans to succeed I now need some new form of leverage. Poor little Ascuasenya is perfect for my purposes."

She sat back and relaxed. "I said you were the second most gullible person in my experience. Coronadas Ascuasenya is the first. She believed me when I told her that you had already left the Barge for Bayfast. She believed me when I told her that our spies had discovered new information which you had to have to avoid disaster. She believed me when I said that with the proper credentials she could get into the castle. Those credentials are very good counterfeits, by the way. When she is finally discovered, the Regent's men will believe they have foiled a serious espionage attempt."

Svir stepped back from the desk, as shocked by her hostility as by what she was saying. For an instant she didn't seem human; Grimm sat in the middle of an infinite complex of scheme and counterscheme. Every detail of the last ten days had pushed him according to her whim. *And still*

*she is driving me. Only now she has a whip that
could really make me die for her.*

"Do you know what Tar Benesh does with spies,
Svir Hedrigs?"

The astronomer shook his head dumbly. Grimm
told him.

"And when they get done, the spy is generally
burned alive," she added. "So, Svir my love, run
to your cabin, get Ancho, and come back here. The
briefing's going to take a while; and you will find
that the only way you can rescue Cor is to save the
Fantasie collection in the process."

Svir had never before wanted to kill anybody.
He wanted to now—very much. This creature
had imperiled the two lives he valued most. He
took a deep breath, fighting dizziness. Grimm
watched, her smile as mocking as her words. When
he finally spoke, his tone was almost mild: "You
hate us that much?"

There was a change in the other's eyes. The
smile broke for an instant, then returned. "I hate
stupidity, something you all have in such *excess*."

Chapter 10

Six hours later, Svir Hedrigs emerged from the offices of the Tarulle executive deck and descended to the debarkation levels. He wore a baggy suit and carried a *balsir* cage disguised as a suitcase. Ancho sat comfortably within the cage; he wore the mysterious clicker on his back.

The barge had reached its pier space and was so firmly tied in that it was difficult to tell where barge ended and pier began. Seraph cast a bright, cheerful twilight across Bayfast. The clashing colors of the city were transformed into pastels. Here and there those pastels were highlighted by yellow and green sparkles where people had uncovered their evening lamps. This shimmery, glowing pattern stretched up to the edge of the seaward cliffs and around the bay to the inland cliffs, which cut off the Monsoonal Drag and made Bayfast a placid spot even at this time of year.

Svir left the barge and walked along the waterfront. The Festival of the Ostentatious Consumption was not due to begin for another six hours, but the citizens of Bayfast were already competing for the best sites along the waterfront from which to watch the events on Sacrifice Island. Svir knew he looked strange walking so dourly among the happy people. His severe costume contrasted sharply with the plaids and monocremes of the Bayfastlings. But he had his special reason for not wearing the costume Tatja had suggested.

The people of Crownesse were happy, confident, and nationalistic. Their ancestors were mainly from the Chainpearls. The hardships of The Continent had forced a dynamism on them. Their bureaucracy was talented, flexible, and—above all—devoted to the crown. In the centuries since they declared their independence from the sea, their culture had spread far: from Sfierro and Picchiu—the old Llerenito colonies in the north—all the way around the coast to the southern tip of the Continent. For the most part (and as such things go), the crown's rule had been a beneficial thing. That changed abruptly twenty-five years ago, when the implacable Tar Benesh appeared in the King's Court. The king had died and Tar Benesh had become the regent. Shortly after, the king's children had disappeared in a sea wreck.

Since that time, Tar Benesh's rule had been a study in expanding tyranny. He had, with the faithful help of the bureaucracy, transformed the open spirit of the Bayfastlings into an aggressive barbarism which could embrace things like the Ostentatious Consumption, and which would enslave the world rather than lead it.

Svir was walking east, toward the keep. That

enormous polyhedron loomed black over the warehouse roofs. Even the ingenious Bayfastlings had needed seventy years to build this ultimate protection for the crown. Nothing short of a year-long artillery bombardment could breach that artificial mountain—and the keep had artillery of its own.

Svir stopped before he reached the plaza that surrounded the keep. He slipped into the entryway of a closed shop and covertly inspected the castle port. Once more the horrible fear rose in him, making every movement slow and clumsy. He was going to die. The whole plan was so complicated, and depended so heavily on Ancho and the tenuous information Tatja had about the keep's design. But he knew he wasn't going to back out. Tatja had discovered a motive strong enough to make him take the risk. It had worked with Cor and now it was working with him.

A figure dressed in the uniform of a guard captain walked across the plaza toward the port. That was the signal to begin. The "captain" was a Tarulle agent whose job it was to tip the guardsmen at the door to look sharp because the crown's inspector general was expected momentarily. In truth, Inspector General Stark *was* supposed to visit the keep at this time, but he had been detained by other Tarulle agents. In any case, the guardsmen at the door were prepared to assume that the next authority figure they saw was the inspector general.

Svir fumbled open the suitcase and lifted out Ancho. The animal responded nervously to his obvious anxiety. Svir tried to reassure him. As per instructions he depressed the tiny button on the box strapped to Ancho's back. The contraption immediately began making a *click-clock-click* sound.

What if the device were a bomb hooked up to a clock, timed to explode after they were in the keep? For a moment, he considered ripping the machine off Ancho's back. But there were limits to paranoia, even when it involved Tatja Grimm. Since his survival was necessary for the salvation of the *Fantasie* collection, the device probably had some beneficial purpose.

He stood up, put the dorfox on his shoulder, and petted him. The animal began radiating immediately. His first target was a middle-aged merchant—one of the few people who were not yet at the waterfront. As the man passed Svir and Ancho, his eyes widened and he performed the nodding bow reserved for members of the bureaucracy. Svir smiled and walked onto the open area before the Keep. In some peculiar way, when Ancho used the effect on others, it made Svir feel confident, competent. And this feeling of authority actually seemed to feed back to the animal, making him perform even more effectively. Svir strolled briskly across the plaza.

The two guardsmen came to rigid attention as he approached. One of them saluted. Svir offhandedly returned the gesture. He passed his credentials to the guardsman. At the same time he spoke the ritual words. "The crown's agent to inventory the prizes."

The senior guardsman looked up from the papers. "Very good, sir." Both men wore ridiculously ornamented dress uniforms, but there was nothing ornamental about their weapons. In a single glance, the guardsman gave Svir a thorough once-over. His alert and active mind checked for the minor details that would give an impostor

away. Unfortunately for the guardsman, his own
mind made him see the details he was looking for.
If questioned later, both guards would swear they
saw the crown's inspector general enter the building, not Svir Hedrigs.

The fellow returned Svir's papers to him and
turned to a speaking tube that protruded from the
black stone of the castle wall. Except for the words
"Inspector General," Svir couldn't hear what was
said. But that was enough. He had passed the
second hurdle. At each checkpoint, the word would
be passed back as to who he was supposed to be.
With a greased sliding sound, a thirty-ton cube of
stone lifted into the ceiling of the entrance. Beyond
was darkness.

Svir walked in, striving not to look up at the
mass of stone above him—or back at the city which
would soon be blocked from his view. The stone
cube slid down smoothly. He stood in the dark for
almost five seconds. Ancho chirped nervously, and
the device on his back continued its *click-clock-
click*. He rubbed Ancho's neck, and the little dorfox
began radiating again. None too soon. A second
block of stone was lifting. Algae-generated light
flooded the chamber. He stepped into the hallway
revealed and handed his papers to the guardsman
standing there. Two were right by the entrance,
while a third stood on a crenelated balcony. All
three wore unadorned uniforms of bureaucratic
black. They weren't nearly as formal as the fellows
outside, but they seemed just as competent. Svir's
identity was passed by speaking tube to the next
checkpoint.

He walked on. The hall was well lighted and
ventilated—even though it was within a mass of

stone four hundred feet high. In some places the stonework was covered by wood paneling and cabinets filled with the arms of early kings. He passed through three more checkpoints, each of a different design. Whenever he had a choice of routes, he took the middle one—he was following a radius straight to the center of the keep, to the crown room vault.

Some of the outer passages were almost crowded. Bureaucrats were making final arrangements for the evening. Svir walked aloof from these, and hoped that none of them compared notes on exactly who they thought he was. As he approached the center, however, there were fewer and fewer people. Besides the guards, he encountered only an occasional very high-ranking bureaucrat.

Here the identification procedures became more complex. The walls were always paneled and the floors heavily carpeted. Svir wondered at this strange luxury in the most secret part of the keep. Besides the usual paintings and displays, there were small glass windows at regular intervals. Beyond that glass, Svir could see only darkness. Probably there was someone back there watching, guarding the guards. Svir was suddenly very glad that Tatja had had Ancho practice at deluding hidden observers. Now he knew the reason for the luxurious trappings. Besides hiding the observation posts, they probably concealed a variety of weapons and deadfalls.

Finally he reached the last checkpoint: the doorway to the crown room itself. It was conceivable that at this moment only the inspector general and Tar Benesh himself had authority to enter this storeroom of the nation's greatest treasures and most secret documents. Here the clearance process was especially difficult. For a few uncomfortable moments, Svir thought they were going to take his fingerprints and run a comparison right there. Would the illusion extend to fingerprints? But apparently that procedure was used in special cases only, and Svir was not subjected to it.

As they opened the outer vault door, he casually turned to the officer in charge. "Captain, I have instructions to move some of the prizes out to Sacrifice Island right away. I'd like to have a couple of squads ready when I finish the general inventory."

"Very good, sir," she answered. "We have about twenty people with the proper clearance for that job. I can have them here in fifteen minutes." She handed Svir an algae lamp. "Don't forget this, sir."

"Uh, thanks." He accepted the lamp uncertainly. "If everything's in order, my inventory shouldn't take that long."

He turned and walked quickly into the lock area between the double doors. The outer door slid shut, the inner lifted open, and he stepped into the crown room.

The vault was a disappointment. The room was large and without ornamentation. Svir's lamp provided the only illumination. Over all hung a musty smell. The treasures were not heaped in some spectacular pile, but were neatly catalogued on racks that filled most of the room. Each object had its own classification tag. A row of cabinets along one wall housed the personal records of the Royal Family. Svir walked along the racks. He almost didn't notice the Crown Jewels and the 930-carat

Shamerest diamond; in the dim light everything looked dull. Finally he reached the red-tag area—the prime sacrifices for the festival.

And there it was: the *Fantasie* collection. Its sheer bulk was impressive. The thousands of volumes were stacked on seven close-set racks. The racks sat on dollies for easy handling. Obviously Benesh thought of *Fantasie* as an article of portable wealth rather than a source of philosophical pleasure. But—as Tatja had so cynically pointed out—the collection was also the vehicle of Cor's salvation. Even in this dim light, he could read some of the binding titles. Why, there was the last *obra* of Ti Liso's zombie and golem series! For the last three centuries, Chainpearl experts had been trying to find that issue. The series had been illustrated by Inmar Ellis, probably the greatest artist of all time. Svir noticed all this in passing. No matter how valuable this collection, its physical dimensions were more important to him now. There was indeed enough room between the third and fourth racks to hide a human body.

Now he had to find the correct passage to the prison tier. If Tatja had lied about that . . . But if she lied, then she couldn't possibly get the collection. Not by Svir's efforts, anyway.

The vault doors were so well constructed that Svir did not notice that he had been discovered until the inner door lifted and he heard the raging voice of—

Tar Benesh.

The regent advanced into the room. A look of astounded shock came to his face as he saw Svir. Svir wondered briefly what authority figure the dictator saw in Ancho's illusion.

Benesh was less than five feet tall. He weighed more than two hundred pounds. Once that weight had been slab-like muscle, but now he was as soft as the velvet and flutter-feather costume he wore.

He raised his arm shakily and pointed at Svir. "Take that—man," he choked. The black-uniformed guardsmen swarmed toward Svir, their momentary confusion replaced by professionalism. Svir felt only confidence as they approached. He was in trouble, true, but he could work his way out of it.

The confidence vanished, replaced by sudden terror.

Then the guardsmen had him. He felt a needle thrust into the base of his neck, and his entire body became a single charley horse. He couldn't move, he could scarcely breathe, and what he saw and heard seemed to be far away, observed through a curtain of pain. He felt his person being searched, and heard Benesh say, "A dorfox, that's the creature you saw."

"But M'Lord Regent, that's a mythological creature."

"Obviously not! Search the crown room." An unprecedented order. "No one enters or leaves this vault till we find—" He paused, realizing that this was impractical. It would tie up the guard situation in the whole Keep. "No, forget that. But I want that creature, and I want it alive." There was a lustfulness in his voice. "Check everyone and everything that passes through these doors."

Svir felt himself picked up, moved swiftly toward the door. Of all the humans in the room, he was the only one who noticed the dorfox seated on the shoulder of Tar Benesh.

As they rushed him through the keep, Svir

wondered what had given him away—though he really didn't care now. Nothing could save Cor and himself. And soon this paralysis would be replaced by the ultimate agony of interrogation.

Finally his captors stopped. There was a creaking sound. Then he was sailing through the air. His hip struck the hard stone floor, adding extra fire to his pain. His head and shoulders were resting in a pile of straw. He smelled rot and blood. The door swung shut and he was in darkness.

There was a shuffling, and someone touched him. Cor! She held his shoulders and whispered what seemed a complete irrelevancy. "I'm sorry, Svir! I tried to warn you but they got me." She was silent for a second, waiting for some response. He longed to put his arms around her. "Svir?" she whispered. "Are you all right? Svir!" He was so thoroughly paralyzed he couldn't even croak.

Chapter 11

"—realize we're sitting beneath the keep artillery. To get out, we have to go around the peninsula past the entrance guns. And now you want me to send twenty people on a raid! When Benesh connects us with this scheme, we'll be blown out of the water—if we're lucky!" Kederichi Maccioso slammed his fist down on Tatja's desk, jarring her drafting instruments an inch into the air.

"Relax, Ked, we aren't suspected of anything. It's still a state secret that the collection is one of the sacrifices. There's—" She broke off and motioned Maccioso to be silent. Barely audible against the thrumming crowd sounds, there was scratching at her office window. Tatja pushed the window open and pulled a shivering, croaking Ancho into the room. She held him close, comforting him with low sounds. Maccioso sat down abruptly and stared at them, shocked.

"The dorfox wouldn't come back alone unless Hedrigs had been taken." It was an accusation.

Tatja smiled. "That's right. Svir never had a chance, though he lasted longer than I thought he would."

"So Benesh knows. We've—" Then he realized what Tatja had just said. "You knew all along he would fail." His voice became flat, deadly. "For all that you've done for Tarulle, I knew there'd come a time you'd sacrifice the barge. Don't think I haven't planned for it."

"Shut up, Ked," Tatja said pleasantly. "You're disturbing Ancho. I know all about the coup you and Brailly have had in reserve the last three years." She set Ancho on her desk. "You know," she said with apparent irrelevance, "I've studied dorfoxes. If they were just a little smarter or a little more mobile, they could take over the world. As it is, I can manipulate them—much to Hedrigs's surprise, I'm sure. With him out of the way, Ancho will accept me as his new master." She undid the clicker and laid it carefully on her desk. "Hand me that bottle of lacquer, will you?" She accepted the bottle and screwed an atomizer onto its cap. She inserted the nozzle into the clicker's keyhole and puffed the volatile lacquer into the box. In spite of himself, Kederichi Maccioso leaned over the table to watch. Ancho moved to the corner of the table and munched the *klig* leaves that Tatja had thoughtfully provided.

"That should fix it." She undid hidden catches and lifted the top off the box. "You know that picturemaker we've been using in our latest issues? I've made some refinements."

Maccioso looked at the machine's innards. It did

resemble the picturemaker Tarulle used. In that device, light was focused on a cellulose plate coated with a special green dye. Wherever light fell on the plate, the dye faded toward transparency. If the plate were properly coated with fixing lacquer, a permanent picture resulted.

Tatja pointed. "See, this clock movement pulls the tape through the central area. Once every two seconds, this shutter flicks open. On alternate seconds, the shutter on the other side of the box takes a picture. So we have a record covering nearly three hundred degrees, a picture every second for ten minutes." She pulled the reel out of the clicker and began to examine it under a large magnifying glass. Maccioso had a distorted view of the pictures through the same lens.

The first thirty pictures covered Svir's approach to the keep. Every other picture was reversed, since it had been made on the opposite side of the cellulose. Despite this and the fact that the pictures weren't as clear as ones made with one-shot devices, the sequence gave Maccioso the strange sensation that he was sitting on Svir's shoulder. On every second frame, Svir's head blocked out part of the picture.

Tatja carefully inspected each picture, becoming increasingly excited as they showed the interior of the keep. Here the exposure she had chosen was more effective and the pictures sharper. "See, the paneling, the paintings—they weren't in any of the reports. And here, I'll bet this is what snagged Hedrigs."

Maccioso squinted at the tiny picture. It looked no different than the three or four previous. "That rectangle on the wall—it's some kind of window.

My guess is the guards have heard of those poison gases we saw in the Sutherseas. That little window is one end of a periscope, and the observer is in another room, protected from the gas, and apparently beyond Ancho's range." They looked at the rest of the pictures, but the last ones were badly underexposed, showing nothing but vague green blurs. They saw something of the crown room. In one of the pictures, Tatja claimed she saw a group of men.

She reached for tiny dividers. "We discovered that Ancho can broadcast through almost twenty feet of porphyry." She made some rapid measurements of relative sizes on the tape. "That periscope window is about three inches by three." She sat back and her eyes unfocused for a moment. "Now assuming their optics are no better than elsewhere, that periscope can't have a resolution better than half an inch." She looked up and flashed Maccioso a dazzling smile. "I'm all set!"

Tatja got up and began to take off her clothes. Maccioso stood up too. Admiral, barge captain . . . helpless little boy. For almost five years he had loved and feared this woman. She had worked miracles for the Tarulle Company, magic that he knew must one day turn on them. As Tatja laid her shirt on the chair, he reached out a huge hand to grab her shoulder, forcing her face close to his.

"You never intended this scheme to save *Fantasie*, did you?"

Tatja shrugged. "You know the saying, Ked. 'Things are not as they seem.'"

"What are you after, damn you?" He shook her, but received no answer. "Well, if you think we're going to sit still for this, you're mad!"

"Poor Ked," Tatja said gently. Her hand moved softly up his arm, found a nerve in his elbow. As he jerked back, she slipped from his hold. "It's true. We've come to a . . . parting. And I have put you all at risk." She reached into an alcove and drew out a full suit of black armor. The crown's inspector general was about her height, but the armor had been designed for a male. In places it chafed tight, but she managed to get it on.

She slipped a steel-edged rapier into its sheath and picked up Ancho from the desk. At the door she turned to face him. "Your chances are good if you keep Brailly on a leash. And go through with the diversion. You really have no choice."

Kederichi Maccioso stared at her for a moment, then nodded slowly. His voice came almost gentle. "That's right, you . . . bitch."

Seraph was in its last quarter, and the evening wake period was ending. Nearly a million people— the entire population of the capital—were crowded along the water's edge. In the waning blue light the crowd was a mosaic carpet covering the streets and the roofs of the lower buildings. The festival was its noisiest as the Bayfastlings cheered the first sacrifices being towed into the bay. These were the secondary sacrifices, the appetizers. The barges formed a continuous train out to Sacrifice Island. They were stacked high with worked jade, optical devices, paintings. Hanging from the stern of each, an oil-wick torch lit the sacrifices.

A twisted smile crossed Tatja's lips as she regarded the scene.

She descended to the sub-pier passageway reserved for official use, and five minutes later emerged on the city side of the crowd. There were plenty of people here, but there was no need to push through crowds. She spoke quietly to Ancho, petted him just so. According to all her theories, Ancho would accept her as his new master, but this was the critical test. She couldn't tell whether he was radiating or not. Certainly the signal was having no effect on her. Then she noticed that people came to attention as she walked past. Good Ancho.

She reached the keep without incident. The guardsmen looked her over very carefully, this being the second inspector general they had seen that day. But they let her through. As she stood in the darkness between the two doors, she moved the dorfox to her waist. The armor plates gave him good purchase, and now he was below the view of the periscopes.

As she came to the doors of the crown room, Tatja spoke in a low, masculine voice to fool any listening tubes. Even with her visor up, she knew the armor would deceive the hidden observers. And of course the guardsmen in the hall didn't have a chance. With Ancho's help, even her fingerprints passed inspection.

Once in the crown room she moved quickly to the royal records. She lifted out the drawer she wanted, thumbed through it, and pulled out a single sheet of vellum. Good. It was the same form as had been publicly displayed at the Assignation of the Regency. From her pouch she drew a seemingly identical paper, smudges and all, and slipped it into the file. She smiled to herself; she had spent hundreds of hours crafting the forgery. It was the high point of her brief career in the drafting arts—and totally beyond the skill of ordinary humans.

Then she left, ignoring the puzzled guards. They had expected the IG to supervise the removal of the prizes.

Tatja found the stairway to the Conciliar Facet unguarded. This was unexpected good fortune. Perhaps Maccioso's diversion had been more effective than she'd planned.

She removed the black resin armor and set the outfit on one of the display racks that lined the base of the stairwell. This was the most perilous part of her plan. Ancho would be a marginal use, an emergency escape tool at most.

From a cloth pouch she drew a white dress and jeweled sandals. She slipped them on, put Ancho on her shoulder, and ran up the stairs. This stairway wasn't often used, since it was a single spiral ascending four hundred feet. Most people preferred to go by stages. Even so, Tatja kept the rapier. Except for that, and the dorfox clutching her shoulder, she might have been an Island girl at a communion picnic.

She took the steps three at a time, so fast that she had to lean toward the center of the spiral to keep her balance. After she first conceived this scheme, she spent much effort scouting Bayfast, studying the people and the keep. Tar Benesh had created the Festival of the Ostentatious Consumption to draw attention from a much more solemn event that took place every five years at the same time. The top people in the bureaucracy were scrupulously honest, but if she were even minutes late, she would have to wait five years—or possibly forever. Taking the back way would avoid

Benesh's Special Men, but if she were wrong about the bureaucratic *esprit* of the rest, then she would likely die.

Tatja took the four-hundred-foot stairs in a single sprint. At the top of that flight was an entrance to the Conciliar Facet, a pentagonal amphitheater that crowned the enormous polyhedron that was the keep. Beyond the next door was the final test. She slid the door open and crept onto the uppermost tier of the amphitheater. There was a cool breeze, and Seraph blue covered everything. From the city came crowd sounds.

Less than a third of the seats in the facet were filled, and those were down in the center, by the podium and reading lamp. Virtually everyone here wore bureaucratic black. An important exception was the gross and colorful bulk of Tar Benesh, sitting in the first row before the podium.

Tatja glanced around the Facet. Maccioso's diversion must have worked. Few of the guards appeared to be Benesh's bully boys. There were only fifteen or twenty armed men present. Of course one of them might still be rotten, but that was a chance she must take. She noticed one man just five feet from her hiding place. The fellow leaned unprofessionally against the edge of the tier, blocking her entrance. She reversed the hilt of the rapier and moved swiftly forward, ramming the pommel into the base of the man's neck. He collapsed quietly into her arms. She dragged him back, at the same time watching for signs that someone below had noticed.

The speaker's voice came clearly to her. She knew there were about five minutes until the ceremony reached its critical point. She looked at her rapier. It was no longer an asset. Without putting herself in silhouette, she reached up and slid the weapon over the battlement. There was a faint scrape and clatter as it slid slowly down the side of the fifty-foot facet. Tatja set Ancho down, and petted him. Only the most subtle effects would be much use here. They waited.

The ceremony was nearing its end. On the podium stood the Lord High Minister to the Crown, the highest bureaucratic officer of Crownesse. The man was old, but his body was lean, and his voice was clear and strong as he read from the curling parchment. He had the air of a man who was for the thousandth time repeating a fervent and sincere prayer, a prayer that had so often been fruitless that it had become almost perfunctory.

"And so in the Year of the Discovery nine hundred and seven did the Crown Prince Evard II and his sister, the Princess Marget, take themselves aboard the Royal Yacht *Avante* to tour the eastern reaches of their Dominions.

"And on the fifth day of their voyage a great storm sent their yacht upon the Rocks of the South—for so we have the word of the ship's captain and those crewmen who survived the tragedy."

Tatja stood up slowly, out of their view. She fluffed out her skirt and waited intently for the moment that would come.

"The royal children were never found. So it is that the regent continues to govern in their stead, until such time as our rulers are recovered. On this twenty-fifth anniversary of that storm, and by order of the regent, I ask that anyone with knowledge of the royal family step forth." The Lord High Minister glanced about moodily. The ceremony was almost a legal fiction. It had been fifteen years since anyone had dared Tar Benesh's revenge with a story of the lost children. It is not surprising that the minister almost fell off his stand when a clear, vibrant voice answered his call.

"I, Marget of Sandros, do claim the crown and my dominions." Tatja stood boldly on the uppermost tier, her arms akimbo. Behind her, and invisible to those below, sat a small animal with large ears. The startled bureaucrats stared at Tatja, the beautiful woman who had turned a ceremony into a coup. Then their eyes turned to the regent. The gaily dressed dictator advanced six ominous steps toward Tatja. His pale eyes reflected hatred and complete disbelief. For twenty-five years he had ruled the most powerful country on Tu—and now a lone girl was challenging him at the very center of his power. Benesh gestured angrily to the guardsmen—the sleek professionals with thousands of hours of target and tactical experience, the deadliest individuals in the world.

"Kill the impostor," he ordered.

Chapter 12

When they came, Svir was ready.

He and Cor had lain quietly in the darkness, telling each other their stories in frightened whispers. As Cor massaged the numbness from his arms, Svir told her of his one backstop against Tatja's treachery. Brailly Tounse—who seemed to hate Tatja as much as Svir did—had provided him with five pounds of Michelle-Rasche powder. Now that powder lay in the heavy weave of his jacket.

"It's safe until the cloth gets twisted tight," he whispered to Cor. "Then almost any extra friction will set it off."

He struggled out of his jacket. Cor helped him wedge the fabric into the door crack. Though only a small portion of the jacket could be jammed in, it would be enough to set off the rest of the powder. Then they retreated to the far corner of the cell. There was nothing more they could do. He hadn't said so to Cor, but the best they could hope for was a quick death. If they weren't killed in the explosion or by the guards, then the next stop was the torture chambers. Their present cell was a carefully contrived filth-pit, designed to prepare prisoners psychologically for what was to come. Somehow the prospect of torture and death no longer provoked absolute terror in him. Cor was the reason. He wanted to hide his fear from her—and to protect her from her own fears.

He put his arm around Cor's waist and drew her to him. "You came out here to save me, Cor."

"You did the same for me."

"I—I'd do it again."

Her reply was clear and firm. "I, too."

When they came, there was plenty of warning. It sounded like a whole squad. The heavy footsteps stopped, and when they began again, there were only two or three men. Svir and Cor slid under the filthy straw. The footsteps stopped at the door. Svir heard the key turn, but he never heard the door open. For that matter, he never actually *heard* the explosion. He felt it through his whole body. The floor rose up and smashed him.

He forced himself to his feet, and pulled Cor up. Svir was scarcely aware of blood flowing down his jaw from his ear. The doorway was a dim patch of light beyond the dust and smoke. They gasped futilely and ran for the opening.

The blast had destroyed the bottom hinges and blown the rest of the door into the ceiling. In the hallway lay the two guardsmen. Both were alive, but in much worse shape than the prisoners. One, with a severe scalp cut, tried ineffectually to wipe the blood from his eyes. Svir and Cor stepped over them and ran down the hall. Then they saw the men at the end of the passage—the backup section. The two prisoners came to a sudden halt and started to turn in the other direction.

A guardsman smiled faintly and twisted a lever mounted in the wall. A weighted net fell onto the two escapees. As the guard approached, Svir lashed out at his legs, hoping to provoke lethal retaliation. The guard easily avoided the extended hand, and grabbed it with his own. "You know, fella, for someone whose life we're supposed to protect, you're making things damn difficult."

Svir looked back blankly. He couldn't make sense of the words spoken. The net was removed, and the guards marched Svir and Cor down the hall. The couple looked at each other in complete confusion. They weren't even treated to the paralysis the guards had used before. It was a long uphill walk, and the guards had to help Cor the last part. Svir wondered if he had gone crazy with fear and was seeing only what he hoped to see. They came to the final door. The guard captain went through. They could hear him through the open doorway.

"Marget, the individuals you requested are here."

"Fine," came a familiar voice. "Send them out. I want to talk to them alone."

"Begging your pardon, Marget, but they have repeatedly offered us violence. We could not guarantee the safety of your person if you interview them alone."

"Mister, I told you what I wanted." The voice took a tone that brooked no argument. "Now jump!"

"Yes, Marget!" The captain appeared at the door. He gestured courteously to Svir and Cor. "Sir and Madam, you have been granted an interview with the queen."

"The—*Queen?*" Cor asked incredulously. She got no answer. They were pushed past the door and found themselves standing on the top tier of the Conciliar Facet. By the light of waning Seraph they saw a beautiful girl in a full-skirted dress.

Tatja turned to them. "You two look like hell," she said.

Svir started angrily toward her, his fright and pain transformed into hate. There was a scuttling sound on the floor, then a tugging at Svir's clothing. A soft wet nose nuzzled his neck. Ancho! Svir's hands reached up and petted the trembling animal.

"Marget?" asked Cor. "Queen? Really you are the Lost Princess of Crownesse?"

Tatja looked beyond them, at the departing guards. "You might as well know the truth. You can't do anything about it. I was no more Marget of Sandros than you; now I am incontrovertibly the queen. My footprints match those of the infant princess which are kept in the crown room. You should have seen the look on Benesh's face when the Lord High Minister announced that I was heir to the crown. The regent had the royal children murdered twenty-five years ago. The job was botched and he couldn't produce bodies that would pass an autopsy. He knew I was a fraud but there was no way he could prove it without revealing his own guilt."

Svir looked across the curving dome of the keep at the city. The crowd sounds came clear and faint through the air. The crowd had moved away from the waterfront. There would be no sacrifices tonight—the people had been told that the crown had been claimed. Crownesse had a queen. That called for the largest of festivals, a celebration that would go on for many days.

Svir turned to Tatja Grimm. "You had to lie and cheat and steal and—probably—murder to do it, but you certainly got what you wanted. You control the most powerful country in the world. I wondered what could make you as vicious as you are. Now I know. The hidden motive that mystified me so much was simple megalomania. Female 'Tar Benesh' has taken over from male. Is this the end of your appetites," he said, the hate rising in his voice, "or will you one day rule all Tu?"

Tatja smiled at Cor and Svir, the scornful smile that was now so familiar. "You never were very bright, were you? It's possible that I'll take over the world. As a matter of fact, I probably will. It will be a by-product of my other plans. I chose Crownesse very carefully. The country has immense physical resources. If there are large heavy-metal deposits anywhere, they are in Crownesse. The government is talented and dedicated. Most administrative posts are awarded on the basis of civil service tests. And the entire bureaucracy is fanatically dedicated to one person: the legal holder of the crown. They served Tar Benesh and his evil for twenty-five years, and they will serve me just as faithfully. I will not be bothered with coups and elections, as I might be if I took over one of the archipelagates.

"We've reached a critical point in the development of civilization, in case you haven't noticed. In the past century there have been a number of basic scientific discoveries. The pharmacists of the Sutherseas have developed drugs which control most of the major diseases. A physicist in the

Osterlai Archipelagate invented that picturemaker we use. All over the world, revolutionary advances are being made. Rey Guille was right, you know: Organizations like Tarulle are responsible for this. For centuries they spread ideas from island to island until finally scientists stopped thinking of them as fantasy and actually invented what writers described. I'm making a gift of that *Fantasie* collection to Tarulle, by the way."

"How magnanimous."

Tatja ignored him. "These inventions and techniques are going to have effects far beyond what is obvious—just think what that picturemaker will do for parallax astronomy. If they all were brought together and worked over intensively, the changes would be even more spectacular. But you people on the islands are too lazy to do that. The people of Crownesse are not. They've had to work awfully hard just to stay alive here on the Continent. They will take your inventions and use them and develop more inventions, until they control the entire planet."

She looked up into the sky, at Seraph and the bright star Prok. "I've had five years on the Tarulle Barge, enough time to sail the world, enough time to guess what this place really is. Myth and standard archeology agree that we originated somewhere deep in The Continent, that man moved to the islands recently—just before the rise of civilization. What else could explain the absence of prehistorical remains on the Islands? But every year the biologists and the explorers come closer to the true answer. That truth would be known around the world if I published all the stories I am getting at *Fantasie*: the human race *originated* in the islands—and in the historical past.

"Do you understand me? This is a world of shipwreck, where people lost their memories and their minds." Her arm brushed at the sky. "And Seraph is too near; any fool can see that. Out there must be empires so vast they can 'lose' whole planetary systems."

Tatja's voice changed, lost its authority and its spite. She turned to look at Svir and Cor; her eyes were soft. For a moment she wasn't the master of all events, but a young girl, very much alone. "You call me megalomaniac. That is to laugh. What is worth having here? Ruling this world does not interest me, except for one thing: I've never found anyone I can talk to, anyone who can understand the things I often want to say."

Svir suddenly understood the meaning of her scornful smiles: hopeless envy.

"And that is why I am going to turn this world upside down, and make of it a fire so *bright* that someone real will notice."

The fallen goddess turned from the parapet and the gay crowds. She didn't look up as she walked away.

PART III

THE FERAL CHILD

PART III

THE FERAL CHILD

Chapter 13

The astronomer royal was all wet. At Bayfast the Waterfall lasted more than forty days: nearly a fifth of the year. For the last thirty-eight days and nights it had rained without pause. The city's troughed streets were filled with swift-moving water. Behind all sounds was the rumbly hum of myriad droplets striking stone and wood and water. After four years, the astronomer royal was still not accustomed to the monsoon climate of the Continent. At the back of his mind was the irrational thought that when the rain stopped, Seraph might be washed from the sky.

Svir Hedrigs considered returning to his carriage. It wasn't worth it; he was already too wet. By the Bayfast logic, if the rain is warm—why stay dry? With a mixture of irritation and envy, he watched the guardsmen on the pier. They appeared to enjoy being wet to the skin. They wore their black uniforms with a cockiness that said being soaked was the height of fashion.

His carriage was parked on the roadway at the root of the pier. Beyond the roadway were the naval warehouses, constructed of marble bricks and rock paste. The quarries on the inland cliffs seemed inexhaustible, and the Crown's Men had used them to build one of the most beautiful warehouse districts in the world. Architects claimed that this part of port could survive artillery attack and was absolutely nonflammable. Svir wasn't so sure about the first claim, but he was certain that during the Waterfall no fire would start outside the warehouses. The pier had an inch of water on it even though it was more than ten feet above the bay.

Perhaps he should have stayed in the dryrooms of the keep. But as astronomer royal, he felt this was a job which could not be delegated. The fastboat they expected was to bring the latest reports from the Doomsday observatory, four thousand miles upcoast and more than twenty-nine thousand feet above sea level—above the monsoonal precipitation. During the Waterfall, the Doomsdaymen were the most important source of astronomical information the crown possessed. Svir's job was to arrange such reports for Marget's consideration. And since Marget really needed no help in the interpretation of astronomical data, the astronomer royal frequently felt superfluous. So it did his ego good to come down to the most restricted area in the naval district and welcome a fastboat that was—incidentally—from a war zone.

In fact, thought Svir as he glanced around, he was the highest-ranking officer in the area. The only other first-level officer was a vice-admiral from naval intelligence. The broad band on Svir's sleeve identified him as a high minister. He generally tried to conceal the tiny crown above that. The crown indicated he was an appointee rather than a member of the civil service.

The astronomer royal squished unhappily across the pier, toward the admiral. The navy woman saluted. "Good day, m'lord."

Svir suppressed some sarcasm as he noticed there was no humor in the admiral's blue eyes. "I was told the fastboat would arrive by twenty-five hours."

"That's right, sir. But unless the wind is steady, the hydrofoils are useless and the boat is as slow as any other."

Svir didn't point out that, except during the Turnabouts, the Monsoonal Drag always blew right for high-speed travel along the coast. The admiral seemed worried enough. Svir casually covered the crown on his left sleeve with his right hand. Four years ago, who would have guessed that one day the most powerful people in the most powerful country in the world would address him as their superior? Even more fantastic, who would have guessed that he would be married to someone as wonderful as Coronadas Ascuasenya? Ever since that night in Krirsarque, his life had been like the story of the Little Sailmaker: success piled upon fantastic success.

But he did not delude himself. He was riding the bow wave of the most spectacular success story in the history of the human race: the career of Tatja Grimm, aka Marget of Sandros, Queen of Crownesse. Tatja's rise to power had been miraculous, and her progress since even more so. Many of her projects seemed pointless, extravagant, half-witted. But a half-wit she was not. For every person who despised her, there were now three who worshiped her. And that ratio was improving. Her fastboat program had seemed ridiculous. Who wants to know what's happening on the other side of the world within twenty days of the event? But that program had already repaid itself five times over. With a comparatively instantaneous picture of the world's markets, Crownesse merchants came close to their wildest dreams of avarice. Such success gave people an excuse to overlook her other projects. As far as Svir knew, there were only two people besides Tatja who knew her ultimate purpose—and he was one of those two. He often thought his present post was pay for his silence. Marget was merciful.

Svir glanced at the admiral, and wondered what her explanation of the Marget Mystery might be. The officer was staring across the bay at the inland cliffs. On the ridge line stood the signaling mosaic that relayed messages from the seaward cliffs: the Somnai. Through the rain, Svir could barely see the shifting patterns on the mosaic. "That's it, sir!" the admiral said. "The Somnai batteries have spotted the fastboat. . . . It's entering the bay right now." Her relief was plain. The expedition sent to put down the Picchiu rebellion had been lightly equipped. It had been Marget's idea to use fastboats to transport two thousand troops for a surprise pincer attack in cooperation with the Loyalists. This insurrection was the only blot on the queen's record. Forty days earlier, fastboats from the north reported rumors claiming Marget was an impostor and that her accession had been accomplished by fraud. This claim was especially disturbing because it was true. Four years had passed since the accession, and except for the deposed Tar Benesh, no one had protested before (though Svir suspected that the highest members of the bureaucracy guessed the truth). Then the rumors blossomed into armed insurrection. Marget's shock troops had departed just ten days ago. The returning fastboat would bring news of the battle as well as the astronomical reports that Svir was interested in.

A half-hour passed. The fastboat appeared in the rain-grayed distance. The bay was comparatively windless, and the boat's crew was rowing it slowly toward the pier.

Svir shook his sleeves, hoping to free the sticky linen from his skin. He had had about enough of feeling like a drowned rat. He squinted, trying to get a clearer view of the fastboat. Its boom masts were in the vertical position and its sails were reefed, but there was something strange about it, nevertheless. Then he realized that the boat's port side had only three masts while the starboard had four. He could see the stub of the amputated boom still hanging in the extended position. The boat listed slightly to port.

He pointed to the boat. "Admiral, that boat's been shot up."

The old woman stared for a few seconds. Then she glanced back at the astronomer royal, noticed the crown on Svir's sleeve. "So it has." Apparently the admiral reserved "sir" and "m'lord" for her real superiors: civil service people. She turned and walked quickly away, toward the end of the pier. Svir followed.

There were two large holes in the fastboat's hull, barely above the water line. A suspicious brown stain covered portions of the foredeck. The Guardsmen made way for Svir as he walked to the edge of the pier. Now he was only a yard from the little craft. A sickly smell came from below-decks. He looked at the sailors. They were busy making the boat secure. They moved quickly, efficiently, but their faces were strained and their eyes fixed.

Finally the main hatch opened and the commanding officer appeared on deck. His uniform was as sharp as fatigues ever are, but his arm was in a sling and the left side of his face was a smear of medicant and blood. Following close behind him came a sailor carrying the strongbox that was the fastboat's cargo: the reports from upcoast, from the war zone.

Svir felt a bit nauseated. He knelt to give the wounded man a hand up. The fellow saw the gray band on his sleeve, came to attention, and saluted.

"Lieutenant Mörl reports return Fastboat One Nineteen, m'lord," he recited.

"Gods, man, what happened?" Behind him, Svir felt the admiral trying to maneuver him away from the edge of the pier. High minister or not, Svir's question was a substantial breach of protocol—if not security. But the wounded Lieutenant Mörl was too exhausted to notice much beyond the rank on Svir's sleeve.

"The Rebels have artillery, sir. I don't know how. They wiped out our main force in half a day. My recon group followed the Rebels into Doomsday area. They fought the Loyalists at Kotta-svo-Picchiu. The city was razed. We left then. Appar-

ently they saw us. Overtook us in one of our own
fastboats."

The admiral gasped, and Svir could imagine her
surprise. *Artillery?* Reliable, accurate artillery? So
the Crownesse military no longer had a monopoly
on the ultimate weapon.

But the admiral was shocked by the wrong thing.
Kotta-svo-Picchiu had housed the second-largest
telescope in the world. The insolent Doomsdaymen
often insisted that the queen use the Kotta Eye for
her projects, rather than the High Eye at the top
of Heavensgate Mountain. Marget was not going
to be happy about this turn of events.

Chapter 14

Svir leaned forward, delighted by the feel of a dry shirt sliding across his back. Thank goodness these ministerial conferences were held in a dryroom—at least the Bayfastlings wanted their maps and documents kept dry. The room was deep within the Crown Keep. Along the walls were racks of maps and overlays—one of Marget's innovations. The ten top ministers of Crownesse sat at the table. All wore plain black uniforms. Sometimes Svir thought these bureaucrats were ostentatious in their worship of the utilitarian. Only once in a generation did they all wear their dress uniforms.

Tatja Grimm stood at the head of the table, a pointer in her hand. As Queen of Crownesse she was expected to dress lavishly at all times, but at cabinet meetings she could get away with a jeweled semiskirt and silk blouse, her red hair combed smoothly over her shoulders. The ruler of half the civilized world appeared to be around thirty years old. Svir knew that was due to artful makeup. In fact, she was not much past twenty, and in some ways still younger than that.

The report from upcoast had seriously disturbed her, though Svir might be the only minister who saw this. When she was truly upset, she often lost her ability to gauge the understanding of her audience; sometimes her speech became so elliptical only a mind reader could follow. Other times—as in the present case—she went to great lengths to explain the obvious. At the moment she was lecturing them about the Upcoast situation map. It showed the Continent stretching west and northward from Bayfast. The four-thousand-mile-long Doomsday Mountain Range separated a narrow coastal strip from the Interior. That coastal strip was the breadbasket of Crownesse. Now the northernmost province, Picchiu, had revolted against the crown.

"Fortunately, Sfierro Province remained loyal to our rule, and has raised a large army to oppose the Insurrectionists. Ten days ago we sent two thousand troops to land north of the Picchiui—here." She tapped the pointer on a spot some ten miles south of Kotta-svo-Picchiu, at the border of the Doomsday Province. "Doomsday refused to supply troops," she grimaced, "but we hoped to trap the Insurrectionists between our well-trained troops on the north, and the Sfierranyii on the south.

"Gentles, we were stomped. Our so-called shock troops were decimated. If not for the 'undisciplined' Sfierranyii, the Insurrectionists would have it all now. Instead, the Loyalists chased the Rebels north, to the Picchiu River. In the most recent battle we know of, Kotta-svo-Picchiu was destroyed.

We are now fighting a war on the very borders of Doomsday Province.

"In its way, this is as bad for us as if the Picchiui had been victorious. The Doomsdaymen need little excuse to declare their independence of us. Their lands are beyond the effective range of our military forces. The destruction of Kotta-svo-Picchiu—a Doomsday city, despite its name—gives them excuse. The forty-inch telescope just outside the city was destroyed." She took a deep breath. "Gentles, you know I have my . . . quirks. One of them is a profound love for things astronomical. I needed that telescope. I also need the good will of the Doomsdaymen to give me access to their other telescope—the High Eye. We *must not* lose the Doomsday area." She looked at the bureaucrats, and Svir knew she saw the signs of amusement and relief on the ministers' faces. Doomsday Province was important to them for its metals production, not its astrological/astronomical cult. It was good news that her commands did not conflict with national interest. The bureaucrats were loyal, but some monarchs had set the nation back years with fanatical hobbies. It was nice to have a queen with innocuous interests. Tatja smiled back at them, and turned to the Minister of Information. "All right, Wechsler, what do your spies say?"

Haarm Wechsler stood and moved to the head of the table. Wechsler barely topped five feet, and weighed not more than one hundred pounds. But as Minister of Information, he was a man with a long lever; he controlled the most extensive espionage operations in history. He bowed spastically to Tatja. "Thank you, Marget. I've reviewed the reports Lieutenant Mörl brought from my agents

Upcoast. They mosaic an interesting picture. All we've known till now is that the Picchiul Assembly simply passed a resolution declaring that Your Majesty—your pardon—achieved power through fraud. This was so obviously ridiculous that we ignored it—until the assembly further resolved to sever its connections with what it claimed was an unlawful government here in Bayfast. Now my agents report this is all the work of one Oktar Profirio. Profirio is an elusive individual—and a preternaturally talented one. He is a member of the Provincial Assembly—an appointee, replacing a member who died last year. That appointment was on, uh, 17 Summer 936. Before that date he had no fame whatsoever." Wechsler set his notes on the table and looked about the room impressively. "In fact, I suspect the name is an alias. Though Profirio sounds like an Upcoast name, there is no clan in Picchiu which bears it."

Tatja interrupted. "It could indeed be an alias, Minister Wechsler. But about thirty years ago a family of poor nobles named Profirchte moved from the Tsanart Islands to Picchiu. I understand they changed their name to Profirio."

The Minister of Information flushed. It was well known that he had the ego (and raw talent) of ten. Rarely was he bested. It was this occasional display of omniscience that more than anything else kept the ministers of Crownesse personally loyal to Tatja Grimm.

"Um, yes, Marget, I was not aware of that. However, and be that as it may," he rushed ahead, "Oktar Profirio is the behind the Rebel use of artillery. He designed accurate and stable gun tubes. Your Majesty is aware that, of all things, this is what makes artillery the deadly weapon it is. It took us nearly half a century to develop such tubes. Profirio achieved the same in less than half a year. He is either a magician or a defector from our own military. Personally, I have never believed in magicians." No one laughed. "The troops we sent Upcoast were lightly armed—no art'ry, no cavalry, no weapons heavier than the standard crossbow. It is no surprise that they were smashed, now that we know the enemy's advantage. Profirio's men may be provincial rabble, but his guns are damn accurate.

"Fortunately, the Loyalists have some artillery, too. The most recent reports are from my Picchiul agents; they aren't too specific about the Sfierranyii. Apparently the Loyalists managed to steal some of Profirio's guns. Without this theft, the perfidious Profirio would now control all Picchiu Province. Instead, the Loyalists chased him north, to Kotta-svo-Picchiu. The Rebel command took refuge in rooms beneath the observatory. Loyalist fire destroyed that complex, and parts of the city. We know Profirio escaped with a large part of his army—"

"Excuse me, Minister Wechsler," said Svir.

"Certainly. Don't hesitate to ask your question, my man."

Svir ignored Wechsler's tone. "About the men who report from some vantage point on the accuracy of the artillery fire—"

"You're thinking of the Forward Art'ry Observators."

"Yes, that's who I mean. With all this rain, how can they report back to the artillery batteries with fire control directions? I mean, isn't there some new communication technique involved here?"

Wechsler stared for a moment; obviously, the question hadn't occurred to him. Without FAOs, artillery was blind, and therefore useless. Then he saw the answer and smiled. "I fear you have been studying the stars so long, you've forgotten the state of things on the ground. At the fortieth parallel, the latitude of Kotta-svo-Picchiu, there are a number of clear days, even during the Waterfall. So heliographs may be used efficiently and—"

"Besides," spoke Tatja as she stood up, "we're talking about the foothills of the Doomsday range. That's rugged country. If the Sfierranyil art'ry were based on the highlands south of the river, the gunmen would be in line of sight of Kotta-svo-Picchiu—they wouldn't need Forward Observators." She walked swiftly to the head of the table and motioned Haarm Wechsler to be seated. Her comment had an absentminded tone.

Usually Tatja let cabinet meetings drag on and on, till the ministers actually thought the plans decided upon were their own. But when she was truly impatient, she would let the ministers talk for a bit, then break in and tell them—in great detail—how to do their jobs. This was exactly what she did now. "I think we have the facts. You've seen the other reports that the fastboat brought back. Through no fault of your own, we were smashed. According to the reports, Profirio still has thirteen thousand men and two hundred gun tubes of six-inch caliber. Apparently the Sfierranyii have something like eight thousand men and perhaps one hundred and fifty gun tubes. North of Profirio are the uncommitted Doomsdaymen.

"We've three goals: to prevent the destruction of any more astronomical artifacts, to destroy Profirio's army, and to capture Oktar Profirio himself." There was uneasy shifting among her audience; the high ministers saw no particular necessity for the first and third.

"Now, here is how we will accomplish these goals." She sat down and spoke more rapidly and with less inflection. "In four or five days the Waterfall will end, and we will be in the Turnabout. Before that happens we will dispatch every fastboat in our command Upcoast. I will accompany the expedition." Around the table, Svir saw the incredulous faces; the Crown never went on military expeditions. "We won't bother with ships of the line. They're too slow and would be caught in the Turnabout. I figure we can transport something like fifteen thousand men with supporting equipment and art'ry by fastboat alone. This time we won't try a pincers. We'll land on the Loyalist side of the lines and depend on the mountains and the Doomsdaymen to keep the enemy from retreating further north.

"Here is the order of operations: the 336th and 403rd Infantry Battle Groups will compose the landing force, with the direct support of the 25th and 50th Art'ry Batteries. At present the following fastboats are available: Five to Eight, Eleven, Thirteen, Seventeen to Thirty-five . . ." The high ministers recovered from their shock and began writing as fast as they were able; stenographers were barred from cabinet meetings. Once before, Marget had rattled off a battle plan like this. The awful thing was that no matter how off-the-cuff her comments seemed, they were consistent with the facts. Marget knew her military establishment like no leader in history. Her orders extended to the third level of organization. It would have taken the military staffs of the various services ten days of coordinated planning to produce the order she was creating now.

The first time this happened, there had been audible snickers from the ministers. They had repeatedly stopped and questioned her. That had been the only time Svir had seen Tatja enraged. Her outburst had equaled the tantrums attributed to the Mad Kings of the sixth and seventh centuries; several ministers had reverted to common status after that incident. Experience is a good teacher, and Tatja's plans *worked*, so this time no one interrupted with questions or suggestions. It was probably the most efficient and one-sided committee meeting in history. Tatja spoke for half an hour.

Finally she stopped. The ministers looked at their notes, and saw with glazed relief that the order was complete. She smiled pleasantly and asked, "Are there any questions?" There was an exhausted chorus of "No" from around the table. It would be several hours before they or their aides could devise any questions. "Very well," said Tatja, "I will be available to answer any questions that do occur to you. If there is to be a deviation from this plan, I want to hear of it immediately. With this matter, I don't believe in delegating decisions. It's another of my . . . quirks. I expect to be on my way by the night wake period on the third. I'll see you then, if not earlier."

It was a dismissal. Svir followed the others toward the door. He didn't know whether to be

relieved or disappointed. The plan did not require
his services. He had rather enjoyed watching the
other ministers sweat a little, especially Wechsler.
On the other hand, it all bolstered his suspicions
that his post was a sop for his silence. With a great
show of courtesy he offered Haarm Wechsler the
door. Wechsler grunted and walked out. Just then
Tatja spoke. "Stay a minute, Svir." From the corner of his eye, Svir saw Wechsler's retreating back
stiffen at these words. He could imagine the other's suspicion and puzzlement.

When the others were gone and the door shut,
Tatja spoke again. "Have a seat, Svir. I didn't
include you in my order of operations because
your duties will depend on factors I can't predict,
while the military situation will probably work
according to plan—though not the plan I just gave
our friends." Svir sat back in the chair, rather
enjoying being the confidant of the most powerful
person in the world. "I have a feeling that we are
going to be dealing with the Doomsdaymen. Os-
tensibly we needed their support in order to keep
this Profirio from retreating further north. As an
astronomer, you're the only cabinet member who
can speak to their priests with sympathy. And I
know they respect your work in astrometry."

"But you would be just as competent to handle
them."

"Sure, and I'm competent to do anything my
cabinet ministers can do. But there's only one of
me. During the next few days, there will be times
when my actions are so contrary to the interests of
Crownesse that the ministers will balk. Since the
Mad Kings, the civil service has found ways of
defending itself against the arbitrary ruler—and

still maintain a tradition of selfless loyalty to the crown.

"There are only three people I really trust. You and Cor are two of them. You know enough of my motives to go along with my plans even when they seem absurd to my faithful ministers." She gave a lopsided smile. "Cor's going to have to take a vacation from her publishing business. I want you two to handle those chores I don't have the time for—and which the others might . . . misunderstand."

Ugh. This was beginning to sound like old times. Still, her frankness was a welcome change. It was nice to be on the inside of a conspiracy for once.

She sat back in her chair. Svir had seen this change before, but it always seemed spectacular to him. At one moment she was taut, intense, directing a mesh of plans that stretched across the planet and beyond. Then, in an instant, she was a relaxed, seductive woman.

"I only wish Ked Maccioso were here too. He has most of your qualifications—and he's a native of Picchiu. By now he's probably gotten over the way I used him and the barge." The Tarulle company had received the Bayfast *Fantasie* collection and much more when Tatja had come into power.

She crossed her long, smooth legs, and leaned back. Her eyes were half-closed, her lips parted in a dreamy smile. Her figure was slender compared to four years ago—but both he and Cor agreed that these curves were *her* curves. Puberty had come late and lasted long, but Tatja Grimm was truly a young woman now, perhaps the equivalent of a fifteen-year-old. Svir felt sudden guilt to be here and watching and . . . *attracted.* He wanted

so much to go to her, put his arms around her—
all the more because he was sure that she wasn't
pretending, that in fact she had forgotten his presence. He hunted desperately for something to break
the spell.

Then he guessed the cause of her sudden mood.
"You really think Wechsler's 'Perfidious Profirio' is
a godling in disguise?"

"Mmmhmm. . . . There's a good chance. He
could be a defector from our own art'ry labs, but I
think Haarm Wechsler's spies would have discovered that. If he's not a defector, then he's probably of my—caliber. There is no straightforward
way to make practical artillery pieces from nonme-
tallics. A rather complete grasp of ceramic and
impregnation chemistry is required. Even then,
several years of trial-and-error experimentation are
needed unless you use optimization techniques
that I've never bothered to write up. And if Profirio
has built all these gun tubes as fast as it seems,
then he's using factory schemes I've never seen
before. If only he is what he seems." A frown
crossed her face, and her business personality nearly
surfaced.

Svir got up and moved toward the door. The
fact that her desire was not directed at him had no
effect on his desire for her. He vaguely wondered
what violence would greet an advance. And that
thought made him feel even more guilty. If he left
now perhaps he could forget the feeling.

As he reached the door, he remembered the
folder he was carrying. Damn. His escape must be
delayed a few moments. He returned and set the
folder on the table before Tatja. "Marget"—he

used the official name-of-address—"here are the latest reports from the High Eye."

Her eyes opened wide, and her back straightened with a little start. She didn't seem irritated at the interruption, just a little bewildered, as if she had been awakened. "Uh, oh yes. Thanks."

He turned to go. "Stick around, Svir. You can have these back." Tatja read the reports faster than he could browse light fiction. She paused only at the last sheet. Svir remembered the report. It was one of the most peculiar he had seen in a long time. He wondered what her reaction would be. He looked over her shoulder. There were the typical salutations which, in the case of the Doomsday astronomers, had to be sarcasm. The Doomsdaymen had always resented the crown, submitting only because that power could protect them from nearer enemies. They hadn't counted on the rise of Tatja Grimm, who exercised an unwelcome interest in all things astronomical, and who required quarterly reports. At first they had patronizingly referred her to the standard journals, where a few of their results appeared. Even now that they sent her complete reports, Svir felt they did it with an air of condescension. The report began:

Summer 52, 936 YD

To Her Most Gracious Majesty, Marget of Sandros, Queen of All Crownesse, High Mayor of Bayfast, Lady Protector of the Coasts and Deserts, Greeting: Herein we present the 129th consecutive astronomical report of our humble search across the Face of God. We beg Your Majesty's indulgence with this unworthy and trivial tabulation entitled:

Six Abnormal Objects in the Constellation of the Running Thief

In the course of a routine sky patrol session, picture plate 2879 was exposed at approximately 1:47 Heavensgate Meridian Time on the 16th of Spring, 936. A new object in the negative first magnitude was revealed by this exposure. Ten acolytes were assigned the task of maintaining a night-round watch on this area of the sky.

(Svir winced at this offhand reference to what must have been one of the most tortuous projects in the history of astronomy. He could scarcely bear to imagine sitting in the cold and rarified air, hours at a time—watching for a barely visible twinkle light-years away. The Doomsday astronomers were famed for this sort of sadomasochism.)

During the next two quarters, the images of five more such objects were captured on picture plates. Data concerning all six objects are tabulated below.

Object Nr	Began (HMT)	Date	RA*	Declination	Max Mag	Duration (Minutes)
0	1:47	Spring 16, 936	206°32′53″	23°14′05″	-1.**	35
1	2:04	Spring 34, 936	206°32′28″	23°14′09″	-0.8	35
2	2:23:06	Spring 52, 936	206°32′17″	23°14′10″	0.5	31
3	2:43:33	Summer 15, 936	206°32′10″	23°14′09″	1.3	31
4	3:06:11	Summer 33, 936	206°32′06″	23°14′08″	2.0	30
5	3:30:46	Summer 51, 936	206°32′04″	23°14′06″	3.5	29

*According to our amended usage, 0°RA is the zenith meridian at the High Eye on the 1st of

Winter, 920 YD, at 00:00:00 HMT. Right ascension increases in the same sense as the sun travels across the Celestial Face.

**The magnitude given for (0) depends on the assumption that the object was uniformly bright during the plate's exposure, which is a reasonable approximation if the light curve of (0) was similar to that of the other objects. As is our custom, error estimates are not provided.

Objects (1) through (5) were subjected to spectroscopic examination. Their light appears entirely due to continuum radiation. The light curves for objects (1) through (5) appear identical except for the overall change in magnitude, indicated above by the column for maximum magnitude achieved.

The 206/23 region will be below our horizon at the critical time of evening on the 14th of Fall. However, a close watch of this area will be maintained in the coming quarters.

This concludes the 129th report of astronomical activities to Your Majesty. It was prepared by Your Majesty's unworthy servant Mikach G., First Archobserver and Chief Instrumentalist to the High Eye.

Tatja stared at the report for a full ten seconds. When it came, her laughter was explosive. She doubled up in her chair and her face became red. Finally she sat up and wiped tears from her eyes. "Talk about 'words writ large upon the sky,'" she gasped.

Svir picked up the report and looked at it once more. He could guess what she meant by that remark, but he couldn't see how the lights described could be a message. It certainly was an abnormal sequence, but did she think that every unexplained phenomenon was evidence of extra-planetary intelligence?

She saw his look. "You mean you don't see it?"

He donned pedant's armor. "With only the information in this report, I don't. Perhaps you're drawing on information I don't have."

"Oh, I suppose that's possible," she said slowly. "But you are an astronomer. At least that's what you keep telling me. Perhaps you aren't aware of the key facts necessary to solve this puzzle: there are four quarters to a year, fifty-five days to a quarter, forty hours to a day, sixty minutes to an hour, and sixty seconds to a minute. Light travels at one hundred and eighty-six thousand miles per second, and what's more—" she pretended to strain after some subtle detail "—oh yes, the world revolves about the sun at a distance of ninety-two million miles, and not vice versa—as you may have been led to believe. Got all that?"

"Urk." Svir felt his face grow hot; he guessed the point. And he a parallax astronomer! "I'll give it another look," he said, backing toward the door.

Chapter 15

Svir was very suspicious of skoats. They were used mainly as draft animals in the Chainpearls. The fat brown quadrupeds were fine for pulling wagons, but now he was riding one! He watched the brown neck and pointed ears warily. Cor claimed this one was gentle; he was not convinced. The animal had the unsettling habit of bringing its head around and taking a so-called playful nip at his legs. And even if the beast was a great humanitarian, the ride was torture. His rear must be one big bruise. His legs ached from being splayed over the tubby animal's back. What's more, the skoat *smelled*, and its acrid sweat mixed itchily with his own.

He lurched forward as the skoat started downhill. The Crown's Men were on a wide, paved road. It was almost ten feet across, the second-best highway in this part of the Continent. But they were well into the highlands south of the

Picchiu River, and the road switched back and
forth more miles than it went forward. Now their
battle group was headed into a narrow valley.
Almost two hundred feet below, he could see the
stream that had—over millennia—gouged this chan-
nel through the limestone. As they descended, the
sunlight filtered through progressively thicker layers
of leaves until they rode through green twilight.
It was cool and pleasant. The air moved slowly and
was laden with the musty smell of hundreds of
years of decomposing leaves. This scent was strange
to Svir, who had never seen a deciduous tree
before.

The tranquillity of the scene barely registered
over his fatigue.

He crossed the stone bridge at the bottom of
the valley, then twisted in his saddle and looked
back. Where was everyone? Only one gun carriage
behind him was visible, yet he *heard* the creaking of
carriage wheels, the snorts and clatter of a thousand skoats. As his mount climbed the north side
of the valley, he finally saw them. The splotch
camouflage rendered the army virtually invisible
in dense foliage, the wagons' outlines like heat
shimmers above a fire.

There was a louder clatter, and Svir saw a rider
overtaking him. Cor. She urged her animal up the
slope with baby talk and lots of enthusiasm. He
couldn't get over the fact that she was actually
fond of the creatures—even thought she could talk
to them. He put her superior riding ability to the
fact that she had grown up on the Llerenitos,
where skoats were popular.

"Hi, Cor," he said. He leaned out to touch her

shoulder. Kissing a girl on skoatback is virtually impossible.

Cor held his hand for a moment. Svir continued, "I thought you were supposed to stay in Marget's wagon with Ancho." Cor had been under strict orders to remain in the wagon, but he was happy she'd chosen to mutiny.

She retorted, "No, she tells me to stay with Ancho, period. And if you can't see that's what I'm doing, then perhaps I'll take up some other male." Svir looked more closely and saw that there was a bulge under her blouse where no bulge should be. A second later, brown eyes and a pair of pointed ears pushed out of that bulge.

"Besides," said Cor, "we wanted to get some exercise, and be with you."

"Um," Svir felt a little jealous. No doubt she'd had some sleep this afternoon. The expedition from Crownesse had landed in Picchiu Province just after sunrise—nearly twenty-five hours ago. It had taken many hours to get equipment, troops, and skoats off the fastboats. They—Tatja and her generals—had decided to ride straight through the afternoon without sleep: in these longitudes there was no Seraph to twilight the night. The sun was still five hours above the horizon. Svir wondered whether he could hold out till dark. He was falling asleep in his saddle, a feat he would have sworn impossible just ten hours earlier. How the infantrymen kept going he couldn't guess.

But the crown's strategy was sound. Soon they would meet the Loyalists—and incidentally come under Rebel art'ry fire. How exciting.

Now they were moving up a gentle slope. The crest was about four hundred yards away. The tree cover was light, but there was still shade. To the east he saw the foothills of the Doomsday Range, green and gray. Beyond them, so far away and yet so clear against the sky, stood the great peaks of the range. On He'gate, the highest one, was the Doomsday observatory. The view brought him wide awake.

"Svir, look up front." There were riders clumped together. Svir squinted. It was Tatja and the colonel in charge of point security. At least it was the colonel's skoat. But what was that officer doing this far back? They were talking to someone on the ground. The dismounted fellow was suited in maroon, and wore a strangely plumed hat. A Loyalist.

The colonel wheeled and waved to the troops. The command was immediately translated by the sergeant driving the nearest team of art'ry skoats. "Hard hats!" the little sergeant shouted as she donned her own. Svir reluctantly reached for his own reinforced-web-plastic helmet, set it on his head, and fastened the chin strap. He had once thought the head armor looked rather dashing; well, everyone makes mistakes.

Around them, the column was changing into an extended rank, about fifty yards from the crest of the hill. This would take a while. He and Cor dismounted. *Heaven!*

Two hours later, they were back in the saddle. The expedition's fifteen thousand troopers were assembled. For two miles in either direction the irregular line of skoats, guns, and men stood waiting to plunge into the field of enemy observation.

A whistle sounded. The army surged over the crest. Ahead of them the road descended gently, then rose toward a second ridge two or three miles away. Miles beyond the second, he could see another. But the peaceful scenery extended just four hundred yards to their front. Beyond that, the green was broken by craters and patches of blackened earth. On the far hill, a stretch of burnt trees stood like monstrous black mold. The usually pleasant smell of charred wood came strongly across the valley. Svir looked at his wife. She was gently talking her skoat forward. Ancho had disappeared inside her blouse.

The army descended rapidly, and Svir found himself praying they could escape enemy observation and gain the blackened hillside. Soon they would be out of sight to anyone beyond the next hill.

Then the sky exploded. Two hundred yards to the front, a line of orange-red fireballs hung forty feet in the air. A second later Svir's head was snapped back and his helmet clanged. He reached up and felt a quarter-inch shrapnel fragment imbedded in his helmet. He watched glassy-eyed as the fireballs become innocent black puffs of smoke and blew away. What would it be like when the enemy got the range and timing?

The army broke into squares, one battle group forward, the next back, so as to avoid complete catastrophe if the curtain of fire ever came on target.

The corrected fire was thirty seconds coming. The nearest burst was high explosive, and it made the shrapnel sound like a popped paper bag. He felt the blow through his whole body. His skoat staggered to its knees. Svir was tossed backwards, out of the saddle. He grabbed air, his mind filled with visions of landing on the ground and being trampled. Then his mount surged to its feet and he found himself on its rear, behind the saddle. He scrambled forward as the animal broke into a gallop.

Cor! He looked wildly around and saw her riding out of the smoke. Her lower face was covered with blood. She came abreast of him and shouted, "You hurt bad?"

"That's what I was going to ask you," he shouted back. His jaw was bloody, too. They both had nosebleeds. "Come on." They were falling behind their battle group. They swerved around a brushfire and regained their positions. The formation finally reached the bottom of the valley, where they would be hidden from enemy observation. The air cleared, and Svir no longer choked on dust and smoke. At their far right flank an impact-fused H.E. shell went off next to an art'ry piece. Svir watched in amazement as the gun tube rose high in the air.

They learned later that casualties had been light, that the whole affair lasted less than fifteen minutes.

His ears buzzed from the punishment they had received, and all sound came muffled. The land was black except for flickering halos of flame around tree skeletons. There was blue sky somewhere above the haze. They were now eighty yards from the crest. Shells still burst, but the enemy's aim, at least for Svir's battle group, was wildly inaccurate. Of the other battle groups, he could not be so sure. The ridgeline was cut by numerous defiles that made it hard to see cross-slope. The group's forward motion ceased. Supply vehicles moved to the guns they were to feed. The air was filled with the sounds of whining skoats, creaking wagons, shouting men. These last were not confused sounds, but the efficient direction of officers who knew exactly what they wanted and were working with well-trained troops.

The group was preparing for art'ry battle. A gun carriage pulled up near Svir and Cor. The driver leaped down and raced to the front of her skoats. She unfastened their harnesses and led them away from the piece. The gunmen on top of the carriage moved just as efficiently. They were performing a much-practiced task, and there was no talk or wasted motion. Two of them unlashed the weapon as the other two passed a six-inch shell up from the supply wagon. Infantrymen ran past, their crossbows at port arms. Svir couldn't imagine how they could run after the long day's march, but the troopers were really moving. In seconds, they were gone in the smoke. Evidently that smoke was not due to enemy action—Svir could hear grenades popping. He looked back at the gunmen. The piece was loaded and the heavy plastic breach closed. A courier from the FAOs called out fire control directions. The greenish barrel was cranked up. Through the haze, Svir could see other gun carriages, and hear their breeches being slammed shut. The enemy was about to get a devastating reply. Then came a pause. The crown's war machine awaited the command that would set it in motion.

Three minutes passed, and still no action. Through the buzzing in his ears, he heard Cor say something. He turned to her. "What's that?"

"I ask, where are the Sfierranyil Loyalists?"

A good question. Everyone here wore Crown camouflage. The only provincial he'd seen all afternoon was the one talking to Tatja and the point colonel. What sort of trap . . . he looked around, half expecting to see enemy bowmen spring from hidey-holes.

Just then, an officer rode down the line, shouting indistinct commands. The gunmen looked up in surprise, then began unloading their weapons. As they did, the forward infantrymen came back down the hill. Svir gaped. This reminded him of stories about recruits commanding training units. Apparently, the people at the top could not make up their minds.

The troops reformed and resumed their march—though now they were moving east, parallel to the ridgeline. Svir sighed and urged his animal forward. It was at least an hour till sunset, and at this latitude twilight would last three hours.

He sidled toward the nearest gun carriage and called to the driver. "What's the story?" The woman looked down at him—his camouflage bore no rank insignia. Her answer was an obscenity, roughly equivalent to "We were shafted."

He fell back and walked beside a carriage. The gunman sitting there was more talkative. "That's right. We got it up to here." He motioned. "There's only one decent reason for racing over that hill in daylight, and that's to get our pieces in range and give the enemy a taste of our rock. If we weren't going to engage, we should've stayed back there—" he waved at the hill to the south "—until dark, and then come across. Instead we lost men—*for nothing!*" The gunman seemed to realize he might be talking to someone in authority. "Somebody made a stupid mistake," he finished.

Svir found himself nodding. Perhaps Tatja was

out of action, but the Crownesse generals themselves were competent men. That left provincial treachery the most likely cause of the debacle.

Behind them, the sun sent rose and orange across the sky. The high peaks of the Doomsday Range stood bright, the world's ragged edge. They left the burning land, and soon there was only the smell of grass and living trees. If Svir hadn't been in the saddle for most of the last twenty hours, he might have enjoyed the scene. He slumped forward, trying to keep his balance in the waves of sleep that swept stronger and stronger over him. Cor rode beside him; he was thankful she didn't try to make cheerful conversation.

The sky was dark now. Only the Doomsday peaks were still in daylight. They formed a jagged red band, hanging in limbo above the darkened, nearer lands. Somehow he had missed the sunset. . . .

Then Cor was pushing at his shoulder, calling to him. He sat up and looked about. Twilight was nearly past. There were lots of stars, but Seraph's familiar light was missing. "We're here," Cor said.

At first glance the forest around them seemed uninhabited. Then he saw the tents hidden in the brush. Further away he could hear the *grunchunch* of browsing skoats. The Crown's Men had finally reached the Loyalists. Svir slipped from his saddle and leaned against the skoat. A shadow approached.

"*Svo keechoritte bignioru?*" it asked.

Svir was about to croak, "*Sagneori Sfierro,*" (I don't speak Sfierro) when Cor cut in with, "*Attrupa bignoro chispuer, sfiorgo malmu.*" Sfierro was quite close to Cor's native Llereno.

"*Traeche ke,*" the other said, and led them some

hundred paces into the brush. The Sfierranyi stopped, pointed to an open space, and gabbled something more. "He says we can put our tent up here," Cor said. Svir felt like crying. At this point he could scarcely unpack his skoat. The Sfierranyi solved that problem by unhitching the pack and dropping it to the ground. Then he grabbed the skoats' reins and led them away.

Svir looked stupidly at the gray patch that was the folded tent. Itchybites buzzed in the moist, cool air. The tiny bastards would feed well tonight. He fell to his knees and tried to unfasten the tent buckles. Cor joined him. Soon they had the tent spread flat on the ground. He slipped the center pole through the tent fabric and hoisted it. Cor crawled inside and set the floor rods.

Then they were both inside. The ground seemed so soft. He reached for Cor, and she came easily into his arms. His kiss became a snore and he was asleep.

Cor grinned in the darkness. "This is no good, friend. Tomorrow, you get more sleep during the day."

Chapter 16

"Listen, you pack of traitors. You cost us thirty-five men and three art'ry pieces this afternoon. We're going to have an explanation or we're going to have your heads!" In the flickering torchlight, Haarm Wechsler's face was even paler than usual. "For the last two hours you've led us a merry chase all over this camp. But now we've found you." He stopped and stood a little taller. The guardsmen behind him came to attention. "Now you can answer for your infidelity to Marget herself."

Everyone in the room—Provincial and Bayfastling—came to his feet. Tatja entered the Sfierranyil command tent and looked around. Close behind her came three general officers. Her lips parted in a faint smile and she murmured to Wechsler, "Got'em softened up, Haarm?" She advanced to the table and sat down. "Please be seated, gentles." Behind her, the Crownesse people uneasily took their seats. On the other side of the table the

181

182 *Vernor Vinge*

Sfierranyil commanders seemed equally upset. Most of the provincial commanders were old men. All but one she recognized from Wechsler's dossiers. These weren't the best campaigners in the world, but they should have been loyal.

Her tone remained pleasant. "Now that we are all together, perhaps things can be cleared up. You deceived us this afternoon. Your courier told us you needed immediate artillery support. When we came to your aid, we found you were moving away from us. This misunderstanding cost us men and equipment, and I ask for an explanation." Her reasonable tone took some of the edge off Wechsler's previous statement of the question.

A militiaman stood and bowed, his chest of medals glinting in the torchlight. He wiped his hand through tangled white hair, the picture of a general disgraced; even his epaulets drooped. His Språk was excellent, however. "Marget, what you say is true. There was deception. We can only beg your mercy. We deceived you because we were deceived ourselves. We, uh, our training is not as thorough as might be desired by Your Majesty. We are operating far outside our province. To the north is our enemy and the Doomsdaymen—which latter refuse us aid. To the south is Picchiu Province—whose army is our enemy." The old man paused. His rambling had taken him so far afield he couldn't remember his point. Tatja grabbed Wechsler's elbow before that worthy could make some cutting comment about Sfierranyil mental acuteness. After all, she found normal people almost as dopey as this one.

The militiaman had regained the thread. "Marget, the campaign has taken us further and yet further

inland, as we followed the forces of the Rebel
Profirio. We never guessed that your aid would
come to us from the south—or that it would arrive
so soon. We mistook you for Picchiul reinforce-
ments pretending to be Crownesse troops. Thank
the gods that you were so numerous that we could
not attack you—only trick you into Rebel fire.

"So. That's why we deceived you. And that's
why, even when you arrived here, we were cir-
cumspect in admitting you to our command area."
The fellow's head bobbed up and down miserably.
Behind Tatja there was some easing of tension: the
explanation was credible.

Tatja nodded. "Where is Profirio's main force
now?"

"Uh, we believe it's across the river, about five
miles upstream."

She raised an eyebrow. "How is that possible?
This afternoon we were attacked by his artillery—
and that was almost fifteen miles downstream from
here." She produced a small piece of parchment
and wrote rapidly upon it.

The young provincial sitting opposite Tatja
touched the militiaman's sleeve and said, "*Deche
mau*, Sam." The old man nodded gratefully and
sat down.

As the young man stood, Tatja handed the parchment to a messenger and whispered something to
him. The courier nodded and left. She turned back
to the provincials. The young fellow was dark, his
beard close-trimmed. The expression on his narrow face was unworried, almost sardonic. He wore
the uniform of a full general in the provincial
militia, but his chest bore not a single medal—

which was unusual, since the Sfierranyil Militia gave medals for things like having clean fingernails.

"And who are you?" came Wechsler's voice.

"Marget, I am Jolle. Until present difficulties I was a commercial chemist, but war makes different things of people, and the Provincial Assembly elected me military commander of this expedition." There was a faint snort of disgust from the Crown's Men. They had a saying in the civil service that a nation which elects its generals elects defeat.

Jolle spoke rapidly. He had the right words and syntax, but there was a Sfierro lilt to his pronunciation. "You see, Profirio has split his art'ry from his infantry. So, in fact, our misunderstanding this afternoon may give us a decisive advantage over the Rebels."

"Hmm, that would take some explaining."

Jolle nodded. "This Profirio fellow wants desperately to reach the mountains. We think he figures on persuading the Doomsdaymen to join his cause. After today's encounter, we know the man has decided to gamble, to leave his art'ry behind and gain himself speed. I suspect he intended to put his troops between us and O'rmouth, so our artillery fire would provoke the Doomsdaymen to enter the contest on his side. At the same time, his own art'ry could follow both armies, along the Riverside Road. Thus he would end up with his art'ry on our flank and the Doomsdaymen against us, too.

"Unfortunately for him, the scheme hinged on our ignorance of it. This is why our misunderstanding of this afternoon is for the good: Profirio's art'ry commander was flustered by your appearance. He opened fire, and destroyed his master's plan. Knowing that his art'ry is hopelessly far behind, *we* can use the Riverside Road with impunity. Thus we can get inland the faster, and achieve just the position he wanted for himself."

Tatja considered. Profirio's gamble had the ingenuity and daring she expected. It had failed because of a subordinate's mistake and the unexpected appearance of her troops. There were still edges and ends that didn't fit, but the more she saw, the more she was convinced that her goal was near.

How quiet everything was. It was late, and the animals of these lands had no Seraph to light their nights. The only sounds were insects creaking. It was hard to believe they were sitting in the midst of an armed camp. Inside the tent, things were quiet too. Even the officers who pretended to be awake sat with their eyes glazed. A sound suspiciously like a snore came from behind her. These poor weak people—given thirty hours of hard work, they were dead on their feet.

She looked up and found Jolle's dark eyes gazing back. There was something unnatural about this one's accent. Her next question was not directly related to the events of the day. "Have you any idea where the Rebels got their art'ry in the first place?"

Jolle shrugged. "No. Though he raided the ammunition stockpiles Your Majesty keeps in the provinces. I've heard the man is a foreigner."

"Yes, I've, uh, suspected that. But where did you Loyalists get your artillery?"

"Well, the ammunition as Profirio did."

"And the gun tubes?"

Jolle spread his hands in self-deprecation. "I am a chemist. I beg forgiveness if it displeases the crown, but I designed most of the artillery you see among the Sfierranyii. Without it we would have had no chance to protect Your Majesty's interests."

In that instant the silence seemed complete. One dark face filled the sensory universe; time itself slowed as she considered one fantastic possibility and then another.

Svir came awake with the lightheaded alertness that follows a short, uneasy sleep. He swallowed painfully, trying to remove a nauseous taste from his mouth. "What do you want?" he heard Cor say to the figure silhouetted in the entrance to the tent.

The shape whispered, "Ma'am, I have a message for you." The courier reached forward, fumbled a parchment into Cor's hand. Svir hunted about in his pack and came up with matches. The light was almost painfully bright.

The courier blew the flame out. "We're under light security, sir. You can't do that," he said.

Svir's voice was as close to a scream as a whisper can be. "How the hell can we read this without a light!"

"I didn't make the rules, you—"

Svir was speechless for a second. Then he remembered that he was a person of authority and pulled rank. The messenger backed out of the tent, cowed. Svir carefully unsealed the flap, then lit another match, shielding it with his hand. The message was cryptic and simple: "Azimuth 30°. Do it now—T."

"Oh, boy. Tatja wants us to go ahead with the

Plan." He began assembling the tripod and signaling equipment. Meanwhile Cor woke Ancho and fed him. The dorfox was not lively; they could expect trouble with him. Finally Cor convinced the little animal that there was a job to do. Ancho clung to her neck as she crawled out of the tent. Svir followed, dragging tripod and signaler.

For the moment, every sensation seemed intense. But his balance was poor and he still had that awful taste in his mouth. This was actually the middle of the night wake period, as practiced in Bayfast. In fact, for him it was nearly lunchtime. The long daylight march and the different sleeping customs of the Upcoast people had inverted his normal schedule. He felt alert only because his natural time sense told him he should be.

The trees were close set. Insect sounds were loud and there were no signs of human activity. Svir peered up through the branches at the stars. He couldn't see enough sky to recognize constellations. He and Cor moved cautiously along an indistinct path. The air was cool, but his uniform was still damp with sweat. He couldn't remember having felt more dirty and chilled.

He guided Cor—northward? Upslope, anyway.

There was a man-sized blotch about fifty feet away. He touched Cor's shoulder, pointed the fellow out to her. He felt her nod. She reached to caress the dorfox. When she was satisfied that Ancho was alert and radiating, they resumed their walk. Svir breathed a nearly audible sigh of relief as they passed the sentry unchallenged. They were almost thirty yards past the hallucinated soldier when a low, determined voice spoke. "Halt. Who goes there?"

Svir froze. Damn. The first sentry was a decoy. They were lucky the second guy bothered to challenge them at all.

"I said, 'Who goes there?' Respond or I shoot."

Svir gulped and said, "Erl Bonnip, trying to find the latrine." As he spoke, Cor turned and walked toward the voice in the bush. Now that Ancho had noticed the other fellow, he was radiating I'm-not-here. Since the sentry was already alerted, the signal couldn't cover Svir's existence; he must stand exposed.

"Advance and be recognized."

Svir moved cautiously toward the voice. At best he would be turned back—and that only if the sentry didn't notice the tripod and signaler he was carrying. . . .

There was a dull *thunk* and a muffled groan. Then Cor emerged from the thicket.

"It's okay," she whispered. "I didn't hit him hard, but Ancho gave him a good dose."

They continued along the trail. The night no longer seemed particularly tranquil. He knew this job was not the trivial errand Tatja had made it sound. If they weren't shot by Sfierranyil or Crownesse sentries, there was always the possibility that Rebel infiltrators might get them. The ground sloped down now. Technically they were in the Picchiu River valley. A darkness at the bottom of the sky was the far side of the valley, seven miles away. Svir thought he could see the river itself, glinting here and there between trees. A fatbat cooed somewhere near. How many human eyes watched this scene?

The forest thinned, and they moved quietly into the open. Their first objective was to get far enough

from the camp so its position wouldn't be given
away. He swore silently. If Tatja were sure of her
theory, why bother? She'd gone over the plan in
mind-numbing detail during the voyage from
Bayfast. She thought an alien was marooned here,
was using native materials and native armies to
attain its incomprehensible goals. Now the pre-
sumed alien must be contacted, and since this was
an operation at cross purposes with the crown's
official goal, he and Cor must do it on their own.
They could get killed, all for an unsupported
speculation.

He led Cor into a thicket; they settled down.
He looked into the sky, found the Hourglass, and
extended its base to intersect the long bar of the
Northern Cross. Now that he had north fixed, he
could find the azimuth in Tatja's message: the
azimuth of the Rebel camp.

As he set the tripod on the ground and screwed
the signaler on it, Cor took out paper and pen,
ready to record any answer. He pulled the starting
strip and felt the box warm. He grasped the shutter trip and recalled the exact words Tatja wanted
sent. The message was in Savoy Mercantile Code,
the most common signaling code of Crownesse:
AS THE ISLAND APE SAID TO THE SHIP-
WRECKED SAILOR: MAY I AID YOU? Since
island apes are brainless, only a very peculiar person
would get the point.

He began tripping out the message. The lamp's
shutter flew open and shut with barely audible
clicks. The air was clear, and the box was well
shielded. He saw no sign of the beam he was
casting across the valley. He had barely finished
the third word when he saw a light flicker down

by the river. He ignored it, concentrated on his own message. Behind him, Cor whispered the letters she was recording from the other signal lamp: "KZTPQ MPAPF RPTOZ DZRNR."

He finished the message and folded the tripod. "Let's go. I'll bet you iron that was one of our own spies reporting that someone was signaling the enemy from here. If Profirio doesn't land a shell on us, we'll be shot by our own people."

They scrambled out of the brush and trotted across open ground. Svir dropped the signaler; they were no longer red-handed. He guided Cor by the waist. She paid little attention to the ground, but kept her face turned toward the river valley. On her shoulder, Ancho made whimpering noises.

Cor stopped, and Svir followed her gaze. Across the valley, at the top of the far crest, a signal lamp winked on and off. Cor took her book out and recorded every letter. The message was short: just two words, and the first was nonsense. More military signals? He felt Cor shrug. "I think the friend yonder plays Tatja's game; maybe she can translate." They watched for nearly half a minute, but there was nothing more. Further up the hill they were stopped by a party of guards. Ancho was either asleep or afraid, because he didn't radiate anything effective. Svir identified himself as the astronomer royal and demanded to be taken to the command area to report a "disgraceful breach of security."

Fifteen minutes later they walked through the light trap of the command tent. Though large and well appointed, the interior had a crudeness that labeled it provincial. A single oil lamp hung from the center pole. Svir and Cor walked past the officers and guards who sat bleary-eyed behind the queen. Tatja's face was strangely slack. She glanced up and didn't seem to recognize them. What had happened? Svir looked at the provincials. Nothing strange there. Apparently she had been talking to the young underofficer who faced her across the camp table.

Cor handed her the notebook. She stared at the message for a long moment: JOLLE JESTS. Her slack expression was replaced by a faint smile. She looked up at them, then at the fellow standing on the other side of the table. She spoke very softly. "We were wrong, Cor. There are two of them."

Svir looked more carefully at the other man. There were enough bars on his sleeve to make him very high ranking. His chair was set ahead of the provincial generals. He returned Svir's gaze with a puzzled frown. Then he smiled and leaned forward. His voice was low. "How many more are there like you three?"

Tatja replied just as softly, "How many more are there like you two?"

"Just we two. You see, I'm a gendarme, a policeman. The thing called Profirio is—a monster."

Chapter 17

It was said Riverside Road in Picchiu Province passed through the most beautiful country in the world. Svir did not dispute the assertion. The road ran along the Picchiu River, straight through an open forest whose trees often extended their branches to form a roof across the road, a roof that scattered green and gold highlights on the pavement.

They were nearly ten thousand feet above sea level, and though the air was thin, it was wonderfully crisp, and dry. For the first time since they had left Bayfast, Svir felt really clean. That morning, he and Cor had taken a quick swim in the icy waters of the Picchiu. Even now, he could hear the river rolling by just a few feet away. That sound would come louder as they moved upstream, as the valley became a gorge and the riverbed steepened.

It was when the forest roof parted that things

got really impressive. Still miles away, the main peaks of the Doomsday Range rose thousands of feet above the road. Except for a cloud band at the fourteen-thousand-foot level, every detail was visible. Much of the flanks were free of snow, and the bare bones of the young mountains stood black and gray and yellow and brown. Svir thought he could see every crystalline striation there. In the nearer distance, rugged hills ranged on either side of the river valley. Downstream those hills were gentle, covered by the same deciduous forest as the valley proper. Here they bore dark-needle looproot trees. And they were fast becoming too rugged for the looproot—great sections of bedrock were visible. The hillsides would soon become cliff faces.

But no matter how formidable the valley walls might seem, Svir knew there were paths there. And somewhere up there, the enemy's infantry and supply trains made their slow, difficult way. By now those forces must be several miles behind the Crownesse–Sfierranyil army, since the Crown's Men were using the wide, straight Riverside Road.

Through the trees bordering the road, Svir could see foot soldiers paralleling the cavalry and art'ry. The Sfierranyil battle groups had been annexed to the crown's, summing to nearly twenty-four thousand men and five hundred art'ry pieces. From their position in the second group, Svir and Cor couldn't even see the head of the column—some thousand yards ahead. Before and behind them was the line of creaking supply and art'ry wagons, puffing skoats, and silent infantrymen. The line stretched nearly nine miles. It wasn't the biggest army in the world, but the crown's battle groups comprised the best men and equipment from the best military organization in the world.

And of all the people marching along this road, only four knew the real reason they were here. Last night he had witnessed the strangest revelation of his life.

Tatja had adjourned the conference in the tent. This was a relief to most of those present. They had been up all afternoon. Not even Haarm Wechsler had noticed that Tatja and Jolle stayed behind when the others left. Empty, the tent was like a cave. The flickering torch lighted four faces; everything beyond was darkness. Then Jolle revealed the secret behind all recorded history. *Humans were not accidental castaways on Tu. The world was a breeding farm. Slaughtering operations would begin as soon as the creature called Profirio regained contact with his superiors.*

There had been a long silence. Svir felt himself caught in a nightmare that would disappear if he could only show its implausibility. "For food?" he asked.

The other shook his head. Svir wondered if Jolle were his real name. Profirio was certainly an alias, since it had a distinctive Upcoast flavor. "Well, then what does he want to kill us for?"

Jolle spoke a single word. "Golems."

Svir looked blank.

Jolle stared at them for a moment. Then he spoke to Tatja. "There's really only one of you, right?"

She nodded. "Yes, and I've looked."

"Tough," Jolle commiserated. He waved at Cor and Svir, and Tatja replied, "Fingers."

"Hmm," said Jolle, "perhaps I should have, too."

"But surrogate pain. Is there?"

"No. Ten trillion. Human too." He nodded. "You're it and foxily burnt."

Tatja smiled shyly.

Svir's jaw dropped. What were they talking about? Occasionally Tatja would carelessly address him in this fashion, but his blank look had always forced her to be silent or to make sense. Now she had found someone on her own level, and there was no need for "redundancy."

He was about to ask for a translation, when Jolle said, "Excuse me Minister Hedrigs, Miss Ascuasenya. If you're going to be in on this, you should know what's going on. I just assumed from the way you worked together that you. . . . Perhaps golem is not the right word, but what shall I say? Have you ever heard this term?" He made a meaningless sound. "No? Well, not much Anglic would survive their processing, especially a term without referent. So I'll use 'golem' to mean thinking machine. If your technology were just fifty years more advanced, you would think you knew exactly what I mean. . . . As it is, I am constrained to the vocabulary of superstition. Perhaps that's for the best. A word like 'golem' will never give you the false sense of understanding you might have if. . . . The golems I refer to are much more like magic than any science you can imagine. Even you, Marget. Until you have training, I suggest you accept the magical connotation. Then you won't be fooled by false analogies with the thinking machines that you are capable of inventing. . . ."

Jolle had little accent, and he ordered his words properly. Nevertheless his speech was strange. He

spoke rapidly, running one sentence into another.
If a sentence were especially long, his voice would
drop and he would mumble the ending, as if the
words were a redundant, painful ritual. His hands
never stopped moving. The overall effect was impressive. Svir could imagine how the provincials
had been overwhelmed by a man who spewed
forth ideas faster than he could speak them.

Sometimes Tatja sounded like this, though she
was perfectly capable of slow, natural exposition—
after all, she had grown up here. Was Jolle's manner an affectation, or was he unable to slow down?
It had never occurred to Svir that it might be
difficult to act stupid.

Jolle continued, "Though they are necessary to
the function of society, golems are expensive to
construct. There is, however, a cheap—and highly
immoral—way of improvising golems. That method
is to, hmm, destroy the souls of lesser creatures
and so reduce them to golems. Pröfe—Profirio—is
in the employ of an . . . organization that has
spent two thousand years preparing this planet as
a cheap golem-production plant. First they chose a
resource-poor planet far from civilization. Then
they seeded it with your ancestors, Minister
Hedrigs, people they kidnapped from the backwa-
ters of civilization. They wrecked your minds and
bodies, dumped you here, and waited. My type
lives a long time and can afford to be patient.
Every so often, the organization sent a scout
vehicle—crewed by the likes of Profirio—to ana-
lyze your population, technology."

"Yes," broke in Tatja. "Even without me, people would soon guess parts of this."

"Really?"

"We observed one of your vehicles enter our system last year," said Svir.

"You saw our drive stutter. You're further along than they planned. But that was one of the reasons for these scouting missions. They want the planet's population to reach a billion before they start harvesting; but just as important, they want you planet-bound—even an interplanetary flight technology would mean a drastic increase in the cost of operations. In one sense, their motivation is quite understandable: they want the maximum gain for the least effort."

"What would then happen," asked Cor, "if Profirio were successful?"

"Once he tells his superiors that you are ready for . . . harvest, they will set up a slaughterhouse on Thriy—Seraph you call it. One percent of your population will be spirited away every year. There is no escape from such abductions. It will all seem quite supernatural. Technological progress will stop; inventions will disappear, experiments explode. Other than that the organization will have no interest in what you do. As long as your population growth rate remains constant, the operation will show a profit." He spread his hands in a gesture that seemed to put the prediction in the subjunctive.

"Their plans have come perilously close to success. But no matter how expensive artificial golems, and no matter how necessary golems are to our activities, only a small fraction of my kind are warped enough to buy ones produced by the slaughter of innocents. My friends and I have known for nearly a thousand years that Profirio's organization was planning something like this, but we didn't know where they were operating. I have spent four hundred years ingratiating myself to these criminals. Finally my efforts were rewarded. I was hired to accompany Profirio on the present survey of your world.

"Things went well at first. We left our . . . scoutboat in orbit about six hundred thousand miles out. Any closer and if you had good telescopes—as it turns out you do—you would spot the thing immediately. We landed in the outback of Sfierranyi Province. I won't go into the gruesome details, but I botched things and Profirio caught on to me. We had quite a fight out there in the hills last spring. I'm a little surprised the pyrotechnics were not observed—but a typhoon was moving inland at the time and I guess everybody was too busy to notice. Our battle destroyed almost all the equipment we had brought down for our survey.

"Our scoutboat is still out there, and the man who communicates with it will be victorious. I have one instrument left—it's similar to your signalers. But to use it, I must know the exact position of the boat. I need a large telescope to accomplish that. We've continued the struggle with local resources.

"We both needed armies. We are persuasive individuals—but the natives need some excuse to provoke them to war. Profirio chose to revolt against your central government. I did the logical thing and led the local militia on a campaign against the Rebels. It is blind luck that it worked out this way; that your forces and mine met as allies. But I apologize for using your army this afternoon to trick Profirio's art'ry into revealing itself.

"Unless you people are hiding something, there are only two large observatories in this part of the

world. That's why we had the battle at Kotta-svo-
Picchiu. Profirio got there first and was hoping to
hold out until dark. I had to destroy the scope to
keep him from using it. With that gone, we are
forced to go after the High Eye."

"Excuse me," spoke Svir, "but why did you
bother with armies? On a good skoat you could
have made it to O'rmouth in just a few days. Then
you could have applied your powers of persuasion
directly to the astronomers."

Tatja answered that one. "Jolle and Profirio view
armies as you might a shirt of armor. If one of
them took off alone, the other could grab an army
and use it to destroy a single unarmed opponent.
It's a question of balancing the speed with the
risk."

"That's right," said Jolle. "Eventually, Profirio
may be reduced to personal action, but it will be a
sign of desperation. He'll have to persuade the
Doomsdaymen to cooperate with him rather than
us, and his identity will be clearly . . ." Jolle took
a deep breath, interrupting his own rushing flow
of speech. "One of us will control the High Eye—
and the future of this planet will be determined."

Chapter 18

The call to dismount brought Svir back to the present. It was late morning, and they had been on the road five hours. It was time to water the skoats. The place was right, too: Here the road swung close to the Picchiu River. There was a three-hundred-yard stretch where it was easy to bring the animals down to the water.

He and Cor scrambled off their skoats and waited for further directions. Water call was conducted with more precision and ceremony than most supply functions. He had read somewhere that the efficiency of a mounted command could be measured by observing water call. He had to admit that watering a battle group was not simple; they could be here all day if things got out of hand.

Finally it came time for them to go to the river. The art'ry skoats were released from their gun carriages, and animals and men moved over the rocky ground to the river. Behind them, gun crews loaded their weapons and received fire control directions. Then came the concussive *crump, crumpcrump* as the battery lofted six-inch shells into the sky. Ten miles downstream, those shells would tear wide the road they had so recently traversed; the enemy's artillery would not be allowed to catch up. Too bad about the road. The expeditionary force had already stopped five caravans bound for the coast—caravans carrying hundreds of ounces of copper and iron from O'rmouth. Such interference with Doomsday commerce was not going to win the crown any friends, but Tatja intended to stay ahead of the news of her vandalism.

The Picchiu River was one hundred feet wide here. The water foamed and showered as it moved through a rapids; only a canoe could have navigated the torrent. Quartermasters had assembled several hundred watering troughs, since water directly from the river was much too cold for the animals. The skoats had to be urged to the troughs, but when they began drinking, it was with characteristic greediness. Svir examined the animals critically. It was amazing how much they had changed. They were no longer sleek and furry. Now their bodies were covered with superficial cuts and gashes. Though they were fed four times a day, tendons and bones showed clearly through their skin. He commented on this to Cor.

"Yes, I know," she responded in a subdued voice. "On the fastboats I thought the collars seemed small for the animals. Now I understand. This march burns the flesh from them. Most of the collars are now too big for the creatures. We lost thirty of them in the artillery attack, but three times that many have died from exhaustion. See—"

She pointed at a quartermaster veterinarian. The
fellow walked slowly down the rank of skoats, lifting their blankets and painting antiseptic on the
raw sores and cuts he found. The Loyalists' animals were in much poorer shape than the crown's
skoats—they had been in the campaign five times
as long. Even with all the quartermaster's care,
this was still killing work. By the time he reached
the end of the watering line, the vet had marked
three skoats to be dropped from the train. Those
animals were in no shape to continue with the
expedition, even as unburdened reserve. "For no
fault of their own and for no gain of their own,
they lose their lives."

For the first time, Svir felt affection for the poor
animal that had carried him so far.

This was a rest stop for the humans, too. Behind
the skoats, the troops of the battle group lay or sat
on the ground. Most of the Provincial Loyalists lay
motionless. They had been part-time militiamen,
yet they had been on this campaign forty days.
Their uniforms were tattered. Their boots were
held together with ragged cloth bands. In some
cases, blood and pus discolored the cloths. The
Crown's Men had better equipment and were
fresh—besides, they were trained for this sort of
thing. They kept apart from their unprofessional
counterparts. But even among the professionals,
there was evidence of strain. There was little of
the good-natured talk of earlier rest stops.

The hospital wagon arrived with the last of the
battle group. Since they were moving through
wild lands, the Crown's Men were forced to carry
their casualties with them, at least so long as those
casualties weren't too numerous. At present there

were probably a hundred wounded—and about twelve in this battle group. The wagon had its cloth sides rolled up so that the occupants were exposed to the open air. Svir found it difficult to look away from that wagon. There was nothing repulsive about the interior, no gore. Everything looked clean and comfortable. Some of the patients were even sitting up, and these looked better than most of the "ready" troops. But others in the wagon lay quite still, with only their heads exposed. They might have been corpses except for the trouble the crown was taking to bring them along.

Two medics moved to the back of the wagon and drew one of those long white forms off the platform. They carried it to the far side of the wagon. A colonel and three enlisted men followed the medics into the brush. The enlisted men carried entrenching tools. Svir recalled that a field grade officer was required to participate in the burial of all combat victims.

Cor made a strange laugh. "I used to like stories of fate and the gods. It made Rey so mad. 'We are no one's doormat!' he would say at me so fierce. . . . Strange, that fantasies should be the greater truth. They use us up like the skoats." She looked at Svir levelly. "It is *wrong*."

"Don't think fuzzy, Cor." The voice came from behind them. Svir felt Cor start with surprise. They turned and saw Tatja. Instead of her usual camouflage uniform, she wore a feminine outfit which wouldn't have been out of place in Bayfast— but which here seemed as appropriate as a jester at an execution. The oppression that clouded everyone's mind did not touch her. Never before had she seemed quite so callous to the problems of the people she used.

"What's fuzzy about it?" he said angrily.

"You seem to think that people would live in peace if left to themselves. That's rarely true. If you study history you'll find that most wars occur because the *people* see some personal advantage in victory. I imagine that most Sfierranyii figure their support of the crown will get them Picchiul lands after the war. Many of these militiamen thought they would win booty in this adventure— though I doubt they feel that way now."

"Hell, Ta—" The exclamation came out a shout. He lowered his voice and continued with quiet intensity, "So what? We're not talking about the general case. If it weren't for your kind, we *would* have peace."

Tatja smiled. "It's true that Jolle and I are manipulating everyone. But don't forget the *reason*. Our men and the militia believe they die for a cause that we know is trivial, but in the final analysis, this war is more important and more just than *any* in the history of this planet. If we fail, the future will be darker than any war could make it." She had him there. The sacrifices seemed necessary—even if the people who made them were ignorant of the ultimate justification. But he wondered if this argument would appeal if he were one of those who was going to get cut to pieces.

The last skoats were being led from the troughs. Some squads were already being assembled. The art'ry fire had stopped. Soon the next battle group would arrive. No one came near Cor and Svir and Tatja. Unless the Queen wished otherwise, she had privacy—even when she walked in the open.

Cor spoke. "But Marget, how do you know that you aren't also being used?"

"What?" Tatja seemed nonplussed, but Svir had the feeling his wife had uncovered a bombshell.

"Why should we believe the story of the monster and the gendarme? Grant the story, how do we know that Jolle, rather than Profirio, is the gendarme?" The bombshell detonated with soundless violence. "Wouldn't the criminal tell us the same story as the one who tries to save us?"

Tatja shrugged. "I suppose so. But there is no way we can test the story except by sitting tight and watching things develop. Besides—" and now she was smiling again "—I trust my judgment and intuition much more than I trust yours." She looked around, evidently dismissing the problem. "You'd better get your skoats. This battle group is moving out and I want you to stay with it." She turned and walked toward the command wagon of the next battle group, which was just creaking into the clearing. In her short skirt and lacy blouse, she might have been at a picnic instead of a war.

What had happened to Tatja? For the first time in four years, they didn't have a friend who had all the angles figured, who could solve virtually any problem. He looked at Cor, and saw the same thought on her face. They had a life-and-death problem—and if they didn't solve it, no superior being was going to bail them out. There was a monster loose; somehow they must discover who it was.

Chapter 19

The sun was halfway to the horizon when they made their move. Svir sat up and pushed aside the insect netting which hung over their sleeping cots. The loud, unwavering hum of a three year cicada was an overpowering soporific. The generals had finally recognized the fact that people need some sleep in the day (or perhaps it was simply that they could move as easily along the Riverside Road by night as by day, so it was possible to permit a reasonable sleep schedule).

No human sounds could be heard: apparently the sentries were in static positions. But all around them were the insect and bat sounds, and the river burbled in the near distance. Pink flowers crowded between the leaf needles of the looproot about them, and the scent was nearly overpowering in such concentration. Through gaps in the branches he could see the walls of the river gorge rise thousands of feet overhead. They had nearly reached the mouth of the glacier. O'rmouth was hidden beyond the northern wall, above the glacier. The gorge was so deep that they couldn't see He'gate's summit—their ultimate goal. Near the top of the gorge Svir saw a broadwing daybat soaring lazily back and forth across the updrafts as it scanned the ground with its sharp eyes.

Cor sat up. "Ready?" he whispered. She nodded. "Now remember how we're going to play this. I think we'll be safe even if we're discovered. The key is to have Tatja nearby, so Jolle can't kill us without her knowing it. You're going to go to her tent while I take Ancho to Jolle's wagon. I've got a noise bomb. If you hear it, bring Tatja as fast as you can—I may still be in one piece." This recapitulation was needless, but it put off action for a few more seconds.

She squeezed his arm. "Let's . . . let's have me go to Jolle's wagon instead. After all, I can now handle Ancho better than you."

He blushed, shame and courage mixed. "No," he finally said. "If we need Tatja, you can talk to her better than I. C'mon, Love." They stood beside their cots and looked about. Svir felt a little faint. They were twelve thousand feet above sea level, and he was learning firsthand the symptoms of hypoxia. The only good thing about the altitude was that even in the middle of the afternoon it was not particularly hot.

As they walked through the looproot grove, Ancho scrambled back and forth across Svir's shoulders. The little animal was normally most active at this time of day, and for once his large friends weren't trying to make him keep still so they could sleep. During the day, security was less strict than at night. Unless they tried to leave the bivouac, they would probably not even be challenged. They parted company near the center of camp. Cor took the path that led to Tatja's tent, and Svir walked toward the provincial headquarters area. Here the thick arches of the looproot were more closely set. In places the branches and needle leaves reduced the sunlight to a gray-green twilight. The underbrush was shaded out. Tents and cots were scattered at random through darker portions of the grove. The scene was quite different from the display bivouacs he had seen back in Crownesse, where tents and vehicles were set in pretty rectangular formations that looked so neat and military.

The moment he left Cor, he began working on Ancho. It seemed that as the years went by the animal became better and better at responding to the tactile instructions of his masters, and Svir was pretty confident that Ancho would not fail him now. He tried not to think what happened the last time he invaded a godling's privacy. This was different: get some information and split. With luck, Tatja would protect them later.

The first sentry he passed came to attention and saluted. Good. The sentry probably identified him as Jolle. Fifteen feet ahead, the grove thinned and sunlight flooded a mossy clearing. Parked at the edge of the clearing was the camouflaged hulk of Jolle's wagon. The wagon's tent had been pulled out and assembled. If Jolle were in the tent, would it rupture the sentries' credulity when another Jolle appeared outside the tent? He would know in a moment.

He walked briskly toward the wagon's rear entrance. The guards around the wagon saluted. No

one attempted to stop him. He had been identified as Jolle again. He walked purposefully to the
little doorway. The entrance had a standard leverlatch. He pulled at the latch. It didn't budge. He
pulled again, harder. He found himself sweating
as he wondered what the sentries thought of his
inability to enter "his own" wagon. Perhaps one of
the guards had a key, but he didn't dare ask.
Besides, he noticed on closer inspection that no
lock mechanism was visible. He had no chance of
getting in here.

He leaned against the side of the wagon and
pretended to admire the flowers drooping from
the branches that sheltered the wagon from snoop-
ers further up the gorge. There was only one other
place he could try; the tent entrance. Jolle probably wasn't there; but if he were, he might react so
abruptly that Svir wouldn't be able to set off the
noise bomb.

Well, he had come this far; it seemed ridiculous
to back out now. He reflected with some irritation
that in general his courage derived from the fear
that he might be taken for a coward. He walked to
the tent at the other end of the wagon. The vents
were open, but it was too dark for him to see
anything inside. The guard at the entrance saluted, addressed him as Jolle.

He took a deep breath and decided to commit
himself. "I'm going to be in and out all afternoon.
I don't wish to be disturbed." That might help
take care of inconsistencies if the sentry later saw
Jolle outside the tent.

"Very good, sir," the woman replied.

Svir pulled back the entrance curtain and stepped
into the dimness. All was quiet. It was warm, but

not hot. There was even a faint breeze. Sunlight
lay on the carpeted floor, and after a few seconds
he could see the interior clearly. No one home.
The room was lavishly appointed; Jolle had a pen-
chant for the good life. From one corner came the
pleasant odor of burning perfume. Beside the tent
mast stood a low couch and a table supporting a
coolchest and bottles of drink.

He moved quickly across the room to the wagon's entrance. The deep carpet made his movements silent: the loudest sounds were the cicadas
and the daybats. Even in the dimness, he could
see that this entrance was different from the one at
the rear. When the troops were in march, the tent
was stowed in the front of the wagon, behind a
pair of clamshell doors—which now stood open.
Beyond those doors, a beautifully painted partition
of fine-weave spider silk was stretched taut from
one side of the wagon to the other. A doorway was
mounted at the center of the partition. The spider
silk was so fine that Svir would be clearly visible to
anyone behind it.

He pulled at the leverlatch on the little door.
This one didn't move either. Again, there was no
evidence of a locking mechanism. The only explanation was that the door was barred from the
inside. But this would imply that there was someone in there. What now?

Then he heard Tatja's voice outside the tent.
Jolle was with her. They were coming into the
tent. Even now Jolle was telling the sentry at the
entrance to move away, that secret matters were
to be discussed. Svir stood frozen for a moment,
and Ancho echoed his discomfort, whimpering
where he crouched on the astronomer's shoulder.

Svir's only chance was to hide and hope that the dorfox would give him some protection with his I'm-not-here signal. If Jolle were like Tatja it was indeed a slim hope, but Ancho might be able to dull the godlings' senses to merely human levels. He ducked behind the ornate stand that supported the burning perfume. The stand was directly in front of the door into the wagon.

Ancho had barely changed the illusion he broadcast when Tatja and Jolle entered the tent. He couldn't risk looking around the corner of the stand. He held his breath and waited to be discovered. Although the perfume was pleasant in small doses, in high concentrations it brought a nearly overpowering desire to sneeze. He heard them sit on the low couch, and wondered how the interior of the tent could ever have seemed dim. The sunlight coming down from the ceiling vents splashed over the blue-green rug. Why, his footprints might still be visibly impressed in the pile!

"Feral or sport?" Tatja's soft voice came from the area of the couch.

"Feral. Shipwreck, maybe an ambush." Jolle's voice sounded perfectly calm. Perhaps Svir hadn't been detected. On impulse, he reached behind him and pulled again at the leverlatch. It moved smoothly downward and the door swung open. Svir came close to squeaking his surprise. He looked through the little doorway. There was no one in the darkness beyond. Now he had an unpleasant choice: he could remain behind the perfume stand or he could sneak into the wagon. If he moved quickly and quietly, he could probably make it. The doorway was hidden from the couch by the high perfume stand. He would never have dared it without Ancho. Ordinarily Tatja seemed able to hear the faintest sounds. Without the dorfox broadcasting a signal that would put a battle group out of action, she—and probably Jolle—could have heard his heart beating.

In the final analysis it was his curiosity that decided him:

He turned, slipped through the entrance, and quietly shut the door. No alarms sounded. Except for the blood singing in his ears, there was no sound in the wagon. The spider-silk screen provided an almost transparent window on the more brightly lit tent area. Tatja and Jolle were sitting on the couch, and were facing almost directly away from him. There was no sign that he had been discovered. He felt Ancho purring against the side of his neck as the little animal continued to broadcast deception.

Tatja was dressed even more gushily than that morning. A party shawl of virtually transparent silk covered her shoulders. Svir could see the top of her low-cut blouse. Jolle wore a militia uniform. He was pouring drinks. Svir pulled his attention away from the tent and inspected the wagon. It was hot, poorly ventilated. Except for the perfume drifting through the silk screen, he smelled nothing. But it wasn't completely dark here. Along the length of the wagon, red and orange prisms had been set in the roof. A dim, hellish light filtered through. Everything was a jumble. Along one side he saw a bed and bath. The rest of the room was filled with books and ornately carved cabinets. This seemed more like a wizard's den than the quarters of a man from the stars. It was hard to believe that just twenty inches away the sun was shining, bats were flying, and pink flowers scattered blue mist through cool mountain air.

Svir looked back through the silk screen. Jolle handed Tatja a goblet of clear wine. They sipped in silence. Then Jolle spoke. "It was sloppy language. But—" he waved broadly "—we're all the same species. They just don't have the benefit of engineering of self."

"Natural state?" Tatja sounded incredulous.

"Sure. My grandparents even. No. Call it magic."

"Please?"

Jolle laughed sympathetically at the pleading tone in her voice. He reached out to caress the smooth, clear skin of her neck. She moved closer, and even through the silk screen she seemed dazed.

"Well," replied the alien, "I can try. But it will just mislead you. You're asking for an education, not an explanation. There's drugs, genetic manipulation, and direct amplification. The last was first because it's easiest, but the deadliest—as the first discovered."

Svir followed every word closely. He was almost onto what they were talking about. When he filled in the blanks, it made sense.

"Why deadly?" she asked.

"Last last, please," he answered, and extended his arms around her shoulders, drew her against his chest. She came slowly but without reluctance. Her body had none of the tension that was her usual armor.

Now Jolle's voice was low, barely audible. His black hair mixed with Tatja's red. "First first: information?"

"Hmm." Tatja seemed half asleep, but after a moment of thought her voice came muffled against

Jolle's chest. "Something like the log inverse probability of the signal."

"Okay. What about noisy, ah, channels? It's possible to reduce the error rate to arbitrarily low levels with clever coding. True?"

A long silence. She appeared more interested in his neck than the question. Finally her voice came, so low pitched it hardly seemed her own. She was obviously thinking of more important things. "Yes, though it's more complicated than that. I never thought about that before . . ."

Svir came near groaning aloud. The conversation had passed beyond intelligibility just when he thought he might be able to follow it. He looked at the door that had opened so conveniently for him. Perhaps there was some clue as to why it had done so. There was. The door could be locked from the inside by a heavy wooden bar. In a way this was ridiculous, since anyone with a sharp knife could have cut through the silk screen. On the other hand, when the tent was not set up, there was probably a wooden panel fitted over the screen. One end of the bar was enclosed in a metallic collar—an expensive and wasteful ornament. Touching this collar was an (iron?) bar. Around the bar were wound several hundred turns of yellow wire sheathed in transparent resin. There was a fortune in metals here—to what purpose? The wires led away from the bar to a large wooden chest. If he were going to search the wagon, this was the place to start.

He glanced back through the silk screen. The high-powered conversation was over. He couldn't see Tatja at all, but now her blouse was draped over the back of the couch. He looked away from

the screen, blushing. Being a snoop in a good
cause didn't hurt his conscience, but voyeurism
was out of his league. No wonder Tatja was so
dense when it came to discussing the possibility
that Jolle was a bastard. When a goddess is in
love, she's just as irrational as anyone else.

Svir turned and followed the yellow wires to the
chest. It was an expensive Sdan piece. He felt the
ghoulish hardwood faces, hunting for the tongue-
catch the Sdan carpenters worked into their de-
signs. There was a faint buzzing near the box, but
he couldn't see the bug that made the noise. His
searching fingers found the catch and the lid came
up with silent, counterbalanced precision.

A blue glow radiated from that opening. For an
instant he was frozen by the flickering, actinic
gleam. He leaned forward. His first impression
was that the box was filled with treasure: glowing
jewels. The colors and intensities were constantly
changing, so it was hard to know the exact size and
shape of the gems. Silver boxes were set along the
inside walls. The shifting reflections made them
seem almost transparent. After a moment, he noticed that the copper wires from the wagon door
were connected to one of those little boxes. He
looked deep into the pile of "jewels." Though they
were motionless, the changing colors made the
pile shimmer like foam on an island shore.

The buzzing sound was louder now. An alarm!
The buzz reached a crescendo and became a
screeching, inhuman wail. "Master! Help me! I
will be stolen!" From the tent, he heard Tatja's
surprised exclamation and the sounds of rapid movement. Svir scrambled to the other end of the
wagon. From the inside it was easy to flip the

crossbar up and push the door open. As he plunged into the blinding daylight, he heard Jolle enter the wagon.

By luck Svir landed on his feet. As he fell forward, he dug long legs into the ground and sprinted away. Ancho clung to his shoulder and radiated for all he was worth. The nearest guards were more than forty feet away. They knew something strange was happening, but Ancho's efforts kept them from taking effective action. Even so, a couple of crossbow bolts zipped by him as he fled into the forest. He could hear no pursuers. Apparently Jolle was still in the wagon, inspecting his—slave?

Soon he was deep in the grove, the looproots an arched hallway before him. Only dim and shifting pencils of light penetrated the branches and leaf needles above. The ground was covered with a deep, resilient layer of white fungus. The shouting behind him had faded. He was still in the bivouac area—that was more than two thousand feet across—and could see occasional tents and wagons. Ancho protected him from the sentries. It took him fifteen minutes to circle back to his own sleeping area.

Now he moved cautiously. If Jolle had identified him, there would be a welcoming committee here. He stayed in the forest shadows and looked out at the sun-dappled cots. Cor was lying on her cot—next to someone else! He did a double take, and examined the figure beside her. It didn't move. In fact, its face was a brown piece of cloth.

Good girl! When she discovered that Tatja was going with Jolle to his tent, she had done the only thing possible—return to their sleeping area and construct an alibi. He moved quickly out of the shadows, pulled the netting aside, and lay down beside his wife. She jerked with surprise. Her hands were clenched white, and there were tears on her cheeks. Together they disassembled the crude dummy, and Svir told her what he had seen, what had happened.

They lay in each other's arms, and whispered their fears. "He'll kill us, Svir. We've got to talk to Tatja."

They needed protection, but, "We can't talk to her yet. She's probably still with Jolle. And—she's not herself. She's worse than this morning. We'll have to wait until we can get her alone."

"I can convince her; I know I can."

"Look, I don't think Jolle saw me. We'll be safe as long as we play innocent." Ancho wormed his way between them, and Svir petted him. There was really nothing more to say.

Chapter 20

We have to tell Tatja. All through the day, that imperative had driven Coronadas Ascuasenya. And Cor had to be the one to do the talking; she'd made that clear to Svir. After all the years, there might still be a bond from those first days on the barge. Tatja might be willing to listen, and to see out of the trap into which she had fallen. *We have to tell Tatja.* The thought was easier than the deed. For what seemed hours, Cor stood near the back of Tatja's command post, waiting for some break in Marget's schedule. The queen was managing a war . . . and now that she had Jolle, she had no need for her pets.

"—and you can be sure we understand all this, Observer Reynolt. I have no desire to hold your hands under my direct control." The Tatja that spoke was the Tatja of old: composed, persuasive, tactful. She had made no attempt to use her ostensible position as the absolute ruler of all the Continent to overawe the Doomsdayman confronting her.

And every bit of her diplomacy would be required to mollify the angry Doomsday priest. In the starlit darkness, his triple-pointed mitre made him look more a seven-foot obelisk than a human being. He spoke with the sarcastic servility of a subordinate who thinks he has the upper hand. "Your Majesty must know that we Doo'd'en would never ascribe such motives to Your Sacred Person. But in our ignorance, we beg to know why you destroyed parts of the Riverside Road, why you razed Kotta-svo-Picchiu, why you destroyed the sacred eye there, and why you now set an army on the farmlands beneath our capital."

Tatja was a vague shadow by the low field table, but her voice was clear and distinct. "Observer, for all four incursions we tender our apologies, and for the first three we offer reparations. However, when you understand the situation, I believe you will thank us. You reprove us for acts of war, committed to protect your most holy places from the Rebel army, which even now masses below us. Do you realize what will happen if the Rebels are not defeated? They are the ones who first invaded your territories. They are the ones who desecrated the Kotta Eye before it was destroyed. Though I cannot present proof now, the Rebels' ultimate goal is the destruction of the High Eye itself."

The priest had no immediate answer to this. He turned to the window-hole of the stone farmhouse that was Tatja's command post. From outside came the creak and crunch of Doo'd'en wagons carrying bombs and men to their positions, but there was very little for Observer Reynolt to see. Somewhere above them was O'rmouth, capital of Doomsday, and thousands of feet above that, the observatory itself. Two thousand feet below the farmhouse was the Picchiu River, and the mouth of the glacier that fed it. And somewhere down there were twenty-three thousand Loyalists and an unknown number of Rebels.

The crown's generals stood uneasily behind their queen. Cor heard Haarm Wechsler whispering indignantly at Imar Stark, the crown's chief of staff. The military didn't think the Doomsdaymen should be cajoled. If these provincials refused to fight for their queen, they should be ignored until after the battle, and then dealt with as traitors. It seemed a waste of time to stand here debating while the opposing armies took their positions. And it seemed doubly strange that a militia leader should be in charge of that deployment. At this moment Jolle and midrank staff officers were down there in the darkness, deploying crossbow men, ground obstacles, FAOs, and art'ry pieces. Soon there would be nothing peaceful about the night.

Finally Observer Reynolt spoke. Some of the false servility was gone from his voice. "Yes, Marget, we realize this. We are very unhappy about the situation: you have caused us as much damage as the Rebels. But in the past you have been just and have truly protected us. What aid do you require? Your army—if our reports are accurate—is much larger than any trained force we Doo'd'en could field. And we have none of the bomb throwers which both you and the Rebels have."

Tatja laughed softly. "My troops are great. They can whip twice their number—at sea level. But now we're at fourteen thousand feet. I am sure

you understand—even if my own advisors do not—
what these altitudes do to unacclimated troops.
My forces already hold decisive advantages: high
ground, artillery superiority. But to be sure of
victory I want two or three thousand Doomsday
fighting men, uh, Celestial Servants." She turned
to her chief of staff. "How much time do we have,
Immy?"

"The Provincial claims the Rebels won't be in
position for another six hours. Twilight begins about
seven-thirty this morning, so we can expect engagement in six to eight hours."

"Observer Reynolt, it is now thirty-nine-thirty,"
she said. "Can you get a battle group of Celestial
Servants into my command by four-thirty tomorrow morning?"

"Marget, permit me to signal O'rmouth. If my
superiors approve, the Servants will be at your
disposal in less than four hours." The priest gave a
shallow bow which was somehow more respectful
than the extravagant obeisance he had made earlier.

On Reynolt's departure, the generals moved in
to discuss the details of the deployment. Strangely,
Tatja made no move to dominate or even to participate in the conversation.

Soon she left the small stone building. Cor and
Svir followed her. The newly plowed field outside
was steeply sloping, and several times Cor nearly
wrenched her foot in the narrow furrows. Ancho
held tight to her neck. She had never imagined
that ground this rough could be cultivated. Even
though terraced, the fields had twenty-degree
slopes. Only the hardiest vegetation could survive
at these altitudes and in this soil.

Tatja stopped at the edge of the terrace and sat

down. Cor felt Svir clutch her elbow. He wanted to pull her back, set himself in front of her. She disengaged his hand, held it for a moment. They had argued this over and over. If anyone could make the point that had to be made, it was she and not Svir.

Tatja's voice was soft against the creaking of wagon wheels. "Sit down, you two." They sat. "What do you think of the situation?"

Here was the moment they had waited fifteen hours for: Tatja was alert, no longer the soft, yielding girl she had been with Jolle; that was obvious from the way she had just handled the Doomsday priest. They would never have a better chance to try to convince her of Jolle's real objectives. In fact, they might never have another chance. If Profirio were destroyed this night, which seemed likely, Jolle would be left unopposed, and would have no further need of Tatja. Yet now Cor's throat seemed frozen. She remembered what Svir had seen in the tent. Tatja had finally gotten what she wanted, an equal and a friend. How could they possibly persuade her to give up Jolle?

The silence stretched on for an endless moment. Finally it was Svir who answered the queen's question in a voice a bit too high and forced to be natural. "I thought it was really something of a masterstroke, that of convincing the priest to let us use his men."

Tatja laughed for the second time that night. "No," she said softly, "just the natural thing to do. And he really had to do what we asked. They know Profirio has caused much of the damage, and I have treated them fairly in the past. Too bad they're such a bunch of fanatics. I wonder what their reaction will be when they find out that *my* side intends to desecrate the High Eye with its presence. I can just imagine their scream of 'Betrayal.' "

"But Marget," said Cor, puzzled. "You already say that we are poor fighters, even at fourteen thousand feet. We'll be much worse at O'rmouth, and the observatory is nearly ten thousand feet above that. How can you expect success there?"

"You'll see. I assure you, there will be nothing subtle about it. Jolle and I are sure it will work. In the meantime, we have a competent adversary down there below us. I'd give a lot to know what *he* is planning."

So the conversation was back to that. She *must* speak now, Cor realized. Jolle would soon return from the front lines, and then it would be impossible to bring the matter up. Even if the alien didn't kill them before they could finish the story, he could certainly persuade Tatja that it was a fabrication.

She tried to remember Tatja as she had been in her first days on the barge, when she hung on Cor's every word, and her gratitude had been an obvious thing. Over the years, there had been occasional flickers of that, times when she was a confidante, almost a big sister . . . and not a pet. Was there anything left of that? When Cor finally spoke, the effect was strange—like listening to someone else talking or remembering a previous conversation.

"Tatja, you remember our talk yesterday morning at the watering stop?"

"Uh-huh."

Cor didn't lose stride. "We said the possibility

that perhaps Jolle was lying, that Profirio was the gendarme, and Jolle the criminal."

"Yes, I remember all that." Tatja's tone was good humored, if a bit distracted.

"You said that we must wait and watch. Well, Svir and I . . . uh . . . we thought that the situation was so dangerous maybe more could be done. If Jolle were the evil one, maybe he lied about what he salvaged from his fight with Profirio. In fact, if these golems are so popular and if Jolle was the one who . . . uh . . . slaughters humans, then he might even have one with him." There could be no more evasion. If she didn't say it now, Grimm would get ahead of her.

"Tatja, this is exactly what we discovered. Jolle is the criminal. He has a golem with . . ."

"You were the one in the wagon."

"We had to, Tatja! Jolle is the slaver. His golem can even talk, and no machine—"

"You peeping bitch, I'll teach—" In the darkness Cor had no warning. The lower right side of her face went numb and splinters of pain spread through her head. Simultaneously Tatja's other fist buried itself in her middle. The nylon webbing of Cor's shrap vest could not protect her from the ramming force of the blow. It bowled her over the edge of the terrace and she tumbled down the slope. Ancho went flying off into space.

There was the sound of a body block, and Svir's voice, "Don't hit her again! It was me, *me!* I'm the peeper." Cor's head struck a rock, and for a moment all she knew was tiny yellow lights floating lazily before her eyes. She was lying at the base of the terrace slope; Tatja and Svir were scrambling toward her. She coughed back blood and felt the beginnings of triumph. Tatja had used nothing but her fists—and those ineptly. If they could survive just a few more seconds, Tatja would cool off, and Cor might really have a chance to convince her.

From behind her, Cor heard men moving through the darkness. One of them was running. Running? In this dark? The footsteps stopped. Strong hands lifted Cor to her feet, and a calm voice sounded in her ear. "Say friend, what's the problem?" It was Jolle.

Chapter 21

To Svir's amazement, they both still lived. He looked around dazedly. But for how long? This was Jolle's territory:

Though the bunker had been hastily and crudely constructed, it was an effective job. The Crown's Engineers had used a cleft in the terracing. It had been a simple matter to fill the open end with dirt-packed bags and to construct a roof of timber covered with three or four feet of dirt. The occupants of the bunker could survive all but a direct hit from a six-inch shell. Since the enemy was supposed to be without six-inch guns, the bunker should be safe unless it was overrun. There was no real floor to the room, just the curving rocky surface of the cleft. Despite the primitive aspect of the chamber, it was obviously a command post. A field table had been set in the middle of the chamber, and on it were detailed maps and overlays of the area. From the roof over the table hung a peculiar lamp that looked very much like the algae pots used in Crownesse and on the Islands. Its cool blue radiance lit the maps and the men standing around them. Underofficers moved back and forth through a curtained doorway. They were bringing information that was immediately posted on the overlays. Runners occasionally departed through the tunnel to the outside.

Svir felt distant amusement to see that even here, his curiosity was alive: The strange light, for instance. Algae pots were terribly hard to keep alive this far from resupply. Why not use an oil lamp? At night no smoke would be visible to give away their location.

Cor huddled against him, looking even more dazed than he. She had taken the brunt of Tatja's rage. Svir had wiped the blood from her face, but there was a great bruise growing across her jaw. Ancho hung solicitously at her shoulder. No doubt his attention was both comforting and painful.

Cor looked at him, her eyes wide. "Have you seen her . . . or *him?*" she whispered.

He shook his head. "Neither. I . . . I thought Jolle would kill us when he found us with Tatja like that. But he calmed her down, and had you carried here. I don't know what he's planning, but—"

At that moment the subject of their conversation pulled back the curtain and stepped into the room. In the dim light, Jolle's face was shadowed. His black hair glinted metallically. He nodded casually at them and walked to the map table. There they could see his features more clearly. He seemed relaxed—as Tatja did in such situations. His uniform looked freshly pressed. To him, the officers at the table might have been discussing party plans.

Jolle addressed Imar Stark. "We just received a signal from Marget; she is at her command post. Our position is to be the prime command post unless it be knocked out by enemy action. As she mentioned before in your presence, she has delegated immediate command of all operations to me. You may check this reading of her message with your own signalman." He nodded at the curtain.

Stark nodded stiffly. He obviously had no love for the situation, but the queen had been explicit, and besides, this bearded provincial hadn't tried to control the minutiae of operations with the same prickliness that Marget often did.

Jolle continued. "I am putting the militia under you. My generals have already agreed to that, since you are my subordinate in this matter. If our scouts are to be believed—and I suspect some of the signal reports are fakes—the enemy is in position below us. I am saving my artillery until they mass for an assault. When that happens, we'll use the plan discussed before." He glanced at the map. "Good. I didn't know the Celestial Servants were in position. General Stark, we can expect engagement at any moment."

"Yes, sir." The old military man didn't salute, but his voice was respectful. The alien turned, and then walked to the curtain. As if by afterthought, he glanced at Svir. "I'd like to talk with you for a moment, please." His words were mild, but they brought a chill to Svir's spine. Where Tatja had raged, this creature calculated. If he wished them death, then he and Cor would die.

Jolle appeared to mistake the reason for Svir's

immobility. "Miss Ascuasenya is welcome to come, if she feels up to it." He gestured beyond the curtain.

Svir stood, felt Cor's hand tight in his. She came to her feet, and looked into Svir's eyes. "It will be together," she said softly.

Beyond the curtain it was completely dark. No light escaped from the map room, even as they moved past the curtain. The cloth was thick and layered double to prevent leaks. They felt their way to a wooden bench, and sat. There was a long silence. The wall beside him was made of dirt-packed bags. He realized there were slit windows at about chest level. The wall was so thick that he couldn't see the sky. There was only a gray glow and a faint breeze to indicate the night outside. Jolle stood by the windows for a moment and said nothing. From breathing sounds, Svir realized there was at least one other person in the cool darkness, probably behind Cor. He listened carefully, but all he heard now was a fatbat cooing in the distance. At these altitudes even insects were rare and the night silence was profound. The sounds of people talking could be heard for miles, unless precautions were taken. It was suddenly clear why Tatja's meeting with the Doomsdaymen had been held a thousand feet higher up and in the midst of wagon noises.

Finally Jolle spoke—or rather whispered, "Take a break, Captain. I can record any messages incoming." The fourth occupant of the room could be heard standing and walking past the curtain. Then Jolle spoke to Cor and Svir. "We're set. Things are going to rip apart in fifteen minutes unless he anticipates me. I may not have another chance to talk with you before tomorrow—and I want to get this over with before we arrive at O'rmouth."

A cornered animal can only act aggressively, and Svir certainly felt cornered. He hissed back, "That's assuming you win the battle tonight, you bastard." Why didn't the monster make his move?

"Hey, not so loud," Jolle answered quietly. "Part of the reason for this pause is that both sides are making a sound recon. I don't want to get bombed out of my own command post. No. Don't start screaming until I finish my story. Okay?"

Svir felt Cor tense beside him. Apparently she had had the same thought. He closed his mouth, and wondered whether Jolle had seen him preparing to shout or had just concluded that he was likely to try. He might as well forget the idea. Jolle could probably kill him before he could yell.

Jolle continued. "There is no chance we will lose this engagement. We have the high ground, we have the art'ry, and we have some acclimated troops. But this is not the final showdown that our forces think it is. Unless we are lucky, the one called Profirio will survive. This battle is merely an intermediate step, and tomorrow, after our victory, we must move on to the next. That is where I need you."

Cor's words came awkwardly from her injured mouth, but the emotion was clear: "I'll bet it pleases you to pull off the wings of batlets, too. Why don't you finish it? We know you—slaver!"

"You two have jumped to some easy but false conclusions. Have you ever considered that I might have brought you here to kick some sense into your heads?" He didn't wait for a reply. "This is

really my fault, I suppose. I should have picked
you up right after you went through my wagon.
Yes, I knew Svir was the burglar. But we were
very busy, and I hadn't counted on Marget react-
ing as violently as she did to your revelation.
You'll have to forgive her; she's—uh—a little un-
balanced right now. Even I didn't realize how
heavily she's fallen for me.

"But that's passed. I want you back on my side
and I have only minutes. What do you think you
saw in my wagon this afternoon, Svir?"

They weren't to be killed! At least not yet. Svir
straightened. "Well, I saw a golem, and it talked
with a human voice. So Profirio must be the policeman and you the monster."

The alien sighed. "If only your technology were
fifty years more advanced. If only you had more
iron on this world. Svir, what you saw was a
machine, not too much better than what your own
people can make nowadays. It can think only in
the most primitive ways. It displayed abilities that
made it seem alive to you—but actually it performed only a few simple tricks. If that box had
really been humanly intelligent, do you think it
would have let you into the wagon? And consider
the means it used to lock and unlock the wagon
doors. That was a simple—uh—damn, you have
no word for it. Call it an optional magnet. If you
knew anything about—" again he seemed to search
for words "—current changes, you would see the
trick was elementary. Someday I'm going to find
out how you people have such a good theory of
chemistry without knowing about. . . . After all
you have the valence concept. . . ." He was silent
for a moment, as if considering some puzzle.

"And as for the voice you heard calling for my help, that was as mindless as the trip alarms you have in your homes. They make a screaming wail without words. My little box has an alarm that is just a group of words that are repeated endlessly and without consciousness. Look, you already have machines that can record pictures. Why not sound?"

Tiny doubts had been sown by this speech. When he thought back on it, Svir realized that the "golem" had shown no adaptive behavior. Perhaps it was just a mechanical alarm. Now he saw why the alien had insisted on using magic to explain his science. What would sophisticated machines be like if this sentry device were considered primitive? Yet Svir was not convinced. Perhaps *both* Profirio and Jolle were devils and this was all a little game where none of the gods were killed and the locals provided the blood. Everything could be a lie. His mind grasped wildly for some working assumption: the only useful one was to believe the story of monster and gendarme. Until he and Cor could make some decision as to which was which, they should appear to cooperate with the alien.

He was just opening his mouth when Cor said, "I think you've convinced us that we can't be convinced of anything. So what do you want from us?"

"I guess that is all I could hope for. As to your cooperation, I—Listen." Across the night, the sounds came unnaturally clear: voices, occasional screams. The sounds were so precise and yet so faint. They reminded Svir of a miniature painting seen under a glass—small and yet filled with complicated details.

The nylon curtain moved, and someone entered the room. "Sir, we have action at Backtrack Five. We believe more enemy troops are moving into that area."

"Very well, Stark, you may initiate Olive Bat. And send the signal officer in here."

"Right." As the chief of staff left for the map room, Cor struggled to her feet. For a moment she sagged against him, but she wouldn't sit back down. He helped her to the sand-bagged wall, where she leaned against the damp bags and looked out the slits. On the other side of his wife he could hear the signalman taking his position.

The window slits were cunningly constructed to protect against a wide range of art'ry bursts and still allow good visibility. Except for a scattering of stars in the narrow strip of visible sky, there was no light.

"There's nothing to see yet," commented Jolle. "And if we're lucky, the actual fighting will stay below our line of sight."

Svir noticed the flickering light of first one signaler and then another. "The third, fourth, and seventh art'ry batteries acknowledge our command," said the signalman.

Jolle spoke to Svir and Cor. "See, that first flicker was the command from this post. We can't afford to give away our position—in case Pröfe has a suicide squad or a couple of art'ry pieces—so we use runners to take messages from the map room to our signaler. That's about a hundred yards down the hill from here. Then the command is flashed to our units." The explanation had been purely for their own edification, Svir realized.

Then came the *crump* of a single art'ry piece

firing. Seconds passed, and suddenly there was green daylight over the valley. Back in Bayfast Svir had seen art'ry flares fired over the inland cliffs during maneuvers, and this was much the same. The light moved slowly, dimming and then glowing brightly. But this was not Bayfast. Here the mountains extended thousands of feet above the top of the flare's arc. The otherworldly green light illuminated the sides of the gorgelike valley, and in a distortion of perspective the light seemed a tiny green match flickering in a darkened room, casting shadows upon the walls and floor. It was nearly as bright as quarter-phase Seraph, and he wasted several seconds watching the shadows slowly shift as the flare drifted across the sky. But even the flare couldn't reveal the extent of the mountains that shouldered over it. To those hulks it was indeed a tiny match flame. As the light dimmed for the last time, Svir looked at the ground below. The terraced fields stretched down a slope of nearly thirty degrees for a distance of some two thousand feet. Beyond that he could see the road that led from the Picchiu River. The road stretched transversely across the face of the slope. Beyond it, the ground dipped out of sight. Except for the flare moving across the sky and the sounds of battle below, there was no sign of human activity.

The flare dimmed, winked out. All was dark again; Svir couldn't even see the stars now. Signal lamps flickered as the crown's observers reported on enemy positions they had sighted. He judged that most of the signalers were near the edge of the drop-off. In the bunker, the signal officer was scratching away. He spoke to Jolle. "Sir, they say—"

"Never mind, Captain. Just take it into the map room. The men who are going to use this information already have it." As he spoke, the men he referred to took action. In a space of fifteen seconds, the art'ry pieces of the combined crown and provincial forces fired. It was no longer necessary to whisper. Though the firing was a couple of thousand feet away, the racket was loud enough to cover most other noises. As the barrage continued, Svir noticed pale lights flickering in the darkness below their position. Even with flashless powder, the guns emitted a pearly, oval radiance when they fired. It was probably invisible from below the guns' positions, but the command bunker was in line of sight with most of them. They must be well camouflaged; when the flare had shined, he had looked at the road and seen no sign of them. "He's way ahead of the reports," Jolle said mildly.

A second flare went up. This time there was more to see. At the edge of the drop-off, several hundred Rebels were in contact with friendly forces. It was impossible for Svir to tell whether the loyal forces were Provincial, crown, or Celestial Servants. Even after the barrage, the noise of their fighting was loud—they were within fifteen hundred feet of the command post itself, though still considerably below it. He realized that even with the flares, the art'ry wasn't very effective. The flares had pinpointed the enemy, but only after they were almost on top of the guns. In daylight the enemy could have been destroyed while still several miles away, but now the friendly troops had to fight just to protect their guns.

That defense was not entirely successful. There

was an ear-popping concussion, and the floor of the bunker rapped their feet. At same time, a minor avalanche of dirt sifted down through the timbered roof, and fine dust filled the air. Svir and Cor held onto each other, coughing in the smoke-like dust. Ancho cringed at Cor's feet. As the floor steadied, she bent down and picked him up, trying to brush the dust from his coat. Svir could feel heavy dirt in his hair and down his neck; the dust stuck to his skin everywhere.

"Damn," spoke Jolle. "They've captured one of our own guns. Unless—" In the green flarelight, Svir saw him pick up a pair of binoculars and inspected the terrain before them. He didn't look at the fighting men moving toward them, but concentrated on the lip of the drop-off, further away. The flare burned out, but he kept watching. The FAO lights flickered back to the art'ry and command positions.

The signalman stepped back into the room. "Captain," said Jolle, "the enemy has broken our art'ry direction code. The following FAO positions—" he rattled off some map coordinates "—are enemy men pretending to be ours." He paused and watched the messages flickering up from below. "They are directing shells toward our own men. Have those positions shelled."

"Yes sir." The signalman started for the curtain. "We'll throw an acknowledge test at them just to make sure."

"You'll destroy them immediately, mister."

"But sir, if they have the main code, how can you tell who the impostors are? And you're just estimating their position. You at least need a—"

Jolle's voice seemed quiet next to the art'ry fire

below, but it cut through all the random noises with a cool deadliness. "Captain, I gave you an order. Obey it, or join the enemy."

For a moment the captain struggled to find his voice. "Y-yessir. They'll be destroyed immyest." He disappeared.

"That was a clever move," continued Jolle, "though I'm sure Profirio knew it would be obvious to me. But then, what he really wants is confusion, so he can escape from his own forces—which are sure to lose—and insinuate himself into the Doomsday group." Why did the alien trouble to explain these intrigues to mere playing pieces? Did he really think such apparent frankness would convince them of his sincerity?

More enemy forces had cleared the drop-off; now shells were landing on the terraces in sight of the bunker. They lit the battlefield with stop-action flashes. Red, orange, even blue glimmered in the bursting shells—and there seemed to be a fiery structure inside the explosion. The shrap' bombs were less impressive, but from the screams and turmoil, Svir guessed they were doing more damage. A third flare arched across the valley. Several thousand more enemy soldiers had passed the road. They were close! Somehow they had made it to the lip of the drop-off. But this was no unstoppable horde: these men were in the open now. They ran across the terrace, their only cover an occasional tree. Fire fell, burning the fields, torching the trees. The gunmen didn't need any directions to bring their fire directly in on the enemy troops, though many guns were too near to be effective.

And only two men knew what the soldiers were

dying for—knew whether they were dying to save the world or to destroy it.

The army that was now a mob swept past them, and the art'ry fire followed. The shell bursts still cast light across the fields, but they were not directly visible. The noise was muted, coming through the dirt behind them. There was a strange sound he hadn't noticed before. It was a snapping, popping, like the clatter of a broken printer. The sound came from the left side of the front. He leaned forward, and saw a white flashing. It was something like a signaler, but faster and without the dots, dashes, and intermeds of a signaling pattern. Jolle saw the white flickering too. "He's bringing on his secret weapon, but it won't help him."

"Yes, but what is it?" To Svir, the flashing light seemed innocuous.

"It's, uh, a hand-held gun. Pröfe looted the warehouses in Kotta-svo-Picchiu. He got something like a thousand ounces of iron there. Apparently he used some of it to make a repeating gun that's small enough to be carried. I don't think he's actually built a nonmetallic repeater—I tried that, couldn't do it. He has at least five men down there—" He stopped as art'ry shells blossomed over the twinkling lights, outshining them. When the orange faded, the white sparkling was gone too.

The battle sounds were sporadic now. Guns still fired and men still fought, but it was the tempo of grease sputtering in a pan rather than fire running before a strong wind.

"See that?" Jolle pointed to one of the signal lights. "We've destroyed the enemy's main force. The engagement lasted only thirty minutes, and we've achieved complete victory. We'll capture most of the survivors. Things moved so fast, we may have actually caught Pröfe, too." He turned to the signalman, who had just returned. "Captain, go back to the map room and ask Stark to assemble the staff."

Svir looked at Jolle. The shelling had set fire to a nearby tree, and the alien's face was visible in the light. He seemed to be smiling. What if the engagement had destroyed Profirio? Then the whole matter was decided, no matter who was the monster.

"I'll be leaving you in a few minutes," said Jolle. "I want to inspect the prisoners. Marget handled that during the battle, but she would have big trouble if Pröfe were captured.

"Before I go, let me tell you what I want from you. Later this morning, the command group is going to O'rmouth. The Doomsday people think this is all some sort of victory celebration, and we won't say otherwise till we're in conference with the Archobservers. I don't think I've convinced you that Pröfe is the monster . . . but I need you. If you have any questions or tests to put to me, think them over tonight and maybe I can give you some proof before we go up there. When we're actually in conference, I want—"

"Sir?" It was Imar Stark at the curtain. Jolle walked across the room to talk to the general.

Svir stifled a curse, and Cor squeezed his hand. *Patience.* He looked outside, at the burning tree. Its twisted limbs gave it a horrible, manlike appearance. It was a terrible symbol of all this night's suffering. Cor must have thought the same. Ancho stirred nervously on her shoulder, and she pulled at Svir's hand, urging him away from the window slit.

Then the tree spoke. It was a human voice: ponderous, deep, and menacing. The words weren't Spräk or Sfierro. To his Island mind they sounded something like, "*Ter äshe gaul*, Jolle." And he never forgot those words, for simultaneously two other things happened which bent his life out of time.

Jolle's hand jerked Svir back from the slit window. "*Prö*—"

The world ripped open and the light of hell itself shone through. With that bloody light came a painfully loud explosion just inches from his face. Then the rent was mended. He was lying on the ground, and everything was dark except for the painful afterimages floating in his eyes. He felt Cor beside him. Jolle was pulling him to a sitting position. He allowed himself to be raised, then reached for his wife. "C'mon Cor, get up." No answer. Then he was back on the ground, feeling for wounds . . . trying to wake her . . . burning fur . . . Ancho . . .

That stroke of artificial lightning had come through the slit near his left side—where Cor had been standing. And the explosion had been. . . . He still couldn't see anything, but he could hear someone screaming her name over and over. Strong hands pulled him up and someone was slapping his face. The tiny room was filled with people. Or rather he had been moved into the map room. The streak afterimage of Pröfe's weapon still hung before his eyes, but now there was another, fainter light. He was lying on his back, and the room's lamp was shining above him like a broad blue cloud. It seemed so much fainter than before. Everything was dark and blurred.

He rolled over in the dirt. People stood or knelt by something on the ground. Others ran back and forth, but they were irrelevant. The kneeling one was a medic, he could see now. And beside him on the ground—his sight was very blurred, and the impression was vague, but— The explosion at the end of the red thunderbolt had been—Cor's face.

The tired medic muttered, "It was quick at least." The platitude sent Svir into a flat dive that ended at the medic's throat. He was on top of him, then under, and the noise around him seemed bright with surprise and anger. Then everything became dark again.

Chapter 22

The colonization of the West Coast had begun a thousand years before. Llerenito farm settlements were scattered from the twentieth to the fortieth parallel—the seeds whence grew Sfierro and Picchiu. About the same time, people of the Chainpearls founded a major colony at Bayfast. Much later, Chainpearl fishermen began living on the rocky coast north of the fortieth.

In the beginning, these northerners had the same language, the same heritage as the Bayfastlings. The names they laid on their grim land were meaningful to Bayfast ears: Doomsday, Heavengate, Overmouth. But the years passed; hardship and distance brought a parting. After five hundred years, though they still spoke a language understandable to Bayfastlings, their view of the world was utterly alien. These "Doomsdaymen" raised their own religion—which would probably have become Seraph worship if only the Doomsday Range had lain beneath the sky that held Seraph. Instead, the cult's central belief was that the sky of night is the physical manifestation of the most powerful spirit, and that by studying its countenance, all problems can be solved. In the hills near Kotta-svo-Picchiu there were ruins of the astrological temples of the cult's early Observers.

The Doomsday religion would have remained a crackpot cult dominating some minor fishing villages, except for two things. The first was the invention of the telescope, a divine endorsement of the cult's technique. The second was the discovery of copper and iron in the Doomsday Mountains. In one century the fishermen became miners, and very rich ones. Their coastal villages disappeared, except for Kotta-svo-Picchiu, which ballooned into a large port. Scores of mining towns grew in the highlands, and some became cities. The Archobservers found themselves the absolute rulers of one of the wealthiest and most inaccessible countries in the world. Now they had the resources to watch the face of God as befitted that sacred undertaking. As the search for iron carried the ex-fishermen higher into the mountains, the priests noticed that the nights were clearer, the stars brighter.

Thus was born the notion of a cathedral at the top of the world. They would find the highest point in the Doomsday Mountains and construct there the largest telescope possible. The priests guessed the job would take a century and empty their treasure houses; if they had known the truth, even they might have quailed.

It took them fifty years to reach a point ten thousand feet below the peak they judged the highest in the world, and fifty more to build a town there. Overmouth, that "resting spot" was called, since it stood above the largest glacier in the range. In the years that followed, the priests nearly gave up the idea of proceeding higher. Perhaps the heights above were meant for angels, and mere humans should construct their observatory at O'rmouth. Even there, the unacclimated lived less than ten quarters, and most children died in their cradles.

It was only in the last forty years that this terrible thinness of air had been conquered and a means of reaching the top of the world discovered. By then O'rmouth had a population of thirty thousand and rich ore fields had been found in the area, so the city was both the religious and economic center of the region. The drive to the top of the world could be undertaken. It cost thirty more years, and five thousand lives, to set the sixty-inch Eye in its shrine.

"So? We *are* grateful. We are so grateful that we will not ask Your Most Sacred Majesty to pay for the damage her armies did to the Riverside Road, to Kotta-svo-Picchiu, to the Kotta Eye, and to our farmlands below O'rmouth." Mikach the Perceptive, First Archobserver, spoke with unconcealed sarcasm, but with all the dignity of his station. He wore a powder-blue robe, indicating he spoke as a temporal power. A necklace of copper and rubies was draped across his chest. The hair on his face and head was braided into two thick tails, one going down his back, the other down his front. Beside him at the iron-topped table sat other Archobservers. Behind them stood unbearded Observers.

"Yes, and for our part, we are grateful for your help in defeating the Insurrectionists." Tatja spoke quickly but without apparent effort. While the priests had their rubies and copper, her dress was constructed of thousands of tiny gems, each glittering with its own color. Over this were strewn larger gems and curved plates of the principal metals. Spider silk floated about the ensemble. Her shining red hair flowed smoothly from beneath a silver circlet. There must be no doubt who had the greatest wealth here.

Beside her sat the highest advisors to the crown. First on the right was Jolle, still in the uniform of a Provincial militia. Behind them sat military commanders and cabinet officers. No lowlander was standing—at these altitudes, it took some effort just to walk. Except for the Doomsdaymen, the only people who seemed at ease were Jolle and Tatja. All the others struggled with the dizziness and nausea. Just minutes before, Imar Stark had been carried from the room with bloody vomit on his lips.

Tatja continued, "But we do believe that your debt to us is greater than ours to you. We have only a small request of you. You grant me—at least claim to grant to me—the ultimate temporal sovereignty over your lands. I wish to visit the High Eye, and to perform there a simple experiment."

Mikach the Perceptive stiffened, and there was angry muttering among his peers. When the Doomsdayman spoke, it was with deep and frank indignation. "Marget, you know us well, well

enough to know your request is entirely beyond
the limits of hospitality. Only the trained and faithful may approach that sacred instrument. You are
at O'rmouth because of your—titular—sovereignty.
If you insist, we will permit you to use the ten-
inch instrument here—and you must know what a
concession this is. But if you continue to blaspheme, you will be cast down from our heights—by
my temporal power."

As he spoke, Tatja glanced at Jolle, who shook
his head slightly. The others in her party came full
alert at this threat, reaching for the crossbows and
daggers they did not have.

Only the astronomer royal seemed unaffected
by the threat. In fact, he was not listening. His
gaze moved idly around the low room. To the
right, tall windows showed O'rmouth and the glacier. He looked without interest across the narrow
streets. The entire city was crammed into two
hundred acres to take advantage of the avalanche
shade. Nowhere in that low mass of carved stone
and dirty snow was there a bit of green. Every
building, even the lowliest residential coopera-
tive, was built of stone. The granite walls were
decorated with gargoyles, and the corners of larger
buildings were studded with dovetailed stone cylinders. In some ways the Doomsdaymen had no
imagination: The false-log effect was taken as a
sign of ancient nobility. Even now, the roofs were
under several feet of snow. During winter, the
snow covered everything, arching between the
buildings, turning the city's streets into tunnels.

But today, children ran and played in the sun,
unaware that such exertions were impossible for
any but them. The Doomsdaymen believed in large

families. Mortality was high and there was a chronic manpower shortage. One day soon those children would find that arduous labor was the fate of all but a few Doomsdaymen, and they would wear the dull brown uniforms of adult commoners.

Cor. For an instant, the screaming pain drove through his armor. Cor with the smooth black hair. Cor with the brown eyes, the creamy skin. Cor with the strength to support him through all problems, the mind of bright ideas. Cor with the face that—his mind veered from the horror.

It was still impossible to believe that she had gone away and would never come back. Life was like a tree limb growing smoothly in an anticipated direction. Last night the branch was snapped across. Reddish sap oozed out, but the end was dead. Life took a new unrecognized turn, leaving the branch bruised and torn. It would be a time before the new reality seemed inescapable. Until then, he could retreat into the world that was not, and forget what things had become.

And so Jolle's quiet plea of that morning had gone uncomprehended. The words were from a nightmare, perhaps-not world, and he could ignore them. But time passed, and the screaming broke through more often. Eventually he would be pushed into the new reality. Then apathy would become hate. He would destroy the creature who had killed the only girl foolish enough to love Svir Hedrigs. Profirio had tricked many people, but he had here an enemy whose hate could turn back any persuasion. This last thought brought him close to the new reality: His friends, after all, were making plans that would result in the destruction of Profirio.

Tatja, using her most imperial manner, was still working on Mikach. "Very well, Archobserver, if we may not visit the Eye in person, I would like you to conduct an experiment there at our direction."

The Perceptive One didn't answer at once. Perhaps this approach might work. "What is the experiment?"

"A limited sky search."

"How limited?"

"Between one and twenty hours of observation time." In fact, it could take up to three hundred hours if Jolle's intuition were in error by even a small amount.

"And what do you expect to find?"

In this case the truth was the perfect answer. Tatja smiled as she said, "My astronomer believes that the Tu-Seraph system has an external satellite."

"Ridiculous. You've seen our reports. Don't you read them? There is no satellite more than ten yards across nearer than one million miles. I certainly won't allow such redundant use of the High Eye. We have done some experiments for you in the past, but in this request, you go too far."

The Queen sat straight in her portable throne, touched her crown, and spoke flatly to Mikach. This was the last verbal weapon she had. "Subject, I demand your cooperation. Am I not sovereign?"

The other's voice was just as grim. There was no hint of sarcasm, but the tone was unyielding and deadly. "You are sovereign as long as you remain in Bayfast and mind your own affairs. But here you are out of your element. Your forces outnumber ours, but each of us is worth five of you in combat, as you discovered last night. If you give up your demands, we will allow you to depart in peace, friendship, and lealty; we realize that you have the power to control Kotta-svo-Picchiu and the River-side Road, and to choke our commerce. But if you persist in this imperialist heresy, we will destroy you." He half-rose from his seat, then sat down abruptly. Standing in an enemy's presence was bad luck, and Mikach was an Orthodox cultist. Now, the Reformist Observers were more interested in scientific research than past wisdom. They might have been more susceptible to Marget's request; unfortunately, the Reformists were out of power in this decade.

"I am sorry Mikach. I won't try to excuse what we're going to do by calling you a disloyal subject. The overlord ploy was a stunt. I know I can't control your people, at least not for indefinite periods. And we need your metals. So after this is over, please remember that we will always be ready to resume commerce with you."

The Archobserver's anger dissipated before this nebulous attack. He obviously had no idea what was coming.

"Last night you saw our artillery; bomb throwers, I believe you call them."

Several men in Doomsday blue caught the drift, and their eyes widened. Mikach was not so perceptive. "Yes, the catapults."

"They are more than that, Mikach. What you saw last night was a limited demonstration. We were operating at the minimum range possible—about six thousand feet. We can project bombs more than ten miles horizontally with these weapons. And the maximum vertical range is—"

Mikach interrupted with an inarticulate roar.

He lunged to his feet, superstition forgotten. "You'll die for this, infidel! To think we aided you because you ascribed your own treachery to your enemy."

Mikach turned to signal the doorman. There were armed Celestial Servants just outside. If he gave the word, there would be a massacre.

"Sit down, Mikach," Jolle said. His voice was not remarkably loud, nor even tense, but the Archobserver turned back to face the crown.

Tatja took advantage of the break. "We aren't foolish, Mikach. If we don't return, the plan goes into effect automatically. So why don't you do as General Jolle says? Sit down and hear the rest."

Mikach signed to the doorman, but he did not sit down.

"You know the power of a single high-explosive shell. Don't doubt the accuracy of our fire. Though our guns are fourteen thousand feet below the target, my gunmen can put one out of two shells within one hundred feet of the mirror. In fact, the location of your Eye is one of the most precisely measured points in the world; the best mapmakers use its coordinates as a base.

"And I suggest that you do not attack our artillery pieces. They are vulnerable, but there are nearly two hundred of them. *At this moment* they are loaded and aimed. You could not destroy them all before they put out your Eye.

"Under this duress, we ask again: Let our party ascend to the Eye. We will not harm the instrument. Repara—"

"No! Better to destroy it cleanly than by taint." The priest's face was flushed and puffy. Behind him, there was a barely perceptible exchange of glances between Reformist Observers. They preferred taint to destruction.

It was Jolle who answered the dogmatism. "You blaspheme, Mikach. The face of God will still stand a billion light-years beyond your blue, whether your Eye is put out or spat upon. Spittle may be expunged, but if your Eye be destroyed, then you will be lost from God."

It was a Reformist argument couched in Orthodox jargon. For a moment Mikach was silent. He realized that others were thinking what this dark-faced foreigner had just said. The priest's face was calm again; only the trembling of his voice betrayed the struggle within. He neither nodded nor explicitly stated his submission, but asked, "When will you ascend, then?"

Tatja answered, "Sometime in the afternoon. Say twenty-six hours. We'll stay here and rest until that time."

Now the other nodded. "Very well. We'll clear some quarters for you." He leaned across the table, and for a moment his face twisted with the anger of a moment before. "My people will dedicate much of their remaining existence to punishing you."

The generals smiled at this threat, made by the leader of a second-rate military power against the greatest nation in the world. Tatja didn't smile. She respected the determination and technical competence that lay behind the Doomsday religion. Had she been nothing more than the Queen of Crownesse, this would have been a threat to fear. Mikach's promise was the sort which starts crusades.

Chapter 23

Someone had given him a crossbow. It was a powerful model, its cross-spars steeply angled. One full winding could shoot its entire six-bolt magazine. And each bolt contained enough explosive to put a hole through three inches of wood.

At the moment Svir felt no curiosity as to why he, who barely knew how to sight a bow, had been given the weapon. He had not noticed that out of the two-hundred-member party, only Jolle, Tatja, and he were armed.

Jolle and Tatja had originally planned to make the ascent alone, but the ingenious Doomsdaymen had made that impossible. The priests claimed that all the picture-making equipment was at O'rmouth for a general overhaul. This was plausible, since the observatory was too small to contain a machine shop. Unfortunately, more than a hundred Celestial Servants were then needed to carry the gear necessary to Jolle's project. The climb would take two days, with stops at Doo'd'en outposts along the way. So there had been a number of Crown's Men along to watch this mob of potential saboteurs. Everyone was surprised when Marget demanded they all go unarmed. The Servants were pleased with the requirement, the Crown's Men frankly angry.

If he had thought about it, Svir would have understood why only the three of them were armed . . . but he was thinking about very little.

For two days, they had walked up a steep tunnel toward the top of the world. Above the snowpack ceiling, the wind hummed endlessly across the mountain face. Where light holes punctured the roof, the hum became a scream. Sunlight glared brilliant through those holes, splashed whiteness on the figures trudging slowly upwards.

For a thousand feet at a time, the tunnel climbed so steep there were steps cut in the ice. Yet this journey was a walk in paradise compared to the climb that had faced the first explorers. They had gone across the *top* of the snow, through the wind, with no shelters along the way. The atmospheric pressure here was only one-fifth that at sea level. It was difficult to maintain body temperature, much less to work. If it had not been for what the Doo'd'en called the "perfume of life," no amount of sacrifice or faith would have been sufficient to build the observatory and live there.

The perfume of life—to "heathen" chemists, it was simply oxygen. At sea level the partial pressure of oxygen was about three pounds per square inch. At O'rmouth it was 1.4. It had been known for almost a century that the partial pressure of oxygen determines whether the air can sustain life. Thus, though scentless, oxygen *is* the perfume of life. For the last forty years Doo'd'en had used differential liquefaction to produce large amounts of oxygen. The gas was compressed into containers and allowed to slowly escape—as perfume might from an aerator. With some skill, it was possible to raise the partial pressure of oxygen at the observatory from 0.7 to 1.4 pounds per square inch, even though the total pressure inside the observatory was the same as outside. The procedure was simple and effective. No hermetic seals were needed.

Thirty men pulled the carts carrying the oxygen tanks. The aerators could occasionally be heard behind the hum of the wind. For the benefit of the Crown's Men, Tatja had insisted on bringing enough tanks to maintain a partial pressure of 2.0 psi. The enriched air made their climb possible. Barely. And after two days in march, the Celestial Servants seemed as fatigued as the lowlanders; the Servants were carrying the equipment and hauling the carts. Several times the group became so spread out that the aerators couldn't cover everyone. Then, without any warning, walking became impossible, and Tatja or Jolle would push them into a compact formation and move the tanks so everyone was within ten feet of "perfume."

Each step sent bright spurts of pain up Svir's calves. Each breath burned at his lungs. At first, the task of walking had made it easy for him to retreat from the events around him. No more. No more. For the first time in twenty hours, Svir found himself facing reality. Ancho was dead. *Cor was dead.* He believed that. And now that he did, the hate could blossom. Profirio must die—not because he wished to kill millions, but because he had killed the most important person in the universe. By himself, Svir had little chance against the monster. But he had two powerful allies, and he had a weapon. For the moment, he had a purpose.

Where the tunnel cut near the surface, the roof was pearly bright. Elsewhere, the light was fading. The sun would be lowering now, its light shining but indirectly through the roof holes. And in some places, the tunnel was very dark. Algae pots were useless in this cold, and a torch would consume more oxygen than one hundred men. The men around him were shadows, bent to their own pain. He knew that Jolle and Tatja were somewhere behind the whole group. It was a strategic certainty that one of those men who appeared so tired was actually alert, calculating. Walking behind the rest, the queen and the alien could watch with sensitive eyes. If they did not discover Profirio, they at least would not be surprised from behind.

Svir had ended up near the head of the column. Even with good lighting, his two friends would have been out of sight most of the time.

Hmm. If he were Profirio, he would walk up here, too. Svir looked around with new interest. Who seemed a bit too lively? That was probably the wrong thing to look for: Profirio would be a great actor. Under other circumstances these thoughts would have filled him with fear: It was dark, the figures were indistinct, and one of them, perhaps right behind him, was a monster.

Svir was abruptly aware of the cold. He pulled his parka close and tensioned his crossbow.

There was conversation nearby. Low muttering came past the sounds of the wind. There was more than one voice; maybe three or four. Some people can grumble even when they're exhausted. And one of the speakers might be Profirio, gathering supporters. No doubt he could be as fiendishly persuasive as Tatja and Jolle. Svir dropped back till he was even with the sounds. His prospects were in front of the lead cart. Two of them were pulling it. The six-foot tank on the cart emitted its perfume in tiny hisses.

A hand closed on his shoulder. He leaped half a foot into the air, spastically squeezing his crossbow's trigger. But the safety was set and he was spared the mortal embarrassment of shooting himself with an explosive bolt.

"Sorry, friend, I slipped."

Svir turned to look at the other. It was possible the fellow really had slipped. Though the floor was covered with decomposed granite, there were open patches of ice. But at the head of the column, such patches were quite dry. The man released his arm. There was a glimmer from above, and Svir saw that he was fairly old, though muscular. *This could be it!* The other's face showed just a bit too much fatigue. And the man was a Celestial Servant. Profirio would most likely pose as one of them.

Svir made no attempt to start a conversation. He had a dubious advantage over Profirio. The alien must nullify the armed men in the party. Since Svir was one-third of that force, Profirio would either manipulate him with conversation—or kill him. The ploys were limited, and for once it might be possible to compete with a mind like

Tatja's. When the "old soldier" finally spoke, Svir felt a flash of triumph.

"You're one of the Crown's Men, aren't you?" The soldier's voice quavered overmuch, Svir thought.

"That's right," he replied, with as much disinterest as he could muster.

"I don't mean offense, but I see you're armed. You must be important. Maybe you can tell me. Why are you doing this?"

"Doing what?" His reply was not an evasion. The Servant's question seemed disconnected from the dangers that floated through his mind.

"Why do you trespass here? Why do you insult a religion that's never done you harm?" The voice had an innocent, bewildered tone.

The official reason was that this was Marget's whim. To her generals she had presented no more explanation, though some of them were happy to humor her. They thought the Doomsdaymen needed a leash. Certainly Svir couldn't blurt out the real reason for this trip; only Profirio would understand that.

"Perhaps you thought," the Servant continued, since Svir seemed bound to silence, "that we didn't show you proper respect. I love my people, sir, and I love my religion. But I've been south. I know that we're a pretty mean group. We own a beautiful stretch of wasteland and the conviction we're specially blessed by the Almighty. We must be arrogant. If we weren't, we'd have no reason to stay here."

Old soldiers could be this sharp, but no ordinary soldier could express himself so smoothly,

and with such a vocabulary. Svir set his thumb on
the bow's safety.

The Servant continued, "We make a big show of
fierceness, but this was the first time in a hundred
years that Celestial Servants have been in combat.
I always thought military drill was a frivolous,
enjoyable pastime; no one ever died, as they so
often do in mine and construction work. But this
morning my men—"

"Your men?" Svir broke in, trying to keep the
right amount of curiosity in his voice.

"Yes, I'm a Celestial Servant with Stellar Efful-
gence. That's about the same as a colonel in your
army."

Damn. That could explain his diction.

"It was strange to see men die, fighting. We
thought we were protecting people and land. Now
I see it was for nothing. What is the point?" He
sounded hurt, bewildered, almost like Cor had
sounded by the watering stop. Svir turned to give
an honest reply, but the other had dropped back
in the formation. Emotionally, Svir was convinced
of the fellow's sincerity. In a perverse way, that
was the strongest sign that he had been speaking
to the illusive Profirio; when you were sure they
were sincere, then you knew you had been fooled.
He brought his crossbow to port arms, turned,
and let the oxygen cart creak past him. The other
was lost in the mob that walked behind the cart.

Profirio? Maybe that was why the other moved
away. But then, why hadn't he killed Svir and
taken the bow? The alien could certainly have
done so, barehanded and without noise.

Minutes later, the tunnel leveled out, and the
windsound died. The observatory! He tripped on a

stone step. The walls, the floor—they were solid rock now. He saw the carts behind him being pushed over the step. Ahead, the darkness was absolute. If the whole observatory were built this way it must be a pretty dreary place, with no view except of heaven.

Someone brushed past him, moving fast. He lashed out, but his wrist was caught from behind. "It's us," Tatja whispered in his ear. He realized they were moving quietly to the head of the file, to be the first into the observatory. Jolle was taking no chances. Svir tried to follow them, but they were virtually running through the darkness. He had to slow down and cautiously feel his way. . . . Far ahead, Jolle was pounding on a door and shouting.

It would be an interesting bit of treachery if the High Eye Observers chose not to open up; their visitors could never make it back to O'rmouth without more oxygen. But thousands of feet below, where there was still grass and air, the gunners had instructions to fire unless they received helios from Tatja at specified times. This point had been made excruciatingly clear to all concerned.

A trapezoid of sunlight appeared ahead, casting ragged shadows down the rough-cut granite of the hallway. Svir squinted into brilliance. Beyond that doorway, just a few feet away, was the end of their long journey.

Chapter 24

Dazzling sunlight was everywhere. Tall windows marched around the walls, and beyond them was the top of the world. The sky was indigo, as if the sun had already set. Look down and see the Doomsday Range, frozen waves of white tossed on a frozen sea. Here and there, clouds nestled between the peaks. Pale brown clung to one horizon, a trick of the westering sun . . . or the edge of the Central Desert?

The High Eye was not *quite* at the top of He'gate: Some hundred yards west of the dome a scarp rose fifty feet higher, shielding the observatory from the winds that had pursued them here. The limestone stood brown and yellow above smooth snowdrifts. Svir turned; there was the stone hallway they had just been through. The snow lay powdery in the cracks and joints of the yellow masonry. Beyond the windshadow, it whirled with crystal violence around the stonework. Four hundred feet from the observatory, the hallway became a true tunnel, disappearing into the permanent snow pack. A large wind turbine stood north of the tunnel, its snout stuck into the gale; the derrick squatted on a contraption of gears and pistons. A covered trough extended from the turbine back to the observatory. The trough was sheathed by ice. A haze of steam or ice billowed up along its whole length.

A perfectly ordinary doorway was set between two of the windows. It swung open and a heavily clothed figure stepped inside. Though Doomsday born, the fellow swayed drunkenly, gasping for breath. He shut the door and sagged against the wall. Exterior maintenance must have been a killing job.

Inside the dome, a slow fan shuffled at the air. Dead air must be exhausted, and the "perfume of life" be kept properly concentrated. Thus the interior was not partitioned into rooms; the entire dome was visible at a glance. Here there was none of the ornament they had seen at O'rmouth, where there were laymen to be impressed. The floor was divided into sectors. Several were empty, reserved for the newly arrived equipment. Others were piled high with supplies, oxygen tanks, and astronomical equipment.

At the center stood the reason for it all: the High Eye itself. The telescope was the largest in the world; even if it hadn't been set at the top of the world, it would have awed. The sixty-inch mirror was hidden in a plastic and ceramic webbing that extended fifty feet into the air to support the secondary mirror, which was huge in its own right. The secondary sent incoming light back slantwise to picture-making machines next to the main mirror. The entire structure could be turned to follow any point in the sky. Doo'd'en claimed that twenty-five thousand ounces of iron had gone into the steel for the bearings that supported it. No religious ornamentation was necessary to make it seem marvelous.

For a few moments Svir was absorbed by things he'd dreamed of all his life, but thought he'd never see.

Tatja's voice came sharp, tense. "Move into the room slowly. Set down your equipment and line up against the wall." She was facing into the tunnel, her crossbow aimed at the entrance. Jolle was inspecting the astronomers, in particular the fellow who had just come through the outside door.

From the tunnel came a puzzled question. It was Haarm Wechsler. "You refer to the Doomsday porters, of course."

Tatja replied, "I mean everyone. There is a saboteur in the party and we intend to find him." Jolle turned to face the tunnel; where he was standing, he could cover both the Doomsday astronomers and the visitors. Svir raised his bow and flicked off the safety. There was one in particular. . . .

Crown's Men and Celestial Servants stumbled into the light; many were too tired to care what was happening. They came through too fast. Tatja told them to come through in single file, but it was impossible to obey. Most of the carts were drawn by two or three men, and people inevitably walked in clusters behind the aerators. The carts were parked in a ragged formation. Then the visitors stood against the wall, in a single rank. The astronomers remained at the center of the room, their self-righteous anger changing to puzzlement. Why were lowlanders and Servants treated alike? Everyone was beginning to realize there was more here than a fickle queen's whimsy.

Now every face was visible. Nowhere did Svir see that friendly, wrinkled one from the tunnel. Tatja glanced at Jolle. The alien shook his head slightly.

"I don't think so," he said quietly. Then, sharply, to the astronomers, "Where does that staircase lead?" He gestured with his bow. Stairs? Svir realized that what he had mistaken for an unevenness in the floor was something more. And the hole had been lost from view when the main party came into the dome.

"Living quarters, may it please Your Most Illustrious Lordship."

Jolle ignored the sarcasm. "Is there any way from those quarters to the outside?"

"No. The only other entrance is by the Number Three Aerator." Jolle stared at the speaker for several seconds. It seemed to Svir he was considering whether to chase into the basement for Profirio. That would decide things once and for all, but the other might be planning some special ambush. Since he was trapped, it might be best to leave him there.

Jolle glanced at Tatja, and she said opaquely, "No, that would be—wrong." She turned back to the Crown's Men and Celestial Servants. "It is my command that you remove yourselves below. Take two extra oxygen tanks."

The Servants shuffled toward the dark stairway. Several of the crown's generals stood their ground, and Minister Wechsler voiced their feelings. "Marget, you overstep yourself. The Crown's subjects deserve your confidence. Your liaison with this fellow," he waved at Jolle, "is—"

"Haarm, you're in a bind you don't understand. Get below or I'll cut you to pieces." She raised her crossbow.

The crown's officers motioned their men toward the stairs. In three minutes they were all below. Tatja walked to the hole and shut the trap. She rolled one of the supply carts over the door. It might still be possible to open the trap from below, but it could not be done with stealth. She did the same at the other stairway, then walked slowly around the edge of the dome.

Jolle said, "We want you to do two things tonight, Svir. Be prepared to shoot any *saboteur*." He accented the word so that Svir knew he meant one particular saboteur. "And help assemble the equipment." He waved at the carts full of picture-making and analysis equipment.

The second job occupied Svir's time for the next four hours. Even though Jolle and Tatja supervised, and even though the astronomers knew their equipment much better than he, there was plenty for him to do. The Doomsday picture-makers required large quantities of mixed reagents. The optical equipment was both bulky and delicate. At times the astronomers seemed to forget they were working under duress. Then Svir would notice eyes straying to the crossbow slung at his shoulder. These priests were revealing secrets they had sworn to guard forever. If they could think of a way to trick the queen's gunmen below O'rmouth, they wouldn't hesitate to kill him.

The sun set. Outside, the snow went from yellow to orange to red, and the red became deeper and deeper. Svir remembered seeing that red from many miles away, from far down by the Picchiu River . . . so many days ago, when there was still a reason, beyond revenge, for living. The thought almost drove him back into the world of what-might-have-been.

Then the stars were out. This side of the world had a sky much clearer and darker than anywhere beneath Seraph; except when in eclipse, the sister planet dimmed the fainter stars to invisibility. But here, thirty thousand feet above the sea and the mists, the stars were still brighter. They were so bright the snows glittered faintly beneath their brilliance. The wind turbine was shut down. Convection currents around the outside pipes would degrade the seeing. Besides—said the Doomsday archobserver—the building's reservoirs now held enough hot water to support operations through the night. The Eye's lid was pulled back, and aerators were opened full.

Jolle gave the astronomers an area one degree by twenty and specified a search pattern. He was looking for a new object of sixteenth magnitude. Jolle knew the orbital elements of his craft to several digits, but three quarters after having been marooned, he could know the position only approximately. Fortunately, the search area would be visible through most of the night. They would take dozens of pictures and compare them with the Doo'd'en archives brought from O'rmouth.

The Doomsdaymen moved surely about the dome, a tribute to their fanatic regard for their profession. Strange reddish light came from pillars scattered about the room. Another Doo'd'en secret. Svir reached up, touched one of the pillars. The glowing surface was flat, warm. The Doomsdaymen had something that glowed when differentially heated? That might explain their use of hot water.

Finally, the first picture plate was put in the optics beside the main mirror. The clockwork in the base of the instrument was wound, the Eye was aimed, and the exposure began. It would take half an hour for the plate to collect enough light to reveal objects of the sixteenth magnitude. Here was the prime advantage of the Doomsday technique over the greentint method used on the Tarulle Barge. Time exposures were nearly impossible with greentint.

After the first exposure, plates were changed and the telescope was repositioned. The exposed plate was the object of further chemical ritual; after twenty minutes, a priest announced that the picture might be viewed. He set it beside an archive plate of the same sky region, and positioned a double eyepiece over the pair. Svir recognized the procedure. Each ocular gave a magnified view of a separate plate. In this way, small differences between the pictures could be quickly detected. Svir stepped close to the table. The pictures glowed red where the light from the table showed through them. It took a moment to realize that light and dark were reversed here. Then he felt a stab of envy. The plates showed the Batswing Nebula—as Svir had never dreamed it. The gases extended, twisting, beyond the limits of anything seen in greentints taken with the Krirsarque thirty-incher.

Now the search could begin.

*   *   *

The hours passed. There was the routine of setting plates, aiming the Eye, treating exposed plates, and comparing them with previous pictures. But between events, time stretched empty. Jolle and Tatja took positions at the perimeter of the dome. Any intruder would set himself in silhouette against the high windows, unless he crawled along the floor.

It was nearly midnight when the man on the comparator called to Svir, "New object." Svir leaned over the binocular eyepiece and looked at the red and black display. It was an undistinguished star field, nothing brighter than sixth magnitude. There was a whirring by his ear as the Doomsdayman turned a crank. The images flickered as first one and then the other lense was blocked. A faint streak was blinking in one corner of the image. *Hmm.* This wasn't like the earlier ones. The streak was too long to be a reasonable asteroid.

He looked up to call Jolle, and found the other standing beside him. The alien bent over, and studied the scene for several seconds. Then, with the ease of one trained in the use of the instrument, he flipped a reticle into the optics. "That's it. Just the right drift, just the right orientation." There was a hint of triumph in his voice. "No more pictures, Observers. We have found what we came for."

"Then you will leave us now?" came the voice of one of the more recalcitrant priests.

"Not quite yet. We will commit one more small desecration." He glanced at the micrometer settings on the optics, and thought a moment. "Set the Eye back on the coordinates of plate fourteen." He turned, walked quickly across the room. "Give me a hand, Svir."

Above them, the Eye's frame slewed fractionally, bringing the huge tube to near horizontal.

Jolle was already taking equipment out of a cart when Svir caught up with him. The small wooden cabinet was very familiar. Jolle looked up and continued quietly. "I'm going to use what you thought was a golem to operate my signaler." He pushed the cabinet into Hedrigs's hands and pulled an oblong box from the cart. Its smooth sides glittered metallically in the red light. "We've got to hustle. My boat is almost at the horizon; it's already in haze, I think."

Behind them, Tatja was herding the Doomsdaymen to the far side of the room. Just three people were needed now. Any intruder would be Profirio. For once there would be no trouble in penetrating others' disguises and ruses. Everything was very simple.

Svir walked back to the scope, gingerly set the hand-carved cabinet on the floor beside the picturemaker. Above his head, the framework of girders and struts moved infinitesimally, tracking the stars beyond. Jolle opened the cabinet. The jewels glowed even brighter than Svir remembered. The shifting glitter sent blue-green ripples around the room. There was a collective gasp from the Doomsday astronomers, then an even more impressive silence. They had thought they were dealing with madmen. Now the world itself had gone mad.

Jolle drew a cable from the shimmering heap, attached it to the oblong box, and clamped the box to a telescope-alignment strut; evidently this was the signaler. Jolle stood, looked through a sighting scope. In the blue light, his face held a new intensity. "Damn. They didn't leave it tracking properly." He slung his crossbow, and adjusted the tracking wheels. "I could use my machine to do the aiming, but the scope is ready-made for—"

If Svir had not been looking directly into the maze of struts around the mirror, what followed would have seemed like magic. In one flashing motion, Profirio leaped from the scope to the floor, kicked over the glowing cabinet, and shouted, "Jolle killed her!" Svir's weapon was pointed directly at Profirio's middle—killing him was a matter of tightening one finger. But the other's words held him back for a split second; then Tatja screamed *"Don't, Svir!"*

Time slowed to a human pace. In a single second, Profirio had forced a stalemate. Svir realized this as he glanced at Jolle, who had his weapon nearly unslung—and could probably aim and shoot in a fraction of a second. But he didn't move. Svir looked at Profirio, who appeared to be unarmed. This *was* the Celestial Servant who had talked to him in the tunnel. But now his face seemed younger, though very different from Jolle's. Above his beard, Jolle's face was smooth, deeply tanned. Profirio's was paler, and deeply creased with frown and smile lines.

Why didn't Jolle shoot? Svir glanced at Tatja. Her crossbow was leveled and aimed—*at Jolle*. He looked at the glowing pile Profirio had spilled from the cabinet, and realized that at the instant he had accused Jolle of killing Cor, on a different level he had convinced Tatja that things were not as they seemed. Now that Jolle's machine lay exposed, Svir could see there was a shape imbedded in its fiery matrix. That shape was horribly familiar: An oval lump, six inches across. From the lump led a ropelike strand, with finer strands splitting off it. Barely visible, the finest ones touched the silvery boxes that surrounded the pile. How many times had he passed that exhibit at U Krirsarque Museum, and shuddered at the pickled brain and spinal column there? Here the spinal column was bent into a circle to conserve space, but the rest was all the same.

As it lay on the floor, the pulsing treasure whimpered. Broken away from its machine tasks and left for a moment without a program, its high-pitched voice keened over and over, "Where am I, where am I, am I . . ." and the answer was *nowhere anymore.* Several of the astronomers fled outside, preferring hypoxia to the nightmare that had come to their shrine.

So Jolle was the slaver, after all. The revelation had strangely little effect on Svir; it was irrelevant what Jolle had done to strangers. The stock of his crossbow drifted back to the intruder. Svir's universe shrank to Profirio's blue-lit face. *This murderer must die.*

Less than five seconds had passed since the other's appearance. Now he spoke for the second time. "And this is how he did it!" His hand whipped out to slap the side of the signaler. Red lightning. Even at ten feet, the heat of that beam scorched his face—just as it had once before. The beam clipped the dome, and shards of wood and glass showered down. Prompted by this cue, the thing on the floor spoke, its voice suddenly deep and male, *"Ter äshe gaul, Jolle."*

The memory of the last time Svir saw that light

was suddenly very sharp: Jolle had dismissed the signalman just before it happened. He had moved himself out of the way. *Jolle put the golem in the tree and made it use the signaler to kill.* Svir felt his muscles jerk. All men had been puppets to these three. Even now he was being maneuvered as unsubtly as a skoat. That didn't matter. He was remembering a charred face; he would never quite be able to remember how Cor's face had looked in life. His crossbow swung toward Jolle. The bearded one hardly seemed to notice. He was talking low and fast, to Tatja. "We can be. You love—"

Svir's finger pressed the trigger. Jolle reacted with characteristic speed, bringing his weapon down before Svir could shoot. The alien's left leg was blown off as Tatja loosed her bolt. The last thing Svir felt was the explosion as Jolle's bolt smashed everything into darkness.

Chapter 25

The daybat fluttered through the intricately wound branches of the needle tree, settled beside a large pink flower, and folded its blue and orange wings. Its tiny, sleek head moved back and forth as it wiggled between the petals and licked the juices in the base of the flower. This far from human settlement, most animals were not shy of humans—the flower in question was barely fifteen inches above Svir's head.

O'rmouth was one hundred miles away. The mountains dominated the horizon to the east—if one chose to look through the leaves and green branches in that direction. Here the air was thick and rich, just warm enough so that the breeze moving along the ground was pleasantly cool. Here the sunlight was muted by green leaves, not reflected with merciless intensity by snow and ice.

Three hundred feet away, their battle group was setting up bivouac. The universe had chosen to wear its mask of light and love today. Svir recognized the deception. The real world was snow and ice and red thunderbolts that . . .

There was a crackle of branches as Tatja entered the little open spot by the tent and sat down beside him. The daybat jerked its head from the flower and looked warily about, then went back within the pinkness.

They sat in silence for several minutes. Tatja wore a gray fatigue uniform. There was about her none of the purpose or intensity that had driven her before. The Doomsdaymen were far behind them. There were no more threats to face.

Tatja's hand slipped onto his elbow. Then her face was before his and her eyes bore the same quiet, personal interest that he had seen more than four years ago in a certain tavern in Krirsarque—where this dream had begun. "A lot of people died in this adventure, and I am truly sorry it had to be . . . but Cor I miss the most. The most."

He tried to produce an ironic chuckle but all that came out was a croaking sound.

"What?" asked Tatja.

He opened his mouth again. The words came fast, low, slurred. "I was just thinking if Jolle's golem had been a bit more accurate he could have had me too an' maybe saved himself later on."

She raised her hand to his shoulder. "The golem was perfectly accurate, Svir. By killing her, Jolle made you into a tool and eliminated a major threat. Of all the people there, Cor was the only one I might have listened to." Tatja's voice faded. "In all the world, Cor and Rey Guille were the only ones I might have listened to. . . . How I wish I hadn't frightened Rey away. I was just a brilliant animal when I found Tarulle; they made me a person. For a while I had a home, people I could talk to. Rey's telescope was the most beautiful thing I'd ever seen. He and Cor seemed so smart, almost like me. The first days on the barge were the happiest of my life. Now years have passed . . . and those I didn't drive away are all dead. Friends deserve better." She made a peculiar choking sound.

"No, Svir. Jolle meant to kill Cor. And it was only luck that his plan did not work. You see, Profirio was less than one hundred yards from the bunker when the golem shot Cor. Pröfe had already been separated from his supporters. He was trying to move across the no-man's-land to our side. He saw the murder; eventually he learned who had been killed. He talked to you during the walk up the snow tunnel. By the time we reached the observatory, he knew how Jolle was using you, and he knew how to approach you.

"He did sneak below the main floor, as we thought. But you remember that the water from the wind turbines had to go into those quarters. The pipe was too small for him, but the ground around the entrance hole was not rock hard. Pröfe dug his way out during the first hours. Jolle was too near his goal to take everything into account and I . . . I wasn't thinking very straight myself. Anyway, Pröfe got outside, and while you and Jolle were mounting the signaler, he crawled onto the dome and down into the telescope."

Svir looked at her face, saw without comprehension the tears in her eyes. His attention wandered back to the bat on the branch above them. The flower's juices splashed over the petals and a sweet smell drifted down. He had no interest in what had happened in the last hundred hours—in whether the world had been saved or not. His hands clenched and unclenched as he considered what he would do if that bat were so incautious as to come lower.

"Svir, you aren't the only one who had his world kicked to pieces." She laughed, but it was not a happy sound. "I loved Jolle. He manipulated me just as I have all the rest. If I hadn't been fooled, most of this would not have happened. Cor would be alive.

"But this doesn't change the fact that I really loved him. Jolle turned out to be evil, but he was also . . . someone strong, who seemed to like me. Pröfe is a kinder man. But he's not Jolle.

"I'm going to disappear tonight for good. So is Pröfe. I won't go into the details—I'm afraid they wouldn't be completely intelligible—but Pröfe signaled his vehicle last night, and we have transportation now. I imagine Haarm Wechsler will be quite relieved. The bureaucrats will have to find a Crown Surrogate, but after the way I treated them above O'rmouth, I don't think they're interested in having a ruler as unreliable as I. They may even believe I'm something supernatural. Yet everything I did was child's play.

"Now . . . I'm so *scared*. After tonight, everyone I meet will be as smart as I. Once more I'm just a bright animal. Pröfe can't lie nearly as well as Jolle: Pröfe is really not sure if I'll *ever* fit in with his people. I may be lost forever, too bright for this world, too dim for Pröfe's."

She faltered. Then her voice filled with forced enthusiasm. "Svir, things are hard for you just now, but see the good that can come: You are going to live through the beginning of the most exciting time in Tu's history. In the next two hundred years, the people of Tu will move science along to the beginnings of what you have seen with Jolle and Pröfe. No slavers will deny you progress. In three centuries human nature itself will change, and all that went before will have been chrysalis. Your descendents will be like me."

The bat undid its wings and fluttered to the next flower, ten inches from the first. It was less than fifteen inches from his head.

"You will never see me or Pröfe again . . . I guess you're just as happy about that." The bat turned, and one wing draped down so low that Svir could see the individual blue and orange hairs that composed its fur. "But people like us will never be far away. We can't give back what was taken from your ancestors, but we will see that your grandchildren regain it. There are many wrong turnings possible. There are pestilences that could kill all life on the planet—if you misuse the discoveries you will make. We will do our best to protect you—in appropriate, undetectable ways."

Svir's clenched hands became claws as they flashed up. Tatja caught his wrists in the first four inches of motion. Her grip was unshakable. And for once she misunderstood his motives. "Please, Svir. I don't mean protection like you've had the last few days. People were killed and ruined because we were fighting a superman, not someone who could be maneuvered." She looked closely at him. "I hadn't realized how twisted this has left you. You got caught right in the middle, as I did; but I was their equal—and you were nearly destroyed. If Pröfe had any equipment with him, he could cure you, make you realize that there are still ways out. . . .

"I take back one thing I said: I will return. Soon. The cure is simple, and I owe you more than that . . ." She let his hands fall back into his lap, and for a moment her lips brushed his cheek. She stood up slowly, and left the clearing. For several minutes he could hear her moving through the brush, toward the nearest camping area.

His eyes never left the beautiful mammal that moved so delicately on the branch. It had slid along the top of the branch, now edged back under. Its clear black eyes gazed down at him. In a moment . . .

Svir lunged up to catch the bat in a two-handed crushing blow. But the little animal was too fast, and it flashed from between the approaching hands. It fluttered up through the branches and into the blue spaces above.

Here is an excerpt from Vernor Vinge's new novel, Marooned in Realtime, *coming in June 1987 from* Baen Books:

The town nestled in the foothills of the Indonesian Alps, high enough so that equatorial heat and humidity was moderated to an almost uniform pleasantness. Here the Korolevs and their friends had finally assembled the rescued from all the ages. At the moment the population was less than two hundred, every living human being. They needed more; Yelén Korolev knew where to get one hundred more. She was determined to rescue them.

Steven Fraley, President of the Republic of New Mexico, was determined that those hundred remain unrescued. He was still arguing the case when Wil Brierson arrived. ". . . and you don't appreciate the history of our era, madam. The Peacers came near to exterminating the human race. Sure, saving this group will get you a few more warm bodies, but you risk the survival of our whole colony, of the entire human race, in doing so."

Yelén Korolev looked calm, but Wil knew her well enough to recognize the signs of an impending explosion: there were rosy patches on her cheeks, yet her features were otherwise even paler than usual. She ran a hand through her blond hair. "Mr. Fraley, I really do know the history of your era. Remember that almost all of us—no matter what our present age and experience—have our childhoods within a couple hundred years of one another. The Peace Authority"—her lips twitched in a quick smile at the name—"may have started the general war of 1997. They may even be responsible for the terrible plagues of the early twenty-first century. But as governments go, they were relatively benign. This group in Kampuchea"—she waved toward the north—"went into stasis in 2048, when the Peacers were overthrown. That was before decent health care was available. It's entirely possible that none of the original criminals are present."

Fraley opened and closed his mouth, but no words

came. Finally: "Haven't you heard of their 'Renaissance' scheme? In '48 they were ready to kill by the millions again. Those guys under Kampuchea probably got more hell-bombs than a dog has fleas. That base was their secret ace in the hole. If they hadn't screwed up their stasis, they'd've come out in 2100 and blown us away. And you probably wouldn't even have been born—"

Yelén cut into the torrent. "Hell-bombs? Popguns. Even you know that. Mr. Fraley, getting another hundred people into our colony will make our settlement just big enough to survive. Marta and I haven't spent our lives setting this up just to see it die like the under-manned attempts of the past. The only reason we postponed the founding of Korolev till megayear fifty was so we could rescue those Peacers when their bobble bursts."

She turned to her partner. "Is everybody accounted for?"

Marta Korolev had sat through the argument in silence, her dark features relaxed, her eyes closed. Her headband put her in communication with the estate's autonomous devices. No doubt she had managed a half dozen fliers during the last half hour, scouring the countryside for any truant colonists the Korolev satellites had spotted. Now she opened her eyes. "Everybody's accounted for and safe. In fact"—she caught sight of Wil standing at the back of the amphitheater and grinned—"almost everyone is here on the castle grounds. I think we can provide you people with quite a show this afternoon." She either hadn't followed or—more likely—had chosen to ignore the dispute between Yelén and Fraley.

"Okay, let's get started." A rustle of anticipation passed through the audience. Many were from the twenty-first century, like Wil. But they'd seen enough of the advanced travelers to know that such a statement was more than enough signal for spectacular events to happen.

From his place at the top of the amphitheater, Wil

had a good view to the north. The forests of the higher elevations fell away to a gray-green blur that was the equatorial jungle. Beyond that, haze obscured even the existence of the Inland Sea. Even on the rare, clear day when the sea mists lifted, the Kampuchean Alps were hidden beyond the horizon. Nevertheless, the rescue should be visible; he was a bit surprised that the bluish white of the northern horizon was undisturbed.

"Things will get more exciting, I promise." Yelén's voice brought his eyes back to the stage. Two large displays floated behind her.

"As Mr. Fraley says, the Peacer bobble was supposed to be a secret. It was originally underground. It is much further underground now—somebody blundered. What was to be a fifty-year jump became something . . . longer. As near as we can figure, their bobble should burst sometime in the next few thousand years; they've been in stasis fifty million years. During that time, continents drifted and new rifts formed. Parts of Kampuchea slid deep beneath new mountains." The display behind her lit with a multicolored transect of the Kampuchean Alps. The surface crust appeared as blue, shading into yellow and orange at the greater depths. Right at the margin of orange and magma red was a tiny black disk—the Peacer bobble, afloat against the ceiling of hell.

Inside the bobble, time was stopped. Those within were as they'd been at that instant of a near-forgotten war when the losers decided to escape to the future. No force could affect a bobble's contents; no force could affect its duration—not the heart of a star, not the heart of a lover.

But when the bobble burst, when the stasis ended . . . The Peacers were about forty kilometers down. There would be a moment of noise and heat and pain as the magma swallowed them. One hundred men and women would die, and a certain endangered species would move one more step toward final extinction.

The Korolevs proposed to raise the bobble to the

surface, where it would be safe for the few remaining millennia of its duration. Yelén waved at the display. "This was taken just before we started the operation. Here's the ongoing view."

The picture flickered. The red magma boundary had risen thousands of meters above the bobble. Pinheads of white light flashed in the orange and yellow that represented the solid crust. In the place of each of those lights, red blossomed and spread, almost—Wil winced at the thought—like blood from a stab wound. "Each of those sparkles is a hundred-megaton bomb. In the last few seconds, we've released more energy than all mankind's wars put together."

The red spread as the wounds coalesced into a vast hemorrhage in the bosom of Kampuchea. The magma was still twenty kilometers below ground level. The bombs were timed so there was a constant sparkling just above the highest level of red, bringing the melt closer and closer to the surface. At the bottom of the display, the Peacer bobble floated, serene and untouched. On this scale, its motion towards the surface was imperceptible.

Wil pulled his attention from the display and looked beyond the amphitheater. There was no change: the northern horizon was still haze and pale blue. The rescue site was fifteen hundred kilometers away, but even so, he'd expected something spectacular.

The elapsed-time clock on the display showed almost four minutes. The Korolev pattern of bomb bursts was still thousands of meters short of the surface.

President Fraley rose from his seat. "Madame Korolev, please. There is still time to stop this. I know you've rescued all types, cranks, joyriders, criminals, victims. But these are *monsters*." For once, Wil thought he heard sincerity—perhaps even fear—in the New Mexican's voice. *And he might be right*. If the rumors were true, if the Peacers had created the plagues of the early twenty-first century, then they were responsible for the deaths of billions. If they had succeeded with their Renaissance Project, they would have killed most of the survivors.

Yelén Korolev glanced down at Fraley but didn't reply. The New Mexican stiffened, then waved abruptly to his people. One hundred men and women—most in NM fatigues—came quickly to their feet. It was a dramatic gesture, if nothing else: the amphitheater would be almost empty with them gone.

"Mr. President, I suggest you and the others sit back down." It was Marta Korolev. Her tone was as pleasant as ever, but the insult in the words brought a flush to Steve Fraley's face. He gestured angrily and turned to the stone steps that led from the theater.

The ground shock arrived an instant later.

320 pp. • 65647-3 • $3.50

To order any Baen Book by mail, send the cover price plus 75 cents for first-class postage and handling to: Baen Books, Dept. B, 260 Fifth Avenue, New York, N.Y. 10001.